The MOCCASIN MAKER

E. Pauline Johnson, 1897

Photograph by Leary and Co., St. Mary's, Ontario,
courtesy of Brant County Museum, Brantford, Ontario.

The MOCCASIN MAKER

E. Pauline Johnson

Introduction, Annotation, and Bibliography
by
A. LaVonne Brown Ruoff

The University of Arizona Press
Tucson

About the Author

EMILY PAULINE JOHNSON, the daughter of a Mohawk Indian chief and an English mother, has long been regarded as one of Canada's greatest women writers. Born in 1861 on the Six Nations Reserve near Brantford, Ontario, she spent her childhood studying the works of Longfellow, Shakespeare, Byron, and Emerson under the tutelage of her mother. Her earliest poems date from 1879, although few were published before 1892, when she became known throughout Canada for her literary recitals and theatrical performances. After the publication of her first book of poems, *The White Wampum*, in 1895, Johnson traveled throughout Canada, writing numerous stories, articles, and poems for *The Mother's Magazine* and gathering materials for her book of stories about Canadian Indian life, *The Moccasin Maker*. She died in Vancouver, British Columbia, in March of 1913.

Dedicated to

SIR GILBERT PARKER

Whose Work in Literature has brought Honor to Canada

Copyright, Canada, 1913, by The Ryerson Press

THE UNIVERSITY OF ARIZONA PRESS

First printing 1987

Copyright © 1987
The Arizona Board of Regents
All Rights Reserved

Manufactured in the U.S.A.

Library of Congress Cataloging-in-Publication Data

Johnson, E. Pauline, 1861 – 1913.
    The moccasin maker.

    Bibliography: p.
    1. Indians of North America—Canada—Fiction.
I. Ruoff, A. LaVonne.   II. Title.
PR9199.2.J64M6   1987   813'.4   86-6930
ISBN 0-8165-0910-7 (alk. paper)

British Library Cataloguing in Publication data are available.

CONTENTS

Miss Johnson's Mohawk Grandfather

Who was for forty years Speaker of the Council of the Six Nations
Confederation. Fought for the British at Queenston Heights.

INTRODUCTION

by A. LaVonne Brown Ruoff

*B*ORN IN 1861 on the Six Nations Reserve in the Grand River valley near Brantford, Ontario, Emily Pauline Johnson was the daughter of George Henry Martin Johnson, a Mohawk chief, and Emily Susanna Howells, an English-born cousin of the American writer William Dean Howells. Because her father was one quarter white, Pauline was biologically more white than Indian. However, by Canadian law and by heritage she was Indian. The history of her father's Mohawk people and his family's long tradition of leadership within the tribe strongly influenced her life and career. The public's fascination with her unique background as the daughter of a Mohawk chief who descended from an ancient line of chiefs and of an English mother belonging to the Howells family created for Pauline audiences in Canada, Great Britain, and the United States eager to read her work and to attend her performances. She was among the first performers to bring literature to the frontier towns of Canada. Billed as the "Mohawk Princess," Pauline became one of the most popular stage performers in Canada at the turn of the century.[1]

The history of the Johnson family parallels that of the Mohawk tribe, which was originally located in the Finger Lakes region of upper New York. Pauline's ancestor Teyonhehkwea[2] or "Double

1

Life" was a member of the first council of the Iroquois Confederacy. Founded in the late sixteenth century by the Onondaga leader Hiawatha (Taoungwatha), the confederacy initially consisted of five nations: the Mohawks, Onondagas, Cayugas, Senecas, and Oneidas. It later expanded to six when the Tuscaroras joined. Because they supported the British, the confederacy tribes lost much of their land after the Revolutionary War. Many members of confederacy tribes accepted the British government's offer of resettlement on the Grand River, near what is now Brantford, Ontario, as compensation for their support.

Pauline's paternal great-great-grandfather, Teyonehehkewea, was a Mohawk chief who adopted as his daughter Catherine Rollston, a thirteen-year-old Dutch captive. Pauline's father inherited his Wolf clan membership through Catherine. Pauline's paternal grandmother, the strong-willed Helen Martin Johnson (d. 1866) described in "My Mother," was the daughter of Catherine Rollston (Wanowenreteh) and George Martin (Onhyeateh), a Mohawk. The family name of "Johnson" and also the Indian name Pauline adopted as a performer and writer came from her paternal great-grandfather, Jacob Johnson, Tekahionwake or "Double Wampum" (1758–1843). Jacob's son, John, is the grandfather Pauline lovingly portrays in "My Mother." Pauline primarily learned about Mohawk traditions from her grandfather John or Smoke Johnson (1792–1886), respected as a hero of the War of 1812 and as the speaker of the Council of the Six Iroquois nations for more than forty years. The council conferred on him his title of Sakayengawaraton or "Disappearing Mist," from which the name Smoke was derived. Smoke was a member of the Bear Clan.[3]

Helen Martin Johnson (also known as Nellie) and Smoke educated their son George Henry Martin Johnson (1816–84) in the Mohawk language and traditions. Smoke, however, also insisted that his son be given an English education in Anglican schools. As a result of George's mastery of English, he was appointed in 1840 the official interpreter for the English church missions on the Six Nations Reserve. Subsequently, he became a warden on the reserve. George also succeeded to the hereditary chieftaincy as one of the nine Mohawk chiefs on the Iroquois Grand Council, a position carrying the title of Teyonhehkewea. In "My Mother," Pauline described the decisive role played by her grandmother Helen in obtaining this chieftaincy for her son despite the controversy over the propriety of his accepting it while continuing to hold his position as translator.

Pauline Johnson's mother, Emily Susanna Howells (1824–98), was born in Bristol, England, the daughter of a strict Quaker father, Henry Charles Howells (1784 – 1854), and an Anglican mother, Mary Best (d. 1828). Henry was son of Thomas Howells and Susannah Beasley Howells of Hay, Wales, and the brother of Joseph Howells, father of William Cooper Howells. The American author William Dean Howells, William Cooper's son, was Emily's first cousin. After bearing thirteen children, Mary Best died in 1828, when Emily Susanna was four. In 1829, Henry Charles married Harriet

Joyner, who subsequently bore six children. Two years later, when Emily was eight, Henry took his family and his new Quaker wife to America. He settled first in Worthington, Ohio, and then in the village of Putnam, now a part of Zanesville, in southeastern Ohio. A staunch abolitionist, Henry worked zealously for the cause. Life in America brought little happiness to Henry's children by his first wife. Pauline portrays her stern grandfather and her mother's unhappy childhood in "My Mother," a fictionalized account of her mother's life and marriage. At the age of twenty-one, Emily escaped her life of drudgery as a servant and nursemaid in her stepmother's house by accepting the invitation of her sister Eliza Beulah (1819 – 49) and her husband the Reverend Adam Elliot (1802 – 78) to live with them in the Tuscarora parsonage on the Six Nations Reserve at Grand River.

There Emily met twenty-nine-year-old George Henry Martin Johnson, a former student and translator for Elliot who still lived in the Elliot household. The couple's friendship turned to love while Emily nursed George through a serious illness, and they decided to marry. Because both sets of parents, and particularly Helen Johnson, opposed the marriage, the two did not marry until 1853. As Pauline makes clear in "My Mother," Helen did not soften toward her daughter-in-law until after the birth of the first grandchild a year later.

Determined that his new bride should have the best, George bought two hundred acres close to the Tuscarora parsonage and began building an impressive house to be called Chiefswood, which earned for him the Indian personal name by which he was best known on the reserve—Onwanonsyshon or "He Who Has the Great Mansion" (Hale, "Chief George H. M. Johnson—Onwanonsyshon" 140). To emphasize that both whites and Indians were welcome, George had the two-story house designed with one entrance facing the road, used by white visitors who came by horse or carriage, and one facing the river, used by Indian visitors who came by canoe. Two children were born before the family moved into their new home in 1856: Henry Beverly (1854–94) and Eliza Helen Charlotte (called Evelyn or Eva; 1856–1937). Two more children were born at Chiefswood: Allen Wawanosh (1858–1923) and Emily Pauline (1861–1913). The youngest child was named Emily after her mother and Pauline after the sister of Emperor Napoleon of France, George's special hero.

Because she was a sickly child, Pauline spent much time alone while her two older siblings went to school. Her mother stimulated her children's love of literature by reading them Keats and Byron rather than Mother Goose. Pauline and Allen were tutored for two years by an English governess and spent another two years in a reserve school. Both experiments proved unsatisfactory. When her brother entered Brantford Collegiate, Pauline was taught at home by her mother for the next three years. By the time Pauline was twelve, she had read every line of Longfellow and much of Byron, Shakespeare, and Emerson. She had also dipped into the prose writers from Addison to Macaulay. At age fourteen she entered Central Collegiate in Brantford, remaining two years. While there her interest in performing, which had originated in family theatricals, intensified. Pauline returned to Chiefswood in 1879 to live a life of ease, writing poetry, visiting school friends in Brantford, and canoeing on the Grand River.

Her father and grandfather were also strong influences on Pauline. Although her father was frequently away from home on tribal or government business, Pauline nevertheless loved to hear his stories about Hiawatha, the Shawnee chief Tecumseh, and the Ottawa chief Pontiac, as well as those about his hero Napoleon. A gifted orator, George was often away making speeches before Parliament or other audiences on behalf of his people. He was also frequently called upon during ceremonial occasions to represent the liaison between whites and Indians. In 1868, when Pauline was seven, she watched her father ride in full regalia to the Mohawk Church as escort to Queen Victoria's son Arthur, later Duke of Connaught (1850–1942), when he was made a Mohawk chief. Many famous figures visited Chiefswood over the years. The Johnsons established a reputation as gracious hosts, serving even casual guests with fine china, silver, and crystal.

Another strong influence was Smoke Johnson, who, following the death of his wife Helen in 1866, spent much of his time with the family. He thrilled young Pauline with his wartime deeds and those of the Mohawks. As an adult, she deeply regretted that she had not taken the time to learn more of his rich knowledge of his people's culture.

Not all of Pauline's life was idyllic. George's efforts on behalf of his people made Pauline aware from an early age of the problems faced by Indians living in a white-dominated world. On 21 January 1865, when she was four, whites severely beat George when he tried to stop their traffic in liquor and timber on the reserve. Eight years later, on 11 October 1873, six whites beat, shot, and left him for dead in an attempt to end his campaign against the sale of liquor and the robbery of reserve timber. George endured a final beating on 16 April 1878.[4] Despite his declining health, George, now supported by outraged public opinion, redoubled his efforts to curb white lawlessness on the reserve. Never fully recovered from his injuries, he died in 1884. In two stories in this volume, "My Mother" and "Her Majesty's Guest," Pauline describes her father's struggles against illegal liquor and timber traffic. In 1885, as a result of George's death and the family's subsequent financial difficulties, the Johnsons abandoned forever "Chiefswood" and its gracious lifestyle. Emily moved with her daughters Evelyn and Pauline to relatively modest lodgings in Brantford. Smoke Johnson, who had gone to live with a daughter, died the next year. Shortly thereafter, Pauline assumed the Indian name of her great-grandfather Jacob Johnson, signing all of her poems "E. Pauline Johnson" and "Tekahionwake."

Although a few of Pauline's poems were published in the years following her father's death, her career as a poet and performer really began in January 1892 at a Toronto literary evening. Pauline electrified her audience with her recitation of her poem "A Cry from an Indian Wife," based on the first mixed-blood rebellion (1869–70) that Louis Riel led against the Canadian government. The acclaim persuaded her to give several more recitals, where she was billed as "The Mohawk Princess." At the beginning of her career, Pauline wore an evening dress throughout her performance. However, by fall of 1892 she performed the Indian portion in a fringed buckskin dress of her own design and the remainder in an evening gown, a practice she continued throughout her career.

Also that fall, Pauline teamed with Alexander Smily, a veteran of British music halls who provided an additional act for Pauline's program and served as manager. Pauline had persuaded her family that she would perform only until she had accumulated the money necessary to travel to England to find a publisher for her poetry manuscript. By April 1894 she had accumulated enough to finance her trip. Sailing for her mother's homeland, she carried numerous letters of introduction which opened doors of London society to her. Both as a performer and as a guest at many social evenings given by aristocratic London hostesses, she was the hit of the season. According to Keller, the experience had a lasting influence on her life because London spontaneously granted her the status of being "both the cultivated lady and the princess from the primeval forests" that she had been trying so hard to establish in Canada (106). In London she also achieved her goal of finding a publisher for her poetry manuscript when the Bodley Head, foremost publisher of all new English poetry, accepted *The White Wampum.*

After her return home in July 1894, Pauline embarked on a tour of western Canada, an acknowledgment that performing was to become her career rather than a temporary means of financing her career as a poet. Until her retirement in 1909, Pauline traveled across Canada, the United States, and England to perform her own works. In July 1895, her much-delayed *The White Wampum* finally was published. Though the reviews, particularly in Great Britain, were mixed, the publication of the slim volume created even greater interest in her as a performer. To capitalize on this demand, Pauline and Smily toured both western and eastern Canada in 1895. Because western audiences were eager for entertainment and because they had not seen her as often as had eastern audiences, Pauline spent more time in the West than in the East. From 1896 to 1899, the Manitoba Hotel in Winnipeg, rather than the family home in Brantford, became her residence.

The year 1897 was especially eventful for Pauline. That year she broke off her partnership with Smily and met the ambitious but less talented J. Walter McRaye, who in 1901 became her partner and manager. The same year she also met and became engaged to Charles Robert Lumley Drayton, an authority on western property values and an assistant inspector for the Winnipeg office of the Western Canada Savings and Loan Company. The news of the engagement, reported on 27 January 1898 in the Brantford *Courier,* startled the couple's families and friends. Drayton's parents strongly opposed their twenty-five-year-old son's marriage to a thirty-six-year-old, mixed-blood stage performer. Despite his family's opposition and the couple's dissimilar backgrounds, Pauline was determined to marry Drayton. A beautiful girl and woman who never lacked male admirers, Pauline had always assumed that she would marry. Perhaps because of her hero worship of her father and because she could only accept a marriage as ideal as that of her parents, Pauline had not found a suitable husband. Despite the differences in their backgrounds and interests, Pauline may well have realized that Drayton might be her last chance to marry. A month later, Pauline's joy at her engagement was dimmed by the news that her mother was seriously ill. Pauline left Regina by train for Brantford, only to be delayed en route by blizzards. On 23 February she reached home just forty-five minutes before her mother died. In "My Mother," Pauline describes her mother's determination to live until her daughter arrived.

Pauline endured her grief and her own subsequent illness without the comfort of her fiancé. After a separation of seven months, she finally saw Drayton in July, when she attended his mother's funeral in Toronto. Pauline did not see him again until after she completed her western tour in the fall and returned to Winnipeg around Christmas. In early January 1899, she met with Drayton for the last time, when she granted his request to be released from their engagement in order to marry someone else. To recover from her loss, she immersed herself in performances to help raise money for the British effort in the Boer War, which began in January 1899.

Keller conjectures that Pauline's mysterious behavior during the fourteen months following her broken engagement suggests that she sought solace in an affair. During this period, Pauline borrowed five hundred dollars of her share of the rental monies on Chiefswood for the next three years in order to finance a tour of Australia. In June 1900 she engaged Charles Wurz, a German born in Heidelberg, as her new manager. She also placed in Halifax newspapers uncharacteristically large and expensive advertisements for her June performances there. The Australian tour never materialized. By April 1901, Pauline was so desperate for money that she wrote a highly emotional letter to her friend Frank Yeigh begging a fifteen-dollar loan. She described herself as feeling like "an escaped convict—independent, free—everything that is glorious, albeit I am in a network of tragedy—too sad for the human tongue to tell" (quoted in Keller 157).

Pauline alludes to consummated-but-tragic love in "Morrow Land," "Heidelburgh," and "Song," which she excluded from her collected works. From this puzzling letter and these three poems Keller concludes that Pauline became "sexually and romantically involved with the unscrupulous Wurz (160)." Carole Gearson supports Keller's conclusion, pointing out that the original title of "In Heidelburg" was "To C. H. W.," Wurz's initials. Gerson finds additional evidence in Walter

11

McRaye's letters written in 1913 to Newton McFaul MacTavish, editor of *The Canadian Magazine*. In its July issue, which appeared only four months after Pauline's death, the magazine published Charles Mair's appreciation of her. Its advertisement of the highlights of its August issue announced Pauline's "To C. W." and linked this poem to Mair's reference in his article to Pauline's "unfortunate love affair." In response to this advertisement McRaye, who had arranged the poem's sale to the magazine, wrote two letters to MacTavish to preclude the poem's being interpreted as an allusion to Johnson's relationship with Wurz. In a letter probably written in July 1913, McRaye responded angrily that "surely your Office Boy set that up." To throw the McTavish further off the track, McRaye emphasized that "'To C W' is purely an impersonal love poem, as 'The Voyage,' 'The Idlers,' and other love poems are." In addition, McRaye objected to the word "unfortunate" as being suggestive and far from what Mair intended. He informed McTavish that Johnson had changed the title of "To C W" to *"Heidelburg."*[5] In a second letter, dated 19 July, he made clear that the poem did not allude to Pauline's engagement to Charles Drayton in 1896 – 97.[6]

Keller suggests that possibly the death of Pauline's mother "somehow released her from the strict Johnson code of morals; if so, it was a temporary release, for she never again let down the barriers of propriety. On the other hand, it is possible that she was simply overreacting to Drayton's rejection, rebounding into the arms of Wurz" (160). Certainly her poetry and stories written after the end of her engagement to Drayton and her relationship to Wurz reflect great bitterness at the inconstancy of white men toward mixed-blood Indian women. Whatever their relationship, Pauline did not keep Wurz long as her manager. In November 1901 she engaged McRaye as her partner and manager. Although their first tour was shortened by her illness from erysipelas, which killed her father, the two set out again after her recovery. Together, they crisscrossed Canada, especially the West and Northwest Coast.

By 1902, Pauline began to prepare a second volume of poems. Only sixty-seven pages long, *Canadian Born* (1903) contained little new poetry. Of the thiry-one poems, at least ten were composed before the publication of *The White Wampum*. Many were from the Smily-Johnson selection called "There and Back." Although the book increased public interest in her performances, it lowered Pauline's status among critics, who found little in it to praise. From 1904 on, Pauline turned her creative energies to writing prose.

Invigorated by renewed public response to her performances, Pauline undertook another trip to London, arriving in April 1906. Friends such as Sir Gilbert Parker helped her to meet influential people. Among these was Algernon Swinburne, whom she had admired since childhood. Determined not to limit her performances on this trip to social evenings in private houses, Pauline gave a recital on 16 July at Steinway Hall. Both Pauline and her partner McRaye received enthusiastic response from the public and the reviewers. During this trip, she also sought out new markets for her essays and stories. One of the three articles that the *London Daily Express* published that summer was "A Pagan in St. Paul's," later included in *The Moccasin Maker*. However, because the focus of her work was on the contrast between Indian and white societies, Pauline found only a limited market in England.

Far more significant to the future direction of her work was her meeting with the Squamish chief Joe Capilano. With two other Northwest Coast chiefs, Chief Joe had come to London to protest both white encroachments on their land and new game and fishing restrictions that deprived the tribes of needed food. Because the chiefs spoke little English, Pauline, who knew only a little Chinook, was asked to speak to them. Although she left the interview unsure of what the chiefs wanted, she made a fast friend in Chief Joe.

Pauline and McRaye left England in November. The year 1907 was a busy one for Pauline. Not only did she write a series of stories and articles for *Mother's Magazine*, published in Elgin, Illinois, but she also made a third visit to London in April. However, during this trip, she neither performed nor found an English outlet for her writing. By June she was back in Brantford for the marriage of her brother Allen—the only one of the Johnson children to marry. In July she and McRaye joined the Chautauqua circuit, touring primarily in the Midwest and the Plains. They traveled with William Jennings Bryan during part of their tour. For the next two years, Pauline and McRaye toured Canada, concentrating on the West and Northwest Coast. Despite her hectic schedule, Pauline completed a great many prose works for such journals as *Mother's Magazine* and *Boys' World*.

During the summer of 1908 she decided to retire from performing and make her permanent home in Vancouver, where she had both friends and periodical outlets for her writing. However, in order to give McRaye time to build his own following and herself time to accumulate some savings, Pauline postponed retirement until 1909. Settled in an apartment within walking distance of Stanley Park, she plunged into her writing. She also began a collaboration with Chief Joe Capilano that led to some of her best writing. Adding her own sense of imagination and drama, Pauline refashioned the Chinook stories told her by the old Squamish chief, who succumbed to tuberculosis in March 1910. The Vancouver *Province* published the series in 1910 and 1911. Although she did not know it, Pauline herself had only a few years to live. In 1910, she learned that the cancer in her breast was too widespread for surgery. During her remaining years, Pauline worked when the cancer was in remission. Often heavily drugged with morphine, she continued her writing, saw friends, and walked when she had the strength. To assist her financially, friends and members of the Women's Press Club and the Women's Canadian Club of Vancouver arranged to have the Capilano stories published and the profits put in trust for her. Despite Pauline's desire that the volume be entitled "The Legends of the Capilanos," to honor Chief Joe, the volume was published in 1911 under the title *The Legends of Vancouver*. Although thought to be near death, Pauline rallied and began work on a collected edition of her poems entitled *Flint and Feather*. The collection, published in 1912, contained the poems from *The White Wampum* and *Canadian Born* as well as some of the poems written later. The Women's Press Club aided Pauline once more, arranging to publish a collection of her stories written for *Boys' World* in a volume called *The Shagganappi*. They also prepared a second collection entitled *The Moccasin Maker*, which consisted of several of her stories and the essay "A Pagan in St. Paul's." Both books were published posthumously in 1913.

The anguish of her last months was relieved by a visit in September 1912 from the Duke of Connaught, then governor-general of Canada. In terrible pain, Pauline lingered until 7 March. The Canadian Women's Club carried out her funeral wishes. On 10 March her funeral procession, which included a large contingent from Vancouver society, marched past streets lined with people. Christ Church Cathedral was filled to capacity for the funeral service. As she wished, Pauline was cremated in Vancouver. Her ashes, which she had asked to be disposed of as near the Pacific Ocean as possible, were buried in her beloved Stanley Park. Despite her express desire that there be no memorial, the Women's Canadian Club, assisted by the Daughters of the Empire, erected a monument to her in 1922.

II

According to Anne (Mrs. Garland) Foster, *The Moccasin Maker* was originally to be entitled *The Moccasin Makers* because it was to include stories of the Six Nations. However, by the time the collection was put together, Pauline was too ill to carry out her original plan (115). The published volume, consisting of one essay and eleven short stories, focuses primarily on women. Only one of the eleven short stories, "Her Majesty's Guest," does not have a woman either as protagonist or as a major character.

Most of the stories were originally published in *Mother's Magazine*, a journal owned by the David C. Cook Publishing Company of Elgin, Illinois. This firm also owned *Boys' World*, Pauline's primary market for her boys' stories. On 26 March 1907, Elizabeth Ansley, managing editor of *Mother's Magazine*, took Pauline up on her offer to write for the magazine, suggesting that "it occurs to us that you might have something very good to offer the mothers in the way of Outdoor Sports, Mother and Child out-of-doors, Health Exercises, Picnics, Camping, etc., all written especially for the mother, and her family." Pleased with the material Pauline sent to *Boys' World*, Ansley wrote to Pauline on 13 August, encouraging her once more to send material to *Mother's Magazine* and outlining what the journal wanted: "We are endeavoring to lighten the tone of The Mother's Magazine somewhat, and are looking for matter along popular lines. We want to picture only the best and highest; but we do want the good attractively presented. We want some humor and bright, happy stories that will serve as a recreation for the mother when she picks up the Magazine."[7]

From 1907 to 1912, Pauline contributed frequently to *Mother's Magazine*, averaging five pieces per year. During this period, her stories and articles were often the lead features. Her contributions declined as she became terminally ill. Several of the stories in *The Moccasin Maker* appeared in 1909: "Mother O' the Men" (February); "The Envoy Extraordinary" (March); "My Mother" (April, May, June, July). In 1910, "The Nest-Builder" (March) and "Catharine of the Crow's Nest" (December) appeared. "The Tenas Klootchman" was published in August 1911 and "The Legend of Lillooet Falls" in January 1912.

Widely read, *Mother's Magazine* had a circulation of 600,000 in 1910. From 1905 to 1912, it published a great deal of fiction. It also featured articles on wives' rights and mothers' duties, such as knowing one's husband's income and the best methods of child raising; interviews with famous women; spiritual guidance; and numerous pieces on the cultures of foreign countries. After 1915, it printed more articles than fiction, perhaps reflecting American women's increased interest in serious issues during World War I. Around the same time, the magazine also changed from publishing predominantly female authors to predominantly male ones.

Although critics in Johnson's own day praised her powerful treatment of Indian themes and her beautiful descriptions of nature, they ignored her vivid portrayals of women, one of the strongest dimensions of her work. Focusing their attention on the influence of Romanticism on Johnson's work, they have neglected that of nineteenth-century English and American fiction written by women. Nina Baym states in *Woman's Fiction: A Guide to Novels by and About Women in America, 1820–1870* that after the Civil War, women dominated the reading public (13). Most of the American authors at that time were middle-class women who needed money: "only middle-class women had sufficient education to know how to write books, and only those who needed money attempted it" (30). In *A Literature of Their Own: British Women Novelists from Brontë to Lessing,* Elaine Showalter indicates that when the three-decker novel abruptly disappeared in the 1890s because of changes in its marketability, women turned to writing short stories and fragments (30–31). Certainly, Pauline Johnson followed both the tradition of being a middle-class woman who supported herself partly by her pen and of writing short stories rather than novels.

Pauline's stories reflect the themes dominant in women's nineteenth-century fiction. According to Baym, all American women's fiction from 1820 to 1870 shares the same story of "trials and triumph." The heroine encounters mistreatment, unfairness, disadvantage, and powerlessness which result from her status as female and child. The heroine accepts herself as female while rejecting the equation of female with permanent child. Baym suggests that these novels represent a moderate, limited, or pragmatic feminism (18). Showalter finds a similar direction in novels by British women (28–29). American women authors, according to Baym, accepted the popular belief that men and women were essentially different. They were profoundly Victorian in their oppressive sense of reality's habit of disappointing expectations and in their conviction that duty, discipline, self-control, and limited sacrifice were "not only moral but actually useful strategies for getting through a hard world" (18). They were also Victorian in their perception of the self as a social product, "firmly and irrevocably embedded in a social construct that could destroy it but that also shaped it, constrained it, encouraged it, and ultimately fulfilled it" (36). Confronted by those who abuse their power over the heroine or are uncongenial, the heroine endures her lot until she comes of age and matures psychologically so that she can leave the hostile environment and succeed on her own. As a result of meeting the challenges presented by life, the heroine develops a strong sense of self-worth (37–38).

Showalter points out that the women's novel, from Jane Austen to George Eliot, moved in the direction of "an all-inclusive female realism, a broad, socially informed exploration of the daily lives and values of women within the family and community" (29). Feminists challenged many of the restrictions on "women's self-expression, denounced patriarchal religion, and constructed a theoretical model of female oppression, but their anger with society and their need for self-justification often led them away from realism into oversimplification, emotionalism, and fantasy (ibid).

Baym argues that it is erroneous to label as sentimental the novels written by American women from 1820 to 1870 because such judgments are "culture-bound; the critic of a later time is refusing to assent to the work's conventions" (24). Like the novels by their English counterparts, those by American women contain almost no sex and are not graphic about body functions because the authors deplored such experience, wishing to live less brutal lives than had women in the past. Consequently, they idealized "the pretty and tender while representing many other aspects of experience. For the same reason, they assumed a rhetoric that was intended to transcend the pain and crudeness of the things they had to represent" (24–25). Unlike the authors of the novels of sensibility, such as Samuel Richardson, American women writing after 1820 did not emphasize feelings, because they objected to the sexual center of the novels of sensibility which they felt presented woman as inevitable sexual prey (25–26). Showalter finds a similar awareness of, and revulsion from, sexuality in the works of nineteenth-century British women writers.

Most of their fiction, Baym states, was about social relations, "generally set in homes and other social spaces that are fully described" (26). Although home life is almost always unhappy, these novels assume that men and women find their "greatest happiness and fulfillment in domestic relations, by which are meant not simply spouse and parent, but the whole network of human attachments based on love, support, and mutual responsibility." The domestic ideal meant not that woman was to be sequestered from the world in her place at home but rather that everybody was to be placed in the home, so that home and world became one. (27).

Like nineteenth-century English and American women writers, Pauline champions Victorian values. Her heroines in *The Moccasin Maker* inevitably triumph over great difficulty. Both they and her heroes recognize that genuine love between men and women, love that reflects shared values, is the greatest fulfillment in life. Although Pauline clearly feels that, for a woman, domestic life centered around husband and children represents the ideal, many of her heroines are alone—whether as widows or as wives temporarily or permanently separated from their husbands. Even when husband and children are present, Pauline sometimes stresses the isolation that a wife can feel if she follows her husband into the wilderness or when a quarrel separates family members. Her heroines inevitably triumph over difficulties.

Pauline's portraits of white wives and mothers are idealized, even though she places them in realistic situations. In fact, several of her plots are based on true stories Pauline heard. In "My Mother," Pauline gives the fullest description of this ideal in her portrayal of her mother, Emily Susanna Howells Johnson, as Lydia Best. Despite their different racial and cultural backgrounds, Lydia and George Mansion, the pseudonym for George H. M. Johnson, achieve in their marriage a harmonious union in which two hearts and minds act as one. The couple spent thirty years together without ever quarreling because "their tastes and distastes were so synonymous; they hated hypocrisy, vulgarity, slovenliness, imitations" (70). They shared a love of nature, books, beautiful objects, the Anglican Church, and England. Most of all they shared a love of Indians. Lydia's marriage, based on mutual love, respect, and interests, represents the ideal relationship between man and woman celebrated by such writers as Shelley and desired by Pauline herself. It contrasts sharply with the marriages of her two sisters. Elizabeth (Eliza Beulah Elliot) is wedded to a man she does not love; and an unnamed sister (Mary Rogers) is wedded to a man who, as master of his house, commands her obedience. Despite Pauline's decision to become a career woman, she clearly believes that a wife and mother's place is in the home. She portrays Lydia as a strong support of her husband, who went off to "fight the enemy, storm the battlements and win the laurels" while she kept the garrison at home to "welcome... our warrior husband and father when he returns from war" (p. 73). That her husband agreed with this choice is clear from Pauline's comment that her George "felt that his wife had chosen the wiser, greater part; that their children would some day arise and call her blessed because she refused to wing away from the home nest, even if by so doing she left him to take his flights alone" (p. 74). Lydia's own strength is tested when she cares tirelessly for her husband on the occasions when he falls seriously ill and when he barely survives savage beatings and shootings.

The portrait of the mother as her husband's loyal

helpmeet, who exhibits both courage and resource-fulness in caring for her family, is reflected as well in "The Nest Builder," "Envoy Extraordinary," and "Mother O' the Men." The model for the pro-tagonist in the third story, Mrs. Lysle, and for sev-eral wives and mothers in Pauline's later stories, is Mrs. Henrietta Armstrong Constantine (1857–1934), wife of Inspector Charles Constantine (1849 –1912; Keller 200–201). Although Mrs. Lysle, like Lydia Mansion, believes that her place is beside her husband, she also feels great loneliness at being cut off from other women. Both this story and "Nest Builder" celebrate the strength of character that enabled pioneer woman to triumph over great hardships.

What distinguishes Pauline's stories in *The Moc-casin Maker* from short stories by women in the late nineteenth century is her frequent use of Indian heroines. Mother love is as powerful a force among her Indian as among her non-Indian heroines. Her characterization of her Mohawk grandmother in "My Mother" demonstrates the deep love Indian mothers feel for their children, as well as the roles they play as guardians of tribal traditions. Indian mothers' love for children is demonstrated in three other stories in *The Moccasin Maker*. "The Legend of Lillooet Falls" shows how the depth of this love is embodied in the mythology of Northwest Coast Indians. To introduce the story, Pauline uses a technique she also used to good effect in "Tenas Klootchman" and *Legends of Vancouver*— creating a character who tells the story to Johnson. This narra-tive technique enables Johnson to insert into the story the characterization of an old woman cajoled into telling the story of how the Lillooet Falls were created by the earth god when a mother asked him to make the cobweb chains binding her to her child sing of her gratitude for the return of her lost child. Two other stories portray the deep attachment Indian mothers feel for their adopted children, both Indian and white: "Tenas Klootchman" and "Catharine of 'Crow's Nest.'"

In her stories about Indian women, Johnson not only creates memorable characterizations but also dramatizes the traumatic consequences of white contact on Indian life. The consequence she most frequently dramatizes is the tragedy Indian women experience when they fall in love with white men. Charles Mair's comment that "the defeat of love runs like a grey thread through much of Miss Johnson's verse" is equally true of her fiction ("An Appreciation," *Canadian Magazine*, 41 [1913]: 281). Three stories on this theme are included in *The Moccasin Maker:* "A Red Girl's Reasoning," "As It Was in the Beginning," and "The Derelict." Although the prevalence of this theme in her work after 1898 undoubtedly reflects her bitterness over her broken engagement to Charles Drayton, this was not the stimulus for "Red Girl's Reasoning," first published in 1893. The story presents an especially strong feminist perspective for the period because the heroine rejects the security of a prominent marriage in order to remain true to herself and her Indian heritage. In addition to making the story a standard part of her own repertoire, Pauline performed a dramatized version with her partner

Smily. She also considered expanding the story into a play.

Like the other two stories, "A Red Girl's Reasoning" combines the theme of the mixed-blood woman's love for a weak white man with a forceful attack on white religious hypocrisy. The central issue in the story is white refusal to accept the sanctity of Indian marriages conducted in tribal ceremonies. The heroine, Christine Robinson, is the product of such a union. After marrying Charles McDonald, Christine leaves her home at her father's isolated trading post for a new life in a provincial capital. Charles shatters their happiness by rebuking Christine for revealing to their acquaintances that her parents had neither a church nor a magistrate wedding. Christine eloquently defends Indian marriage, reminding Charles that there was no priest present "at the most holy marriage known to humanity—that stainless marriage whose offspring is the God you white men told my pagan mother of " (116). Christine not only leaves her narrow-minded husband to resettle in a small town, but she also firmly rejects his plea that she return to him: " 'neither church, nor law, nor even' and the voice softened— 'nor even love can make a slave of a red girl" ' (124).

This highly melodramatic story emphasizes that in order for a mixed-blood and a white to achieve a happy marriage, each must respect the other's culture. It also stresses the arrogance of the dominant white society which assumes that only its laws and customs are valid. The heroine is temporarily successful in her move into the white world, becoming

the "rage" of the provincial town which is capti-
vated by her beauty, charm, and vivacity (105).
When the two cultures inevitably clash, she must
choose between the Indian and white world. Like
most of the mixed-bloods in American Indian
fiction, she identifies with the Indian world, which
she feels is more virtuous and less hypocritical than
the white.

In "As It Was in the Beginning," the mixed-
blood heroine takes physical as well as verbal revenge against an unfaithful white lover. Here
Pauline uses a first-person narration, which intensi-
fies the dramatization of the heroine's reactions
when she learns she has been betrayed. Pauline's
attack on white religious hypocrisy is even stronger
here than in "Red Girl's Reasoning" because the
French and Cree heroine, Esther, is betrayed both
by her lover and by the priest who took her as a
child from her parents and kept her isolated from
all things Indian. Elizabeth Loosley finds this de-
piction of the white missionary difficult to accept,
"even with due allowance for Victorian melo-
drama" ("Pauline Johnson" 84–85). However, the
missionary reflects the prejudice against mixed
bloods, especially French-Indian mixed bloods,
common in American literature of the period.
William Scheick notes that because of Anglo-
American revulsion at intermarriage between
whites and Indians, "time and again, observations
on the half-blood convey covert attacks on the
French, the French-Canadians (particularly in the
Midwest and the Far West) and the Spanish or
Mexicans (particularly in the Southwest)." Scheick

suggests that in the white American psyche there existed a vague "sense that as long as half-blood were prominent in frontier settlements, the implementation of American Manifest Destiny would be impeded, for the mixed-blood represented the persistence of both an Indian and an alien European presence in America" (5). Through her characterization of the missionary's revulsion at the prospect of Esther's marriage to his nephew, Pauline strongly implies that similar feelings existed among British Canadians. Further, her emphasis on the white clergy's prejudice against Indians reflects a theme present in literature written by Indians since the early nineteenth century, from *The Son of the Forest* (1829) by William Apes (Pequot) to *The Surrounded* (1934) by D'Arcy McNickle (Salish/Cree) and *Winter in the Blood* (1974) by James Welch (Blackfeet/ Gros Ventre).

Despite the tragic conclusions of "Red Girl's Reasoning" and "As It Was from the Beginning," Pauline's stories about liaisons between white men and Indian women do not always end tragically for the women. In "The Derelict," Pauline provides a happy ending in which the weak white man gains from his Indian beloved the strength to oppose the hypocrisy of the Anglican Church.

Pauline's stories reflect her reading of English Romantic writers. In "As It Was in the Beginning," the priest refers to Esther as a snake, an allusion both to the serpent in the Garden of Eden and to the Lamia figure from classical mythology, who entwined herself around her victims in order to devour them. Coleridge used this figure in *Christabel*, and Keats in *Lamia*. Esther is the literary descendant of the Gothic and Byronic heroes as well as of Emily Brontë's Heathcliff. Like them, she is proud. Possessing the capacity for both good and evil, she, like these heroes, seeks revenge for the injustices she suffers. Pauline's reading of Byron is reflected as well in her portrayal of the hero of "The Derelict," Charles Cragstone, as a Byronic hero: a handsome, brilliant outcast estranged from his family in England for committing some unnamed but "inexcusable offence" (212). As a Byronic hero, Charles is equally capable of self-destructive rebellion or great courage in defense of a noble cause. The influence of Romanticism is also evident in Pauline's description of Crow's Nest Pass, which is reminiscent of Shelley's "Mont Blanc."

Pauline's nonfiction prose is represented in *The Moccasin Maker* only by "A Pagan in St. Paul's Cathedral." During the summer of 1906, the *London Daily Express* published this essay, "The Lodge of the Law-Makers," and "The Silent News-Carrier." Keller notes that, although the other two were well received, "A Pagan in St. Paul's Cathedral" especially caught the public's imagination because it described a savage Indian (perhaps an earlier incarnation of Pauline herself). This Indian "is drawn into the midst of the worshippers in the great cathedral and, at the conclusion, finds there is no difference between his form of worship and theirs" (216).

In this essay, Pauline poetically evokes a romantic past in which Canadian Indians lived in harmony with nature. She emphasizes that whites worship in a building, while Indians worship in nature. The cathedral music of the "deep-throated organ and the boys voices" remind her of the Iroquois chants and dances that accompany the "White Dog Sacrifice." Pauline made a similar comparison between Iroquois and white religious worship in her essay "The Iroquois of the Grand River" (*Harper's Weekly*, 23 June 1894, 587–89), in which she also included a brief description of the "White Dog Sacrifice." Pauline's fascination with this ceremony, which she witnessed as a small child in the company of her father and ethnologist Horatio Hale, is relected as well in her more detailed account "The Great New Year White Dog: Sacrifice of the Onondagas" (*The Daily Province Magazine*, 14 January 1911:16).

Elizabeth Loosley comments that the pull between the Indian and white worlds that characterizes so much of Pauline's work is also evident in her attitude toward religion. In her poetry Johnson often presents conventional religious attitudes. "In her prose, she wavers between almost violent antipathy towards orthodox Christianity ('As It Was in the Beginning'; 'Her Majesty's Guest'; and 'The Derelict,' all included in *The Moccasin Maker*) and a more sympathetic attitude towards the Christian faith but without any seemingly deep commitment to it" ("Pauline Johnson" 87). As "A Pagan in St. Paul's" and her stories illustrate, Pauline believed that to worship a higher power, live in harmony with nature, and respect all men—regardless of race or religious belief—were more important than the means by which these were expressed.

III

To dismiss E. Pauline Johnson's work as melo-dramatic romanticism designed to tug the heart-strings of her audiences is to deny her impact as a performer and writer on the development of Cana-dian literature. Her hectic stage schedule and her need to write what could be sold or performed clearly inhibited her growth as a writer. Neverthe-less, her works appealed to the fundamental emo-tions of her audiences, who viewed her not only as an author but also as a vibrant presence who could dramatize these emotions before their enraptured eyes. She was among the first to introduce her fron-tier audiences in the Canadian West to the excite-ment of literature. Her work reflected the popular taste of her age. According to Norman Shrive, while audiences flocked to her performances and bought her books, two genuinely literary magazines of the period, *Canadian Monthly* and Toronto *Week,* died for lack of support, evidence "of the gap between the literary critic, the poet and the popular taste" ("What Happened to Pauline" 30). Seventy-two years after her death, her work continues to be pop-ular, as evidenced by the fact that both her *Legends of Vancouver* (1911) and *Flint and Feather* (1912), the collection of her poems, are still in print.

Both as a performer and as a writer, Pauline is best known as an interpreter of the Indian to non-Indian audiences. Shrive accurately describes her as "one of the few people who saw through the popu-lar image of the Indian and who said so in writing"

(32). During Pauline's lifetime the stereotype of the bloodthirsty savage was vividly reinforced in the public's mind by accounts of the Indian wars in the United States and by the mixed-blood rebellions led by Louis Riel in Canada (1869–70, 1884–85). Fears of Indian uprisings in the United States were fanned in 1890 by the Ghost Dance Movement that spread through Indian reservations and by the massacre at Wounded Knee.[8]

To counteract the stereotypes of the "bloodthirsty savage" and the venial mixed blood, stock figures in the westerns of the period, Pauline creates idealized portraits of Indian and mixed-blood women who possess far more goodness and morality than do the whites who betray them or who are slow to recognize their virtues. However, as Shrive points out, Pauline ironically became part of the artificiality against which she protested in her writing. Although she protested against stereotypical "noble Savages," she also used them in her work. For example, her young mixed-blood heroines are unfailingly beautiful, possessing the best qualities of both the red and white races. They also bear a marked physical resemblance to Pauline herself. Christine, the heroine of "A Red Girl's Reasoning," is described as looking "much the same as her sisters, all Canada through, who are the offspring of red and white parentage—olive-complexioned, gray-eyed, black-haired, with figure slight and delicate, and the wistful, unfathomable expression in her whole face that turns one so heart-sick as they glance at the young Indians of to-day—it is the forerunner too frequently of 'the white man's dis-

ease,' consumption. . ." (104). The heroine of
"The Derelict" possesses similar physical characteristics: ". . . a type of mixed blood, pale, dark,
slender, with the slim hands, the marvelously beautiful teeth of her mother's people, the ambition,
the small tender mouth, the utter fearlessness of
the English race. But the strange, laughless eyes,
the silent step, the hard sense of honor, proclaimed
her far more a daughter of red blood than of white"
(213). Pauline's mixed-blood heroines are unfailingly loyal to the men they love until betrayed.
Her Indian mothers are virtuous to a fault.
However, the situations in which Pauline involves
her heroines are real, and she attempts to make her
heroines reflect their tribal heritages, rather than
relying, as did most non-Indian authors, on artificial
creations that owe more to Chateaubriand's *Atala*
than to existing Indian cultures.

In *The Moccasin Maker,* the primary vehicle
Johnson uses to convey this message is the short
story. However, even her most ardent admirers,
such as Mrs. W. Garland (Anne) Foster and Sir
Gilbert Parker, recognize that this genre was not
her forte. Foster excuses Pauline's lack of sophis-
tication in her short stories by reminding us that
"short story writing was not the highly conven-
tionalized art it is to-day. So that her stories should
be compared with the stories of the period in which
she wrote" (116). Sir Gilbert, in his introduction,
comments that, although she was never without
charm, "mere charm was too often her undoing.
She could not be impersonal enough, and therefore
could not be great; but she could get very near to

human sympathies, to domestic natures, to those who care for pleasant, happy things, to the lovers of the wild" (6). He sees her as a poet rather than a writer of fiction. Nevertheless, Sir Gilbert justly praises her for her picturesque style and her "good sense of the salient incident that always makes a story, she could give to it the touch of drama" (7).

Pauline's literary work belongs to the first renaissance in Canadian literature, consisting of authors born between the years 1860 and 1862. J. D. Logan and Donald G. French note that the work of this renaissance, published from 1887, was marked by a "noteworthy artistic finish in the craftsmanship not noted in the works of earlier Canadian poets" (107). The editors of the *Literary History of Canada* attribute her continuing popularity to the fact that Johnson "is still what she was at the very beginning, a symbol which satisfied a felt need. Like Service and Campbell, she associates a broadly Romantic view of life with the elements of the vast natural landscape. This need to realize topography in terms of life is, of course, the fundamental fact of Canadian experience" (442). Another need that Pauline's work satisfies is the need to portray the experiences and emotions of two minority groups whose voices were little heard in the Canadian literature of Johnson's own day—Indians and women.

Acknowledgments

I am grateful to William W. Howells, professor emeritus of the Department of Anthropology of Harvard University, for sharing with me the information he had gathered about the genealogy and history of the Howells family. I am also grateful to Geoffrey L. Fairs for his assistance in my research on this family. J. Ross Elliot provided information about the Adam Elliot family. Franchot Ballinger, Department of Humanities, University of Cincinnati, located for me the copy of Henry C. Howells's *Letters from Ohio* in the Cincinnati Historical Society. Donald Smith, Department of History, University of Calgary, and Sally Weaver, Department of Anthropology, University of Waterloo, provided material about the Johnson family; Thomas King, Native American Studies, University of Lethbridge, helped search for Lillooet Indian legends. Catherine Brettman, David C. Cook Publishing Company, Elgin, Illinois, searched company archives for information about Pauline's relationship with *Mother's Magazine.*

My research was facilitated by Beth Hanna, Director, Brantford Historical Society and Museum, Brantford, Ontario, and by many American and Canadian librarians who were unfailingly generous in providing information. I am especially grateful to Kathleen Browne, Interlibrary Loan Department, University of Illinois at Chicago. The following assisted me in my research on E. Pauline Johnson and the Johnson family: Michael Doxtater, Woodland Indian Cultural Educational Center, Brantford, Ontario; William Russell, Social Affairs and Natural Resources Records, Public Archives of Canada, Ottawa, Ontario; Bruce Whiteman, Mills Library, Hamilton, Ontario; and Brian A. Young, Manuscripts and Government Records Division, Province of British Columbia; Gladys Zimmerman, Brantford, Ontario. Information about the Howells, Elliot, and Rogers families was provided by Shirley C. Spragge, Library, Queens University, Kingston, Ontario; Ione B. Suppler, Muskingum County Genealogical Library, Zanesville, Ohio; Janet A. Thompson, Ohio Historical Society, Columbus; and Charles Addington, V. P. Cronyn Memorial Archives, Huron College, London, Ontario. My search for information about the Constantines was aided by Benoit Cameron, Massey Library, Royal Military College of Canada, Kingston, Ontario; Michael Dicketts, Kingston Public Library, Ontario; Linda Dixon, Library, University of Winnipeg, Manitoba; Donna Fedorowich, Library Department, City of Winnipeg; S. W. Horrell, Historian, Royal Canadian Mounted Police; Barry Hyman, Provincial Archives, Manitoba. D. Roberta Griffiths of the David Thompson Library, Nelson, British Columbia, provided material about the gold strike on Kootenay Lake.

My husband, Gene W. Ruoff, patiently read through drafts of the manuscript.

Study for this edition was begun under a grant from the Research Division, National Endowment for the Humanities.

The editor's fee has been donated to the fund for restoration of Chiefswood, Six Nations Grand River Reserve.

Notes

1. My primary biographical source is Betty Keller, *Pauline: A Biography of Pauline Johnson.*

2. I have adopted the spelling used by Evelyn Johnson in "The Martin Settlement" (57). She uses the spelling "Teyonkekwen" in "Chief John Smoke Johnson" (110). Other spellings of this title are Teyonhehkwen, Teyonhehkon, Deyonhegweh, and Deyonhehgon. See also Whale 43; Hale, "Chief George H. M. Johnson—Onwanonsyshon" 136; Chadwick 87; Leighton, "Johnson, George Henry Martin" 452; and Weaver field notes.

3. For information about John Smoke Johnson, Helen Martin Johnson, and their ancestors, see particularly

36

Evelyn Johnson, "Chief John Smoke Johnson," "Grandfather and Father of E. Pauline Johnson," and "The Martin Settlement." See also Leighton, "Johnson, John."

4. For a more detailed account, see the notes on the beatings, pp. 85–91 of *MM*.

5. Gerson 17–18. McRaye's first letter to MacTavish about the matter appears to be dated "4/13" but could not have been written before July. Holograph letter in Newton MacTavish Papers, North York Public Library, Ontario.

6. Holograph letter in McTavish Papers, North York Public Library, Ontario.

7. Both letters in E. Pauline Johnson Coll., Mills Lib., MacMaster Univ., F 5. 10, 6.

8. The Ghost Dance Movement that swept the Plains in 1890 was inspired by the teachings of Wovoka, or Jack Wilson, a Paiute who claimed to have received the message from the Great Spirit that the Plains would support millions of buffalo and that the whites would disappear. Within a few weeks, thousands on the northern Plains converted to this movement. After dancing and fasting themselves into states of unconsciousness, Sioux converts described visits with dead tribesmen who spoke of returning to earth. Warrior converts prepared shirts with magic symbols that would ward off white men's bullets. These activities aroused the concern of the government. When a band of Ghost Dancers left their agency, the Seventh Cavalry overtook them and ordered them to turn in all weapons. In the resulting melee, white soldiers killed over 250 of 350 Indians, most of whom were women and children. Only 25 soldiers were killed. This massacre signaled the end of Indians' wars against whites. See especially James Mooney, *The Ghost Dance Religion and the Sioux Outbreak of 1890*. For a brief account see Hagen 129–33.

The stories that follow are a direct photographic reproduction of the 1913 edition published by the Ryerson Press of Toronto, with original pagination retained. The commentary by LaVonne Ruoff has replaced the earlier introductory material.

MY MOTHER

The Story of a Life of Unusual Experiences

[AUTHOR'S NOTE.—This is the story of my mother's life, every
incident of which she related to me herself.   I have neither exag-
gerated nor curtailed a single circumstance in relating this story.
I have supplied nothing through imagination, nor have I height-
ened the coloring of her unusual experiences.   Had I done so I
could not possibly feel as sure of her approval as I now do, for she
is as near to me to-day as she was before she left me to join her
husband, my beloved father, whose feet have long since wandered
to the "Happy Hunting Grounds" of my dear Red Ancestors.]

PART I

*I*T WAS a very lonely little girl that stood on
the deck of a huge sailing vessel while the shores
of England slipped down into the horizon and
the great, grey Atlantic yawned desolately westward.   She was leaving so much behind her, taking
so little with her, for the child was grave and
old even at the age of eight, and realized that this
day meant the updragging of all the tiny roots that
clung to the home soil of the older land.   Her father
was taking his wife and family, his household goods,
his fortune and his future to America, which, in
the days of 1829, was indeed a venturesome step,
for America was regarded as remote as the North
Pole, and good-byes were, alas! very real good-
byes, when travellers set sail for the New World
in those times before steam and telegraph brought
the two continents hand almost touching hand.

So little Lydia Bestman stood drearily watching with sorrow-filled eyes the England of her

23

babyhood fade slowly into the distance—eyes that were fated never to see again the royal old land of her birth. Already the deepest grief that life could hold had touched her young heart. She had lost her own gentle, London-bred mother when she was but two years old. Her father had married again, and on her sixth birthday little Lydia, the youngest of a large family, had been sent away to boarding-school with an elder sister, and her home knew her no more. She was taken from school to the sailing ship; little stepbrothers and sisters had arrived and she was no longer the baby. Years afterwards she told her own little children that her one vivid recollection of England was the exquisite music of the church chimes as the ship weighed anchor in Bristol harbor—chimes that were ringing for evensong from the towers of the quaint old English churches. Thirteen weeks later that sailing vessel entered New York harbor, and life in the New World began.

Like most transplanted Englishmen, Mr. Bestman cut himself completely off from the land of his fathers; his interests and his friends henceforth were all in the country of his adoption, and he chose Ohio as a site for his new home. He was a man of vast peculiarities, prejudices and extreme ideas—a man of contradictions so glaring that even his own children never understood him. He was a very narrow religionist, of the type that say many prayers and quote much Scripture, but he beat his children—both girls and boys—so severely that outsiders were at times compelled to interfere. For years these unfortunate children carried the scars left on their backs by the thongs of cat-o'-nine-tails when he punished them for some slight misdemeanor. They were all terrified at him, all obeyed him like soldiers, but none escaped his severity. The two elder ones, a boy and a girl, had married before they left England. The next girl married in Ohio, and the boys drifted away, glad to escape from a parental tyranny that made home anything but a desirable abiding-place. Finally but two remained of the first family—Lydia and her sister Elizabeth, a most lovable girl of seventeen, whose beauty of character and self-sacrificing heart made the one bright memory that remained with these scattered fledglings throughout their entire lives.

The lady who occupied the undesirable position of stepmother to these unfortunate children was of the very cold and chilling type of Englishwoman, more frequently met with two generations ago than in this age. She simply let her husband's first family alone. She took no interest in them, neglected them absolutely, but in her neglect was far kinder and more humane than their own father. Yet she saw that all the money, all the pretty clothes, all the dainties, went to her own children.

Perhaps the reader will think these unpleasant characteristics of a harsh father and a self-centred stepmother might better be omitted from this narrative, particularly as death claimed these two many years ago; but in the light of after events, it is necessary to reveal what the home environment of these children had been, how little of companionship or kindness or spoken love had

25

entered their baby lives. The absence of mother kisses, of father comradeship, of endeavor to understand them individually, to probe their separate and various dispositions—things so essential to the development of all that is best in a child—went far towards governing their later actions in life. It drove the unselfish, sweet-hearted Elizabeth to a loveless marriage; it flung poor, little, love-hungry Lydia into alien but, fortunately, loyal and noble arms. Outsiders said, "What strange marriages!" But Lydia, at least, married where the first real kindness she had ever known called to her, and not one day of regret for that marriage ever entered into her life.

It came about so strangely, so inevitably, from such a tiny source, that it is almost incredible.

One day the stepmother, contrary to her usual custom, went into the kitchen and baked a number of little cakelets, probably what we would call cookies. For what sinister reason no one could divine, but she counted these cakes as she took them from the baking-pans and placed them in the pantry. There were forty-nine, all told. That evening she counted them again; there were forty-eight. Then she complained to her husband that one of the children had evidently stolen a cake. (In her mind the two negro servants employed in the house did not merit the suspicion.) Mr. Bestman inquired which child was fond of the cakes. Mrs. Bestman replied that she did not know, unless it was Lydia, who always liked them.

26

Lydia was called. Her father, frowning, asked if she had taken the cake. The child said no.

"You are not telling the truth," Mr. Bestman shouted, as the poor little downtrodden girl stood half terrified, consequently half guilty-mannered, before him.

"But I am truthful," she said. "I know nothing of the cake."

"You are not truthful. You stole it—you know you did. You shall be punished for this falsehood," he stormed, and reached for the cat-o'-nine-tails.

The child was beaten brutally and sent to her room until she could tell the truth. When she was released she still held that she had not taken the cooky. Another beating followed, then a third, when finally the stepmother interfered and said magnanimously:

"Don't whip her any more; she has been punished enough." And once during one of the beatings she protested, saying, "Don't strike the child *on the head* that way."

But the iron had entered into Lydia's sister's soul. The injustice of it all drove gentle Elizabeth's gentleness to the winds.

"Liddy darling," she said, taking the thirteen-year-old girl-child into her strong young arms, "*I* know truth when I hear it. *You* never stole that cake."

"I didn't," sobbed the child, "I didn't."

"And you have been beaten three times for it!" And the sweet young mouth hardened into lines

27

that were far too severe for a girl of seventeen.
Then: "Liddy, do you know that Mr. Evans has
asked me to marry him?"

"Mr. Evans!" exclaimed the child. "Why, you
can't marry *him*, 'Liza! He's so ever old, and he
lives away up in Canada, among the Indians."

"That's one of the reasons that I should like
to marry him," said Elizabeth, her young eyes
starry with zeal. "I want to work among the
Indians, to help in Christianizing them, to—oh!
just to help."

"But Mr. Evans is so *old*," reiterated Lydia.

"Only thirty," answered the sister; "and he is
such a splendid missionary, dear."

Love? No one talked of love in that household
except the contradictory father, who continually
talked of the love of God, but forgot to reflect that
love towards his own children.

Human love was considered a non-essential in
that family. Beautiful-spirited Elizabeth had
hardly heard the word. Even Mr. Evans had not
made use of it. He had selected her as his wife
more for her loveliness of character than from any
personal attraction, and she in her untaught womanhood married him, more for the reason that she
desired to be a laborer in Christ's vineyard than
because of any wish to be the wife of this one man.

But after the marriage ceremony, this gentle
girl looked boldly into her father's eyes and said:

"I am going to take Liddy with me into the
wilds of Canada."

"Well, well, well!" said her father, English-
fashion. "If she wants to go, she may."

Go? The child fairly clung to the fingers of this savior-sister—the poor, little, inexperienced, seventeen-year-old bride who was giving up her youth and her girlhood to lay it all upon the shrine of endeavor to bring the radiance of the Star that shone above Bethlehem to reflect its glories upon a forest-bred people of the North!

It was a long, strange journey that the bride and her little sister took. A stage coach conveyed them from their home in Ohio to Erie, Pennsylvania, where they went aboard a sailing vessel bound for Buffalo. There they crossed the Niagara River, and at Chippewa, on the Canadian side, again took a stage coach for the village of Brantford, sixty miles west.

At this place they remained over night, and the following day Mr. Evans' own conveyance arrived to fetch them to the Indian Reserve, ten miles to the south-east.

In after years little Lydia used to tell that during that entire drive she thought she was going through an English avenue leading to some great estate, for the trees crowded up close to the roadways on either side, giant forest trees—gnarled oaks, singing firs, jaunty maples, graceful elms—all stretching their branches overhead. But the "avenue" seemed endless. "When do we come to the house?" she asked, innocently. "This lane is very long."

But it was three hours, over a rough corduroy road, before the little white frame parsonage lifted its roof through the forest, its broad verandahs and green outside shutters welcoming the travellers with an atmosphere of home at last.

29

As the horses drew up before the porch the great front door was noiselessly opened and a lad of seventeen, lithe, clean-limbed, erect, copper-colored, ran swiftly down the steps, lifted his hat, smiled, and assisted the ladies to alight. The boy was Indian to the finger-tips, with that peculiar native polish and courtesy, that absolute ease of manner and direction of glance, possessed only by the old-fashioned type of red man of this continent. The missionary introduced him as "My young friend, the church interpreter, Mr. George Mansion, who is one of our household." (Mansion, or "Grand Mansion," is the English meaning of this young Mohawk's native name.)

The entire personality of the missionary seemed to undergo a change as his eyes rested on this youth. His hitherto rather stilted manner relaxed, his eyes softened and glowed, he invited confidence rather than repelled it; truly his heart was bound up with these forest people; he fairly exhaled love for them with every breath. He was a man of marked shyness, and these silent Indians made him forget this peculiarity of which he was sorrowfully conscious. It was probably this shyness that caused him to open the door and turn to his young wife with the ill-selected remark: "Welcome home, madam."

Madam! The little bride was chilled to the heart with the austere word. She hurried within, followed by her wondering child-sister, as soon as possible sought her room, then gave way to a storm of tears.

"Don't mind me, Liddy," she sobbed. "There's nothing wrong; we'll be happy enough here, only I think I looked for a little—petting."

With a wisdom beyond her years, Lydia did not reply, but went to the window and gazed absently at the tiny patch of flowers beyond the door—the two lilac trees in full blossom, the thread of glistening river, and behind it all, the northern wilderness. Just below the window stood the missionary and the Indian boy talking eagerly.

"Isn't George Mansion *splendid!*" said the child.

"You must call him Mr. Mansion; be very careful about the *Mister*, Liddy dear," said her sister, rising and drying her eyes bravely. "I have always heard that the Indians treat one just as they are treated by one. Respect Mr. Mansion, treat him as you would treat a city gentleman. Be sure he will gauge his deportment by ours. Yes, dear, he *is* splendid. I like him already."

"Yes, 'Liza, so do I, and he *is* a gentleman. He looks it and acts it. I believe he *thinks* gentlemanly things."

Elizabeth laughed. "You dear little soul!" she said. "I know what you mean, and I agree with you."

That laugh was all that Lydia wanted to hear in this world, and presently the two sisters, with arms entwined, descended the stairway and joined in the conversation between Mr. Evans and young George Mansion.

"Mrs. Evans," said the boy, addressing her directly for the first time. "I hoped you were fond

31

of game. Yesterday I hunted; it was partridge I got, and one fine deer. Will you offer me the compliment of having some for dinner to-night?"

His voice was low and very distinct, his accent and expressions very marked as a foreigner to the tongue, but his English was perfect.

"Indeed I shall, Mr. Mansion," smiled the girl-bride, "but I'm afraid that I don't know how to cook it."

"We have an excellent cook," said Mr. Evans. "She has been with George and me ever since I came here. George is a splendid shot, and keeps her busy getting us game suppers."

Meanwhile Lydia had been observing the boy. She had never seen an Indian, consequently was trying to reform her ideas regarding them. She had not expected to see anything like this self-poised, scrupulously-dressed, fine-featured, dark stripling. She thought all Indians wore savage-looking clothes, had fierce eyes and stern, set mouths. This boy's eyes were narrow and shrewd, but warm and kindly, his lips were like a Cupid's bow, his hands were narrower, smaller, than her own, but the firmness of those slim fingers, the power in those small palms, as he had helped her from the carriage, remained with her through all the years to come.

That evening at supper she noted his table deportment; it was correct in every detail. He ate leisurely, silently, gracefully; his knife and fork never clattered, his elbows never were in evidence, he made use of the right plates, spoons, forks, knives; he bore an ease, an unconsciousness of manner, that amazed her. The missionary himself was a stiff man, and his very shyness made him angular. Against such a setting young Mansion gleamed like a brown gem.

* * * * * * * *

For seven years life rolled slowly by. At times Lydia went to visit her two other married sisters, sometimes she remained for weeks with a married brother, and at rare intervals made brief trips to her father's house; but she never received a penny from her strange parent, and knew of but one home which was worthy the name. That was in the Canadian wilderness where the Indian Mission held out its arms to her, and the beloved sister made her more welcome than words could imply. Four pretty children had come to grace this forest household, where young George Mansion, still the veriest right hand of the missionary, had grown into a magnificent type of Mohawk manhood. These years had brought him much, and he had accomplished far more than idle chance could ever throw in his way. He had saved his salary that he earned as interpreter in the church, and had purchased some desirable property, a beautiful estate of two hundred acres, upon which he some day hoped to build a home. He had mastered six Indian languages, which, with his knowledge of English and his wonderful fluency in his own tribal Mohawk, gave him command of eight tongues, an advantage which soon brought him the position of Government interpreter in the Council of the great "Six Nations," composing the Iroquois race. Added to this, through the death

33

of an uncle he came into the younger title of his family, which boasted blood of two noble lines. His father, speaker of the Council, held the elder title, but that did not lessen the importance of young George's title of chief.

Lydia never forgot the first time she saw him robed in the full costume of his office. Hitherto she had regarded him through all her comings and goings as her playmate, friend and boon companion; he had been to her something that had never before entered her life—he had brought warmth, kindness, fellowship and a peculiar confidential humanity that had been entirely lacking in the chill English home of her childhood. But this day, as he stood beside his veteran father, ready to take his place among the chiefs of the Grand Council, she saw revealed another phase of his life and character; she saw that he was destined to be a man among men, and for the first time she realized that her boy companion had gone a little beyond her, perhaps a little above her. They were a strange pair as they stood somewhat apart, unconscious of the picture they made. She, a gentleborn, fair English girl of twenty, her simple blue muslin frock vying with her eyes in color. He, tawny skinned, lithe, straight as an arrow, the royal blood of generations of chiefs and warriors pulsing through his arteries, his clinging buckskin tunic and leggings fringed and embroidered with countless quills, and endless stitches of colored moosehair. From his small, neat moccasins to his jet black hair tipped with an eagle plume he was every inch a man, a gentleman, a warrior.

34

But he was approaching her with the same ease with which he wore his ordinary "white" clothes—garments, whether buckskin or broadcloth, seemed to make but slight impression on him.

"Miss Bestman," he said, "I should like you to meet my mother and father. They are here, and are old friends of your sister and Mr. Evans. My mother does not speak the English, but she knows you are my friend."

And presently Lydia found herself shaking hands with the elder chief, speaker of the council, who spoke English rather well, and with a little dark woman folded within a "broadcloth" and wearing the leggings, moccasins and short dress of her people. A curious feeling of shyness overcame the girl as her hand met that of George Mansion's mother, who herself was the most retiring, most thoroughly old-fashioned woman of her tribe. But Lydia felt that she was in the presence of one whom the young chief held far and away as above himself, as above her, as the best and greatest woman of his world; his very manner revealed it, and Lydia honored him within her heart at that moment more than she had ever done before.

But Chief George Mansion's mother, small and silent through long habit and custom, had acquired a certain masterful dignity of her own, for within her slender brown fingers she held a power that no man of her nation could wrest from her. She was "Chief Matron" of her entire blood relations, and commanded the enviable position of being the one and only person, man or woman, who could appoint a chief to fill the vacancy of one of the

35

great Mohawk law-makers whose seat in Council had been left vacant when the voice of the Great Spirit called him to the happy hunting grounds. Lydia had heard of this national honor which was the right and title of this frail little moccasined Indian woman with whom she was shaking hands, and the thought flashed rapidly through her girlish mind: "Suppose some *one* lady in England had the marvellous power of appointing who the member should be in the British House of Lords or Commons. *Wouldn't* Great Britain honor and tremble before her?"

And here was Chief George Mansion's silent, unpretentious little mother possessing all this power among her people, and she, Lydia Bestman, shaking hands with her! It seemed very marvellous.

But that night the power of this same slender Indian mother was brought vividly before her when, unintentionally, she overheard young George say to the missionary:

"I almost lost my new title to-day, after you and the ladies had left the Council."

"Why, George boy!" exclaimed Mr. Evans. "What have you done?"

"Nothing, it seems, except to be successful. The Council objected to my holding the title of chief and having a chief's vote in the affairs of the people, and at the same time being Government interpreter. They said it would give me too much power to retain both positions. I must give up one—my title or my Government position."

"What did you do?" demanded Mr. Evans, eagerly.

"Nothing, again," smiled the young chief. "But my mother did something. She took the floor of the Council, and spoke for forty minutes. She said I must hold the position of chief which she had made for me, as well as of interpreter which I had made for myself; that if the Council objected, she would forever annul the chief's title in her own family; she would never appoint one in my place, and that we proud, arrogant Mohawks would then have only eight representatives in Council—only be on a level with, as she expressed it, 'those dogs of Senecas.' Then she clutched her broadcloth about her, turned her back on us all, and left the Council."

"What did the Council do?" gasped Mr. Evans.

"Accepted me as chief and interpreter," replied the young man, smiling. "There was nothing else to do."

"Oh, you royal woman! You loyal, loyal mother!" cried Lydia to herself. "How I love you for it!"

Then she crept away just as Mr. Evans had sprung forward with both hands extended towards the young chief, his eyes beaming with almost fatherly delight.

Unconsciously to herself, the English girl's interest in the young chief had grown rapidly year after year. She was also unconscious of his aim at constant companionship with herself. His devotion to her sister, whose delicate health alarmed them all, more and more, as time went on, was only another royal road to Lydia's heart. Elizabeth was becoming frail, shadowy, her appetite was fitful, her eyes larger and more wistful, her fingers smaller and weaker. No one seemed to realize the insidious oncreepings of "the white man's disease," consumption, that was paling Elizabeth's fine English skin, heightening her glorious English color, sapping her delicate English veins. Only young George would tell himself over and over: "Mrs. Evans is going away from us some day, and Lydia will be left with no one in the world but me —no one but me to understand—or to—care."

So he scoured the forest for dainties, wild fruits, game, flowers, to tempt the appetite and the eye of the fading wife of the man who had taught him all the English and the white man's etiquette that he had ever mastered. Night after night he would return from day-long hunting trips, his game-bag filled with delicate quail, rare woodcock, snowy-breasted partridge, and when the illusive appetite of the sick woman could be coaxed to partake of a morsel, he felt repaid for miles of tramping through forest trails, for hours of search and skill.

PART II

PERHAPS it was this grey shadow stealing on the forest mission, the thought of the day when that beautiful mothering sister would leave his little friend Lydia alone with a bereft man and four small children, or perhaps it was a yet more personal note in his life that brought George Mansion to the realization of what this girl had grown to be to him.

Indian-wise, his parents had arranged a suitable marriage for him, selecting a girl of his own tribe, of the correct clan to mate with his own, so that the line of blood heritage would be intact, and the sons of the next generation would be of the "Blood Royal," qualified by rightful lineage to inherit the title of chief.

This Mohawk girl was attractive, young, and had a partial English education. Her parents were fairly prosperous, owners of many acres, and much forest and timber country. The arrangement was regarded as an ideal one—the young people as perfectly and diplomatically mated as it was possible to be; but when his parents approached the young chief with the proposition, he met it with instant refusal.

"My father, my mother," he begged, "I ask you to forgive me this one disobedience. I ask you to forgive that I have, amid my fight and struggle for English education, forgotten a single custom of my people. I have tried to honor all the ancient rules and usages of my forefathers, but I forgot this one thing, and I cannot, cannot do it! My wife I must choose for myself."

"You will marry—whom, then?" asked the old chief.

"I have given no thought to it—yet," he faltered.

"Yes," said his mother, urged by the knowing

39

heart of a woman, "yes, George, you have thought of it."

"Only this hour," he answered, looking directly into his mother's eyes. "Only now that I see you want me to give my life to someone else. But my life belongs to the white girl, Mrs. Evans' sister, if she will take it. I shall offer it to her to-morrow—to-day."

His mother's face took on the shadow of age. "You would marry a *white* girl?" she exclaimed, incredulously.

"Yes," came the reply, briefly, decidedly.

"But your children, your sons and hers—they could never hold the title, never be chief," she said, rising to her feet.

He winced. "I know it. I had not thought of it before—but I know it. Still, I would marry her."

"But there would be no more chiefs of the Grand Mansion name," cut in his father. "The title would go to your aunt's sons. She is a Grand Mansion no longer; she, being married, is merely a Straight-Shot, her husband's name. The Straight-Shots never had noble blood, never wore a title. Shall our family title go to a *Straight-Shot?*" and the elder chief mouthed the name contemptuously.

Again the boy winced. The hurt of it all was sinking in—he hated the Straight-Shots, he loved his own blood and bone. With lightning rapidity he weighed it all mentally, then spoke: "Perhaps the white girl will not marry me," he said slowly, and the thought of it drove the dark red from his cheeks, drove his finger-nails into his palms.

40

"Then, then you will marry Dawendine, our choice?" cried his mother, hopefully.

"I shall marry no one but the white girl," he answered, with set lips. "If she will not marry me, I shall never marry, so the Straight-Shots will have our title, anyway."

The door closed behind him. It was as if it had shut forever between him and his own.

But even with this threatened calamity looming before her, the old Indian mother's hurt heart swelled with a certain pride in his wilful actions.

"What bravery!" she exclaimed. "What courage to hold to his own choice! What a *man!*"

"Yes," half bemoaned his father, "he is a red man through and through. He defies his whole nation in his fearlessness, his lawlessness. Even I bow to his bravery, his self-will, but that bravery is hurting me here, here!" and the ancient chief laid his hand above his heart.

There was no reply to be made by the proud though pained mother. She folded her "broadcloth" about her, filled her small carven pipe and sat for many hours smoking silently, silently, silently. Now and again she shook her head mournfully, but her dark eyes would flash at times with an emotion that contradicted her dejected attitude. It was an emotion born of self-exaltation, for had she not mothered a *man?* —albeit that manhood was revealing itself in scorning the traditions and customs of her ancient race.

And young George was returning from his father's house to the Mission with equally mixed emotions. He knew he had dealt an almost unforgivable blow to those beloved parents whom he had honored and obeyed from his babyhood. Once he almost turned back. Then a vision arose of a fair young English girl whose unhappy childhood he had learned of years ago, a sweet, homeless face of great beauty, lips that were made for love they had never had, eyes that had already known more of tears than they should have shed in a lifetime. Suppose some other youth should win this girl away from him? Already several of the young men from the town drove over more frequently than they had cause to. Only the week before he had found her seated at the little old melodeon playing and singing a duet with one of these gallants. He locked his teeth together and strode rapidly through the forest path, with the first full realization that she was the only woman in all the world for him.

Some inevitable force seemed to be driving him towards—circumstances seemed to pave the way to—their ultimate union; even now chance placed her in the path, literally, for as he threaded his way uphill, across the open, and on to the little log bridge which crossed the ravine immediately behind the Mission, he saw her standing at the further side, leaning upon the unpeeled sapling which formed the bridge guard. She was looking into the tiny stream beneath. He made no sound as he approached. Generations of moccasin-shod ancestors had made his own movements swift and silent. Notwithstanding this, she turned, and, with a bright girlish smile, she said:

"I knew you were coming, Chief."

"Why? How?" he asked, accepting his new title from her with a graceful indifference almost beyond his four-and-twenty years.

"I can hardly say just how—but—" she ended with only a smile. For a full minute he caught and held her glance. She seemed unable to look away, but her grave, blue English eyes were neither shy nor confident. They just seemed to answer his—then,

"Miss Bestman, will you be my wife?" he asked gently. She was neither surprised nor dismayed, only stood silent, as if she had forgotten the art of speech. "You knew I should ask this some day," he continued, rather rapidly. "This is the day."

"I did not really know—I don't know how I feel—" she began, faltering.

"I did not know how I felt, either, until an hour ago," he explained. "When my father and my mother told me they had arranged my marriage with—"

"With whom?" she almost demanded.

"A girl of my own people," he said, grudgingly. "A girl I honor and respect, but—"

"But what?" she said weakly, for the mention of his possible marriage with another had flung her own feelings into her very face.

"But unless you will be my wife, I shall never marry." He folded his arms across his chest as he said it—the very action expressed finality. For a second he stood erect, dark, slender, lithe, immovable, then with sudden impulse he held

43

out one hand to her and spoke very quietly. "I love you, Lydia. Will you come to me?"

"Yes," she answered clearly. "I will come."

He caught her hands very tightly, bending his head until his fine face rested against her hair. She knew then that she had loved him through all these years, and that come what might, she would love him through all the years to be.

That night she told her frail and fading sister, whom she found alone resting among her pillows.

"'Liza dear, you are crying," she half sobbed in alarm, as the great tears rolled slowly down the wan cheeks. "I have made you unhappy, and you are ill, too. Oh, how selfish I am! I did not think that perhaps it might distress you."

"Liddy, Liddy darling, these are the only tears of joy that I have ever shed!" cried Elizabeth. "Joy, joy, girlie! I have so wished this to come before I left you, wished it for years. I love George Mansion better than I ever loved brother of mine. Of all the world I should have chosen him for your husband. Oh! I am happy, happy, child, and you will be happy with him, too."

And that night Lydia Bestman laid her down to rest, with her heart knowing the greatest human love that had ever entered into her life.

Mr. Evans was almost beside himself with joyousness when the young people rather shyly confessed their engagement to him. He was deeply attached to his wife's young sister, and George Mansion had been more to him than many a man's son ever is. Seemingly cold and undemonstrative, this reserved Scotch missionary had given all his heart and life to the Indians, and this one boy was the apple of his eye. Farsighted and cautious, he saw endless trouble shadowing the young lovers— opposition to the marriage from both sides of the house. He could already see Lydia's family smarting under the seeming disgrace of her marriage to an Indian; he could see George's family indignant and hurt to the core at his marriage with a white girl; he could see how impossible it would be for Lydia's people to ever understand the fierce resentment of the Indian parents that the family title could never continue under the family name. He could see how little George's people would ever understand the "white" prejudice against them. But the good man kept his own counsel, determining only that when the war did break out, he would stand shoulder to shoulder with these young lovers and be their friend and helper when even their own blood and kin should cut them off.

* * * * * * * *

It was two years before this shy and taciturn man fully realized what the young chief and the English girl really were to him, for affliction had laid a heavy hand on his heart. First, his gentle and angel-natured wife said her long, last goodnight to him. Then an unrelenting scourge of scarlet fever swept three of his children into graves. Then the eldest, just on the threshold of sweet young maidenhood, faded like a flower, until she, too, said good-night and slept beside her mother. Wifeless, childless, the stricken missionary hugged to his heart these two—George and Lydia—and they, who had labored weeks and months, night and day, nursing and tending these loved ones, who had helped fight and grapple with death five times within two years, only to be driven back heartsore and conquered by the enemy—these two put away the thought of marriage for the time. Joy would have been ill-fitting in that household. Youth was theirs, health was theirs, and duty also was theirs—duty to this man of God, whose house was their home, whose hand had brought them together. So the marriage did not take place at once, but the young chief began making preparations on the estate he had purchased to build a fitting home for this homeless girl who was giving her life into his hands. After so many dark days, it was a relief to get Mr. Evans interested in the plans of the house George was to build, to select the proper situation, to arrange for a barn, a carriage house, a stable, for young Mansion had saved money and acquired property of sufficient value to give his wife a home that would vie with anything in the large border towns. Like most Indians, he was recklessly extravagant, and many a time the thrifty Scotch blood of the missionary would urge more economy, less expenditure. But the building went on; George determined it was to be a "Grand Mansion." His very title demanded that he give his wife an abode worthy of the ancestors who appropriated the name as their own.

"When you both go from me, even if it is only across the fields to the new home, I shall be very much alone," Mr. Evans had once said. Then in an agony of fear that his solitary life would shadow their happiness, he added quickly, "But I have a very sweet and lovely niece who writes me she will come to look after this desolated home if I wish it, and perhaps her brother will come, too, if I want him. I am afraid I *shall* want him sorely, George. For though you will be but five minutes' walk from me, your face will not be at my breakfast table to help me begin each day with a courage it has always inspired. So I beg that you two will not delay your marriage; give no thought to me. You are young but once, and youth has wings of wonderful swiftness. Margaret and Christopher shall come to me; but although they are my own flesh and blood, they will never become to me what you two have been, and always will be."

Within their recollection, the lovers had never heard the missionary make so long a speech. They felt the earnestness of it, the truth of it, and arranged to be married when the golden days of August came. Lydia was to go to her married sister, in the eastern part of Canada, whose husband was a clergyman, and at whose home she had spent many of her girlhood years. George was to follow. They were to be quietly married and return by sailing vessel up the lakes, then take the stage from what is now the city of Toronto, arrive at the Indian Reserve, and go direct to the handsome home the young chief had erected for his English bride. So Lydia Bestman set forth on her long journey from which she was to return as the wife of the head chief of a powerful tribe of Indians—a man revered, respected, looked up to by a vast nation, a man of sterling worth, of considerable wealth as riches were counted in those days, a man polished in the usages and etiquette of her own people, who conducted himself with faultless grace, who would have shone brilliantly in any drawing-room (and who in after years was the guest of honor at many a great reception by the governors of the land), a man young, stalwart, handsome, with an aristocratic lineage that bred him a native gentleman, with a grand old title that had come down to him through six hundred years of honor in warfare and the high places of his people. That this man should be despised by her relatives and family connections because of his warm, red skin and Indian blood, never occurred to Lydia. Her angel sister had loved the youth, the old Scotch missionary little short of adored him. Why, then, this shocked amazement of her relatives, that she should wish to wed the finest gentleman she had ever met, the man whose love and kindness had made her erstwhile blackened and cruel world a paradise of sunshine and contentment? She was but little prepared for the storm of indignation that met her announcement that she was engaged to marry a Mohawk Indian chief.

Her sister, with whom she never had anything in common, who was years older, and had been married in England when Lydia was but three years of age, implored, entreated, sneered, ridiculed and stormed. Lydia sat motionless through it all, and then the outraged sister struck a vital spot with: "I don't know what Elizabeth has been thinking of all these years, to let you asso-

48

ciate with Indians on an equality. *She* is to blame for this."

Then, and only then, did Lydia blaze forth. "Don't you *dare* speak of 'Liza like that!" flung the girl. "She was the only human being in our whole family, the only one who ever took me in her arms, who ever called me 'dear,' who ever kissed me as if she meant it. I tell you, she loved George Mansion better than she loved her cold, chilly English brothers. She loved *me*, and her house was my home, which yours never was. Yes, she loved me, angel girl that she was, and she died in a halo of happiness because I was happy and because I was to marry the noblest, kingliest gentleman I ever met." The girl ceased, breathless.

"Yes," sneered her sister, "yes, marry an *Indian!*"

"Yes," defied Lydia, "an *Indian*, who can give me not only a better home than this threadbare parsonage of yours"—here she swept scornful eyes about the meagre little, shabby room—"yes, a home that any Bestman would be proud to own; but better than that," she continued ragingly, "he has given me love—*love*, that you in your chilly, inhuman home sneer at, but that I have cried out for; love that my dead mother prayed should come to me, from the moment she left me a baby, alone, in England, until the hour when this one splendid man took me into his heart."

"Poor mother!" sighed the sister. "I am grateful she is spared *this*."

"Don't think that she doesn't know it!" cried

49

Lydia. "If 'Liza approved, mother does, and she is glad of her child's happiness."

"Her child—yes, her child," taunted the sister. "Child! child! Yes, and what of the *child* you will probably mother?"

The crimson swept painfully down the young girl's face, but she braved it out.

"Yes," she stammered, "a child, perhaps a *son*, a son of mine, who, poor boy, can never inherit his father's title."

"And why not, pray?" remarked her sister.

"Because the female line of lineage will be broken," explained the girl. "He *should* marry someone else, so that the family title could follow the family name. His father and mother have practically cast him off because of me. *Don't* you see? Can't you understand that I am only an untitled commoner to his people? I am only a white girl."

"*Only* a white girl!" repeated the sister, sarcastically. "Do you mean to tell me that you believe these wretched Indians don't want him to marry you? *You*, a *Bestman*, and an English girl? Nonsense, Lydia! You are talking utter nonsense." But the sister's voice weakened, nevertheless.

"But it's true," asserted the girl. "You don't understand the Indian nation as 'Liza did; it's perfectly true—a son of mine can claim no family title; the honor of it must leave the name of Mansion forever. Oh, his parents have completely shut him out of their lives because I am only a white girl!" and the sweet young voice trembled woefully.

50

"I decline to discuss this disgraceful matter with you any further," said the sister coldly. "Perhaps my good husband can bring you to your senses," and the lady left the room in a fever of indignation.

But her "good husband," the city clergyman, declined the task of "bringing Lydia to her senses." He merely sent for her to go to his study, and, as she stood timidly in the doorway, he set his small steely eyes on her and said:

"You will leave this house at once, to-night. *To-night*, do you hear? I'll have no Indian come *here* after my wife's sister. I hope you quite understand me?"

"Quite, sir," replied the girl, and with a stiff bow she turned and went back to her room.

In the haste of packing up her poor and scanty wardrobe, she heard her sister's voice saying to the clergyman: "Oh! how *could* you send her away? You know she has no home, she has nowhere to go. How *could* you do it?" All Lydia caught of his reply was: "Not another night, not another meal, in this house while *I* am its master."

Presently her sister came upstairs carrying a plate of pudding. Her eyes were red with tears, and her hands trembled. "Do eat this, my dear; some tea is coming presently," she said.

But Lydia only shook her head, strapped her little box, and, putting on her bonnet, she commanded her voice sufficiently to say: "I am going now. I'll send for this box later."

"Where are you going to?" her sister's voice trembled.

"I—don't know," said the girl. "But where-
ever I go, it will be a kindlier place than this.
Good-bye, sister." She kissed the distressed wife
softly on each cheek, then paused at the bedroom
door to say, "The man I am to marry loves me,
honors me too much to treat me as a mere possession. I know that *he* will never tell me he is
'master.' George Mansion may have savage blood
in his veins, but he has grasped the meaning of the
word 'Christianity' far more fully than your husband has."

Her sister could not reply, but stood with
streaming eyes and watched the girl slip down
the back stairs and out of a side door.

For a moment Lydia Bestman stood on the
pavement and glanced up and down the street.
The city was what was known as a garrison town
in the days when the British regular troops were
quartered in Canada. Far down the street two
gay young officers were walking, their brilliant
uniforms making a pleasant splash of color in the
sunlight. They seemed to suggest to the girl's
mind a more than welcome thought. She knew
the major's wife well, a gracious, whole-souled
English lady whose kindness had oftentimes bright-
ened her otherwise colorless life. Instinctively the
girl turned to the quarters of the married officers.
She found the major's wife at home, and, burying
her drawn little face in the good lady's lap, she
poured forth her entire story.

"My dear," blazed out the usually placid lady,
"if I were only the major for a few moments,
instead of his wife, I should—I should—well, I

should just *swear!* There, now I've said it, and I'd *do* it, too. Why, I never heard of such an outrage! My dear, kiss me, and tell me—when how, do you expect your young chief to come for you?"

"Next week," said the girl, from the depths of those sheltering arms.

"Then here you stay, right here with me. The major and I shall go to the church with you, see you safely married, bring you and your Hiawatha home for a cosy little breakfast, put you aboard the boat for Toronto, and give you both our blessing and our love." And the major's wife nodded her head with such emphasis that her quaint English curls bobbed about, setting Lydia off into a fit of laughter. "That's right, my dear. You just begin to laugh now, and keep it up for all the days to come. I'll warrant you've had little of laughter in your young life," she said knowingly. "From what I've known of your father, he never ordered laughter as a daily ingredient in his children's food. Then that sweet Elizabeth leaving you alone, so terribly alone, must have chased the sunshine far from your little world. But after this," she added brightly, "it's just going to be love and laughter. And now, my dear, we must get back the rosy English color in your cheeks, or your young Hiawatha won't know his little white sweetheart. Run away to my spare room, girlie. The orderly will get a man to fetch your box. Then you can change your frock. Leave yesterday behind you forever. Have a little rest; you look as if you had not slept for a week. Then join the major and me at dinner, and we'll toast you and your redskin lover in true garrison style."

And Lydia, with the glorious recuperation of youth, ran joyously upstairs, smiling and singing like a lark, transformed with the first unadulterated happiness she had ever felt or known.

PART III

UPON George Mansion's arrival at the garrison town he had been met on the wharf by the major, who took him to the hotel, while hurriedly explaining just why he must not go near Lydia's sister and the clergyman whom George had expected would perform the marriage ceremony. "So," continued the major, "you and Lydia are not to be married at the cathedral after all, but Mrs. Harold and I have arranged that the ceremony shall take place at little St. Swithin's Church in the West End. So you'll be there at eleven o'clock, eh, boy?"

"Yes, major, I'll be there, and before eleven, I'm afraid, I'm so anxious to take her home. I shall not endeavor to thank you and Mrs. Harold for what you have done for my homeless girl. I can't even—"

"Tut, tut, tut!" growled the major. "Haven't done anything. Bless my soul, Chief, take my word for it, haven't done a thing to be thanked for. Here's your hotel. Get some coffee to brace your nerves up with, for I can assure you, boy, a wedding is a trying ordeal, even if there is but

54

a handful of folks to see it through. Be a good boy, now—good-bye until eleven—St. Swithin's, remember, and God bless you!" and the big-hearted, blustering major was whisked away in his carriage, leaving the young Indian half over-whelmed with his kindness, but as happy as the golden day.

An hour or so later he stood at the hotel door a moment awaiting the cab that was to take him to the church. He was dressed in the height of the fashion of the early fifties—very dark wine broadcloth, the coat shaped tightly to the waist and adorned with a silk velvet collar, a pale lavender, flowered satin waistcoat, a dull white silk stock collar, a bell-shaped black silk hat. He carried his gloves, for throughout his entire life he declared he breathed through his hands, and the wearing of gloves was abhorrent to him. Suddenly a gentleman accosted him with:

"I hear an Indian chief is in town. Going to be married here this morning. Where is the ceremony to take place? Do you know anything of it?"

Like all his race, George Mansion had a subtle sense of humor. It seized upon him now.

"Certainly I know," he replied. "I happened to come down on the boat with the chief. I intend to go to the wedding myself. I understand the ceremony was arranged to be at the cathedral."

"Splendid!" said the gentleman. "And thank you, sir."

Just then the cab arrived. Young Mansion stepped hastily in, nodded good-bye to his acquaintance, and smilingly said in an undertone to the driver, "St. Swithin's Church—and quickly."

* * * * * * * *

"With this ring I thee wed," he found himself saying to a little figure in a soft grey gown at his side, while a gentle-faced old clergyman in a snowy surplice stood before him, and a square-shouldered, soldierly person in a brilliant uniform almost hugged his elbow.

"I pronounce you man and wife." At the words she turned towards her husband like a carrier pigeon winging for home. Then somehow the solemnity all disappeared. The major, the major's wife, two handsome young officers, one girl friend, the clergyman, the clergyman's wife, were all embracing her, and she was dimpling with laughter and happiness; and George Mansion stood proudly by, his fine dark face eager, tender and very noble.

"My dear," whispered the major's wife, "he's a perfect prince—he's just as royal as he can be! I never saw such manners, such ease. Why, girlie, he's a courtier!"

"Confound the young rogue!" growled the major, in her ear. "I haven't an officer on my staff that can equal him. You're a lucky girl. Yes, confound him, I say!"

"Bless you, child," said the clergyman's wife. "I think he'll make you happy. Be very sure that you make *him* happy."

And to all these whole-hearted wishes and comments, Lydia replied with smiles and carefree words. Then came the major, watch in hand,

56

military precision and promptitude in his very tone.

"Time's up, everybody! There's a bite to eat at the barracks, then these youngsters must be gone. The boat is due at one o'clock—time's up."

As the little party drove past the cathedral they observed a huge crowd outside, waiting for the doors to be opened. Lydia laughed like a child as George told her of his duplicity of the morning, when he had misled the inquiring stranger into thinking the Indian chief was to be married there. The little tale furnished fun for all at the pretty breakfast in the major's quarters.

"Nice way to begin your wedding morning, young man!" scowled the major, fiercely. "Starting this great day with a network of falsehoods."

"Not at all," smiled the Indian. "It was arranged for the cathedral, and I did attend the ceremony."

"No excuses, you bare-faced scoundrel! I won't listen to them. Here you are happily married, and all those poor would-be sight-seers sizzling out there in this glaring August sun. I'm ashamed of you!" But his arm was about George's shoulders, and he was wringing the dark, slender hand with a genuine good fellowship that was pleasant to see. "Bless my soul, I love you, boy!" he added, sincerely. "Love you through and through; and remember, I'm your white father from this day forth."

"And I am your white mother," said the major's wife, placing her hands on his shoulders.

For a second the bridegroom's face sobered.

Before him flashed a picture of a little old Indian woman with a broadcloth folded about her shoulders, a small carven pipe between her lips, a world of sorrow in her deep eyes—sorrow that he had brought there. He bent suddenly and kissed Mrs. Harold's fingers with a grave and courtly deference. "Thank you," he said simply.

But, motherlike, she knew that his heart was bleeding. Lydia had told of his parents' antagonism, of the lost Mansion title. So the good lady just gave his hand a little extra, understanding squeeze, and the good-byes began.

"Be off with you, youngsters!" growled the major. "The boat is in—poste haste now, or you'll miss it. Begone, both of you!"

And presently they found themselves once more in the carriage, the horses galloping down to the wharf. And almost before they realized it they were aboard, with the hearty "God bless you's" of the splendid old major and his lovable wife still echoing in their happy young hearts.

* * * * * * * *

It was evening, five days later, when they arrived at their new home. All about the hills, and the woods, above the winding river, and along the edge of the distant forest, brooded that purple smokiness that haunts the late days of August—the smokiness that was born of distant fires, where the Indians and pioneers were "clearing" their lands. The air was like amethyst, the setting sun a fire opal. As on the day when she first had come into his life, George helped her

58

to alight from the carriage, and they stood a moment, hand in hand, and looked over the ample acres that composed their estate. The young Indian had worked hard to have most of the land cleared, leaving here and there vast stretches of walnut groves, and long lines of majestic elms, groups of sturdy oaks, and occasionally a single regal pine tree. Many a time in later years his utilitarian friends would say, "Chief, these trees you are preserving so jealously are eating up a great deal of your land. Why not cut them away and grow wheat?" But he would always resent the suggestion, saying that his wheat lands lay back from the river. They were for his body, doubtless, but here, by the river, the trees must be—they were for his soul. And Lydia would champion him immediately with, "Yes, they were there to welcome me as a bride, those grand old trees, and they will remain there, I think, as long as we both shall live." So, that first evening at home they stood and watched the imperial trees, the long, open flats bordering the river, the nearby lawns which he had taken such pains to woo from the wilderness; stood palm to palm, and that moment seemed to govern all their after life.

Someone has said that never in the history of the world have two people been perfectly mated. However true this may be, it is an undeniable fact that between the most devoted of life-mates there will come inharmonious moments. Individuality would cease to exist were it not so. These two lived together for upwards of thirty years, and never had one single quarrel, but oddly enough, when the rare inharmonious moments came, these groups of trees bridged the fleeting difference of opinion or any slight antagonism of will and purpose; when these unresponsive moments came, one or the other would begin to admire those forest giants, to suggest improvements, to repeat the admiration of others for their graceful outlines —to, in fact, direct thought and conversation into the common channel of love for those trees. This peculiarity was noticeable to outsiders, to their own circle, to their children. At mere mention of the trees the shadow of coming cloud would lessen, then waste, then grow invisible. Their mutual love for these voiceless yet voiceful and kingly creations was as the love of children for a flower—simple, nameless, beautiful and powerful beyond words.

That first home night, as she stepped within doors, there awaited two inexpressible surprises for her. First, on the dining-room table a silver tea service of seven pieces, imported from England —his wedding gift to her. Second, in the quaint little drawing-room stood a piano. In the "early fifties" this latter was indeed a luxury, even in city homes. She uttered a little cry of delight, and flinging herself before the instrument, ran her fingers over the keys, and broke into his favorite song, "Oft in the Stilly Night." She had a beautiful voice, the possession of which would have made her renowned had opportunity afforded its cultivation. She had "picked up" music and read it remarkably well, and he, Indian wise, was passionately fond of melody. So they laughed and loved together over this new luxurious toy, until Milly, the ancient Mohawk maid, tapped softly at the drawing-room and bade them come to tea. With that first meal in her new home, the darkened hours and days and years smothered their haunting voices. She had "left yesterday behind her," as the major's royal wife had wished her to, and for the first time in all her checkered and neglected life she laughed with the gladness of a bird at song, flung her past behind her, and the grim unhappiness of her former life left her forever.

*   *   *   *   *   *   *   *

It was a golden morning in July when the doctor stood grasping George Mansion's slender hands, searching into his dusky, anxious eyes, and saying with ringing cheeriness, "Chief, I congratulate you. You've got the most beautiful son upstairs—the finest boy I ever saw. Hail to the young chief, I say!"

The doctor was white. He did not know of the broken line of lineage—that "the boy upstairs" could never wear his father's title. A swift shadow fought for a second with glorious happiness. The battlefield was George Mansion's face, his heart. His unfilled duty to his parents assailed him like a monstrous enemy, then happiness conquered, came forth a triumphant victor, and the young father dashed noiselessly, fleetly up the staircase, and, despite the protesting physician, in another moment his wife and son were in his arms. Titles did not count in that moment; only Love in its tyrannical majesty reigned in that sacred room.

61

The boy was a being of a new world, a new nation. Before he was two weeks old he began to show the undeniable physique of the two great races from whence he came; all the better qualities of both bloods seemed to blend within his small body. He was his father's son, he was his mother's baby. His grey-blue eyes held a hint of the dreaming forest, but also a touch of old England's skies. His hair, thick and black, was straight as his father's, except just above the temples, where a suggestion of his mother's pretty English curls waved like strands of fine silk. His small mouth was thin-lipped; his nose, which even in babyhood never had the infantile "snub," but grew straight, thin as his Indian ancestors', yet displayed a half-haughty English nostril; his straight little back—all combined likenesses to his parents. But who could say which blood dominated his tiny person? Only the exquisite soft, pale brown of his satiny skin called loudly and insistently that he was of a race older than the composite English could ever boast; it was the hallmark of his ancient heritage—the birthright of his father's son.

But the odd little half-blood was extraordinarily handsome even as an infant. In after years when he grew into glorious manhood he was generally acknowledged to be the handsomest man in the Province of Ontario—but to-day—his first day in these strange, new surroundings—he was but a wee, brown, lovable bundle, whose tiny gossamer hands cuddled into his father's palm, while his little velvet cheek lay rich and russet against the pearly whiteness of his mother's arm.

"I believe he is like you, George," she murmured, with a wealth of love in her voice and eyes.

"Yes," smiled the young chief, "he certainly has Mansion blood; but your eyes, Lydia, your dear eyes."

"Which eyes must go to sleep and rest," interrupted the physician, severely. "Come, Chief, you've seen your son, you've satisfied yourself that Mrs. Mansion is doing splendidly, so away you go, or I shall scold."

And George slipped away after one more embrace, slipped down the staircase, and out into the radiant July sunshine, where his beloved trees arose about him, grand and majestic, seeming to understand how full of joy, of exultation, had been this great new day.

*   *   *   *   *   *   *   *

The whims of women are proverbial, but the whims of men are things never to be accounted for. This beautiful child was but a few weeks old when Mr. Bestman wrote, announcing to his daughter his intention of visiting her for a few days.

So he came to the Indian Reserve, to the handsome country home his Indian son-in-law had built. He was amazed, surprised, delighted. His English heart revelled in the trees. "Like an Old Country gentleman's estate in the Counties," he declared. He kissed his daughter with affection, wrung his son-in-law's hand with a warmth and cordiality unmistakable in its sincerity, took the baby in his arms and said over and over, "Oh, you sweet little child! You sweet little child!" Then the darkness of all those harsh years fell away from Lydia. She could afford to be magnanimous, so with a sweet silence, a loving forgetfulness of all the dead miseries and bygone whip-lashes, she accepted her strange parent just as he presented himself, in the guise of a man whom the years had changed from harshness to tenderness, and let herself thoroughly enjoy his visit.

But when he drove away she had but one thing to say; it was, "George, I wonder when *your* father will come to us, when your *mother* will come. Oh, I want her to see the baby, for I think my own mother sees him."

"Some day, dear," he answered hopefully. "They will come some day; and when they do, be sure it will be to take you to their hearts."

She sighed and shook her head unbelievingly. But the "some day" that he prophesied, but which she doubted, came in a manner all too soon—all too unwelcome. The little son had just begun to walk about nicely, when George Mansion was laid low with a lingering fever that he had contracted among the marshes where much of his business as an employee of the Government took him. Evils had begun to creep into his forest world. The black and subtle evil of the white man's firewater had commenced to touch with its poisonous finger the lives and lodges of his beloved people. The curse began to spread, until it grew into a menace to the community. It was the same old story: the white man had come with the Bible in one hand, the bottle in the other. George Mansion had striven side by side with Mr. Evans to overcome the dread scourge. Together they fought the enemy hand to hand, but it gained ground in spite of all their efforts. The entire plan of the white liquor dealer's campaign was simply an effort to exchange a quart of bad whiskey for a cord of first-class firewood, or timber, which could be hauled off the Indian Reserve and sold in the nearby town markets for five or six dollars; thus a hundred dollars' worth of bad whiskey, if judiciously traded, would net the white dealer a thousand dollars cash. And the traffic went on, to the depletion of the Indian forests and the degradation of the Indian souls.

Then the Canadian Government appointed young Mansion special forest warden, gave him a "V.R." hammer, with which he was to stamp each and every stick of timber he could catch being hauled off the Reserve by white men; licensed him to carry firearms for self-protection, and told him to "go ahead." He "went ahead." Night after night he lay, concealing himself in the marshes, the forests, the trails, the concession lines, the river road, the Queen's highway, seizing all the timber he could, destroying all the whiskey, turning the white liquor traders off Indian lands, and fighting as only a young, earnest and inspired man can fight. These hours and conditions began to tell on his physique. The marshes breathed their miasma into his blood—the dreaded fever had him in its claws. Lydia was a born nurse. She knew little of thermometers, of charts, of technical terms, but her ability and instincts in the sick-

65

room were unerring; and, when her husband succumbed to a raging fever, love lent her hands an inspiration and her brain a clarity that would have shamed many a professional nurse.

For hours, days, weeks, she waited, tended, watched, administered, labored and loved beside the sick man's bed. She neither slept nor ate enough to carry her through the ordeal, but love lent her strength, and she battled and fought for his life as only an adoring woman can. Her wonderful devotion was the common talk of the country. She saw no one save Mr. Evans and the doctors. She never left the sick-room save when her baby needed her. But it all seemed so useless, so in vain, when one dark morning the doctor said, "We had better send for his father and mother."

Poor Lydia! Her heart was nearly breaking. She hurriedly told the doctor the cause that had kept them away so long, adding, "Is it so bad as that? Oh, doctor, *must I send for them?* They don't want to come." Before the good man could reply, there was a muffled knock at the door. Then Milly's old wrinkled face peered in, and Milly's voice said whisperingly, "His people—they here."

"Whose people? Who are here?" almost gasped Lydia.

"His father and his mother," answered the old woman. "They downstairs."

For a brief moment there was silence. Lydia could not trust herself to speak, but ill as he was, George's quick Indian ear had caught Milly's

66

words. He murmured, "Mother! mother! Oh, my mother!"

"Bring her, quickly, *quickly!*" said Lydia to the doctor.

It seemed to the careworn girl that a lifetime followed before the door opened noiselessly, and there entered a slender little old Indian woman, in beaded leggings, moccasins, "short skirt," and a blue "broadcloth" folded about her shoulders. She glanced swiftly at the bed, but with the heroism of her race went first towards Lydia, laid her cheek silently beside the white girl's, then looked directly into her eyes.

"Lydia!" whispered George, "Lydia!" At the word both women moved swiftly to his side. "Lydia," he repeated, "my mother cannot speak the English, but her cheek to yours means that you are her blood relation."

The effort of speech almost cost him a swoon, but his mother's cheek was now against his own, and the sweet, dulcet Mohawk language of his boyhood returned to his tongue; he was speaking it to his mother, speaking it lovingly, rapidly. Yet, although Lydia never understood a word, she did not feel an outsider, for the old mother's hand held her own, and she knew that at last the gulf was bridged.

* * * * * * * *

It was two days later, when the doctor pronounced George Mansion out of danger, that the sick man said to his wife: "Lydia, it is all over

—the pain, the estrangement. My mother says that you are her daughter. My father says that you are his child. They heard of your love, your nursing, your sweetness. They want to know if you will call them 'father, mother.' They love you, for you are one of their own.

"At last, at last!" half sobbed the weary girl. "Oh, George, I am so happy! *You* are going to get well, and *they* have come to us at last."

"Yes, dear," he replied. Then with a half humorous yet wholly pathetic smile flitting across his wan face, he added, "And my mother has a little gift for you." He nodded then towards the quaint old figure at the further side of the bed. His mother arose, and, drawing from her bosom a tiny, russet-colored object, laid it in Lydia's hand. It was a little moccasin, just three and a quarter inches in length. "Its mate is lost," added the sick man, "but I wore it as a baby. My mother says it is yours, and should have been yours all these years."

For a second the two women faced each other, then Lydia sat down abruptly on the bedside, her arms slipped about the older woman's shoulders, and her face dropped quickly, heavily—at last on a mother's breast.

George Mansion sighed in absolute happiness, then closed his eyes and slept the great, strong, vitalizing sleep of reviving forces.

PART IV

*H*OW CLOSELY the years chased one another after this! But many and many a happy day within each year found Lydia and her husband's mother sitting together, hour upon hour, needle in hand, sewing and harmonizing—the best friends in all the world. It mattered not that "mother" could not speak one word of English, or that Lydia never mastered but a half-dozen words of Mohawk. These two were friends in the sweetest sense of the word, and their lives swept forward in a unison of sympathy that was dear to the heart of the man who held them as the two most precious beings in all the world.

And with the years came new duties, new responsibilities, new little babies to love and care for, until a family, usually called "A King's Desire," gathered at their hearthside—four children, the eldest a boy, the second a girl, then another boy, then another girl. These children were reared on the strictest lines of both Indian and English principles. They were taught the legends, the traditions, the culture and the etiquette of both races to which they belonged; but above all, their mother instilled into them from the very cradle that they were of their father's people, not of hers. Her marriage had made her an Indian by the laws which govern Canada, as well as by the sympathies and yearnings and affections of her own heart. When she married George Mansion she had repeated to him the centuries-old vow of allegiance, "Thy people shall be my people, and thy God my God."

She determined that should she ever be mother to his children, those children should be reared as Indians in spirit and patriotism, and in loyalty to their father's race as well as by heritage of blood. The laws of Canada held these children as Indians. They were wards of the Government; they were born on Indian lands, on Indian Reservations. They could own and hold Indian lands, and their mother, English though she was, made it her life service to inspire, foster and elaborate within these children the pride of race, the value of that copper-tinted skin which they all displayed. When people spoke of blood and lineage and nationality, these children would say, "We are Indians," with the air with which a young Spanish don might say, "I am a Castilian." She wanted them to grow up nationalists, and they did, every mother's son and daughter of them. Things could never have been otherwise, for George Mansion and his wife had so much in common that their offspring could scarcely evince other than inherited parental traits. Their tastes and distastes were so synonymous; they hated hypocrisy, vulgarity, slovenliness, imitations.

After forty years spent on a Canadian Indian Reserve, Lydia Mansion still wore real lace, real tortoise-shell combs, real furs. If she could not have procured these she would have worn plain linen collars, no combs, and a woven woolen scarf about her throat; but the imitation fabrics, as well as the "imitation people," had no more part in her life than they had in her husband's, who abhorred all such pinchbeck. Their loves were identical. They loved nature—the trees, best of all, and the river, and the birds. They loved the Anglican Church, they loved the British flag, they loved Queen Victoria, they loved beautiful, dead Elizabeth Evans, they loved strange, reticent Mr. Evans. They loved music, pictures and dainty china, with which George Mansion filled his beautiful home. They loved books and animals, but, most of all, these two loved the Indian people, loved their legends, their habits, their customs—loved the people themselves. Small wonder, then, that their children should be born with pride of race and heritage, and should face the world with that peculiar, unconquerable courage that only a fighting ancestry can give.

As the years drifted on, many distinctions came to the little family of the "Grand Mansions." The chief's ability as an orator, his fluency of speech, his ceaseless war against the inroads of the border white men and their lawlessness among his own people—all gradually but surely brought him, inch by inch, before the notice of those who sat in the "seats of the mighty" of both church and state. His presence was frequently demanded at Ottawa, fighting for the cause of his people before the House of Commons, the Senate, and the Governor-General himself. At such times he would always wear his native buckskin costume, and his amazing rhetoric, augmented by the gorgeous trappings of his office and his inimitable courtesy of manner, won him friends and followers among the lawmakers of the land. He never fought for a cause and lost it, never returned to Lydia and his people except in a triumph of victory. Social honors came to him as well as political distinctions. Once, soon after his marriage, a special review of the British troops quartered at Toronto was called in his honor and he rode beside the general, making a brilliant picture, clad as he was in buckskins and scarlet blanket and astride his pet black pony, as he received the salutes of company after company of England's picked soldiers as they wheeled past. And when King Edward of England visited Canada as Prince of Wales, he fastened with his own royal hands a heavy silver medal to the buckskin covering George Mansion's breast, and the royal words were very sincere as they fell from the prince's lips: "This medal is for recognition of your loyalty in battling for your own people, even as your ancestors battled for the British Crown." Then in later years, when Prince Arthur of Connaught accepted the title of "Chief," conferred upon him with elaborate ceremony by the chiefs, braves and warriors of the great Iroquois Council, it was George Mansion who was chosen as special escort to the royal visitor—George Mansion and his ancient and honored father, who, hand-in-hand with the young prince, walked to and fro, chanting the impressive ritual of bestowing the title. Even Bismarck, the "Iron Chancellor" of Germany, heard of this young Indian warring for the welfare of his race, and sent a few kindly words, with his own photograph, from across seas to encourage the one who was fighting, single-handed, the menace of white man's greed and white man's firewater.

And Lydia, with her glad and still girlish

heart, gloried in her husband's achievements and in the recognition accorded him by the great world beyond the Indian Reserve, beyond the wilderness, beyond the threshold of their own home. In only one thing were their lives at all separated. She took no part in his public life. She hated the glare of the fierce light that beat upon prominent lives, the unrest of fame, the disquiet of public careers.

"No," she would answer, when oftentimes he begged her to accompany him and share his success and honors, "no, I was homeless so long that 'home' is now my ambition. My babies need me here, and you need me here when you return, far more than you need me on platform or parade. Go forth and fight the enemy, storm the battlements and win the laurels, but let me keep the garrison—here at home, with our babies all about me and a welcome to our warrior husband and father when he returns from war."

Then he would laugh and coax again, but always with the same result. Every day, whether he went forth to the Indian Council across the river, or when more urgent duties called him to the Capital, she always stood at the highest window waving her handkerchief until he was out of sight, and that dainty flag lent strength to his purpose and courage to his heart, for he knew the home citadel was there awaiting his return—knew that she would be at that selfsame window, their children clustered about her skirts, her welcoming hands waving a greeting instead of a good-bye, as soon as he faced the home portals once more, and in his heart of hearts George Mansion felt that his wife had chosen the wiser, greater part; that their children would some day arise and call her blessed because she refused to wing away from the home nest, even if by so doing she left him to take his flights alone.

But in all their world there was no one prouder of his laurels and successes than his home-loving little English wife, and the mother-heart of her must be forgiven for welcoming each new honor as a so much greater heritage for their children. Each distinction won by her husband only established a higher standard for their children to live up to. She prayed and hoped and prayed again that they would all be worthy such a father, that they would never fall short of his excellence. To this end she taught, labored for, and loved them, and they, in turn, child-wise, responded to her teaching, imitating her allegiance to their father, reflecting her fealty, and duplicating her actions. So she molded these little ones with the mother-hand that they felt through all their after lives, which were but images of her own in all that concerned their father.

*　*　*　*　*　*　*　*

The first great shadow that fell on this united little circle was when George Mansion's mother quietly folded her "broadcloth" about her shoulders for the last time, when the little old tobacco pipe lay unfilled and unlighted, when the finely-beaded moccasins were empty of the dear feet that had wandered so gently, so silently into the Happy

Hunting Grounds. George Mansion was bowed with woe. His mother had been to him the queen of all women, and her death left a desolation in his heart that even his wife could not assuage. It was a grief he really never overcame. Fortunately his mother had grown so attached to Lydia that his one disobedience—that of his marriage—never reproached him. Had the gentle little old Indian woman died before the episode of the moccasin which brought complete reconciliation, it is doubtful if her son would ever have been quite the same again. As it was, with the silence and stoicism of his race he buried his grief in his own heart, without allowing it to cast a gloom over his immediate household.

But after that the ancient chief, his father, came more frequently to George's home, and was always an honored guest. The children loved him, Lydia had the greatest respect and affection for him, the greatest sympathy for his loneliness, and she ever made him welcome and her constant companion when he visited them. He used to talk to her much of George, and once or twice gave her grave warnings as to his recklessness and lack of caution in dealing with the ever-growing menace of the whiskey traffic among the Indians. The white men who supplied and traded this liquor were desperadoes, a lawless set of ruffians who for some time had determined to rid their stamping-ground of George Mansion, as he was the chief opponent to their business, and with the way well cleared of him and his unceasing resistance, their scoundrelly trade would be an easy matter.

"Use all your influence, Lydia," the old father

75

would say, "to urge him never to seize the ill-gotten timber or destroy their whiskey, unless he has other Indian wardens with him. They'll kill him if they can, those white men. They have been heard to threaten."

For some time this very thing had been crowding its truth about his wife's daily life. Threatening and anonymous letters had more than once been received by her husband—letters that said he would be "put out of the way" unless he stopped interfering in the liquor trade. There was no ignoring the fact that danger was growing daily, that the fervent young chief was allowing his zeal to overcome his caution, was hazarding his life for the protection of his people against a crying evil. Once a writer of these unsigned letters threatened to burn his house down in the dead of night, another to maim his horses and cattle, others to "do away" with him. His crusade was being waged under the weight of a cross that was beginning to fall on his loyal wife, and to overshadow his children. Then one night the blow fell. Blind with blood, crushed and broken, he staggered and reeled home, unaided, unassisted, and in excruciating torture. Nine white men had attacked him from behind in a border village a mile from his home, where he had gone to intercept a load of whiskey that was being hauled into the Indian Reserve. Eight of those lawbreakers circled about him, while the ninth struck him from behind with a leaden plumb attached to an elastic throw-string. The deadly thing crushed in his skull; he dropped where he stood, as if shot. Then brutal boots kicked his face, his head, his back, and, with curses, his assailants left him—for dead.

With a vitality born of generations of warriors, he regained consciousness, staggered the mile to his own gate, where he met a friend, who, with extreme concern, began to assist him into his home. But he refused the helping arm with, "No, I go alone; it would alarm Lydia if I could not walk alone." These, with the few words he spoke as he entered the kitchen, where his wife was overseeing old Milly get the evening meal, were the last intelligent words he spoke for many a day.

"Lydia, they've hurt me at last," he said, gently.

She turned at the sound of his strained voice. A thousand emotions overwhelmed her at the terrifying sight before her. Love, fear, horror, all broke forth from her lips in a sharp, hysterical cry, but above this cry sounded the gay laughter of the children who were playing in the next room, their shrill young voices raised in merriment over some new sport. In a second the mother-heart asserted itself. Their young eyes must not see this ghastly thing.

"Milly!" she cried to the devoted Indian servant, "help Chief George." Then dashing into the next room, she half sobbed, "Children, children! hush, oh, hush! Poor father—"

She never finished the sentence. With a turn of her arm she swept them all into the drawing-room, closed the door, and flew back to her patriot husband.

For weeks and weeks he lay fighting death as

only a determined man can—his upper jaw broken on both sides, his lower jaw splintered on one side, his skull so crushed that to the end of his days a silver dollar could quite easily be laid flat in the cavity, a jagged and deep hole in his back, and injuries about the knees and leg bones. And all these weeks Lydia hovered above his pillow, night and day, nursing, tending, helping, cheering. What effort it cost her to be bright and smiling no tongue can tell, for her woman's heart saw that this was but the beginning of the end. She saw it when in his delirium he raved to get better, to be allowed to get up and go on with the fight; saw that his spirit never rested, for fear that, now he was temporarily inactive, the whiskey dealers would have their way. She knew then that she must school herself to endure this thing again; that she must never ask him to give up his life work, never be less courageous than he, though that courage would mean never a peaceful moment to her when he was outside their own home.

Mr. Evans was a great comfort to her during those terrible weeks. Hour after hour he would sit beside the injured man, never speaking or moving, only watching quietly, while Lydia barely snatched the necessary sleep a nurse must have, or attended to the essential needs of the children, who, however, were jealously cared for by faithful Milly. During those times the children never spoke except in whispers, their rigid Indian-English training in self-effacement and obedience being now of untold value.

But love and nursing and bravery all counted

78

in the end, and one day George Mansion walked downstairs, the doctor's arm on one side, Lydia's on the other. He immediately asked for his pistol and his dagger, cleaned the one, oiled and sharpened the other, and said, "I'll be ready for them again in a month's time."

But while he lay injured his influential white friends and the Government at Ottawa had not been idle. The lawless creature who dealt those unmerited blows was tried, convicted and sent to Kingston Penitentiary for seven years. So one enemy was out of the way for the time being. It was at this time that advancing success lost him another antagonist, who was placed almost in the rank of an ally.

George Mansion was a guest of the bishop of his diocese, as he was a lay delegate accompanying Mr. Evans to the Anglican Synod. The chief's work had reached other ears than those of the Government at Ottawa, and the bishop was making much of the patriot, when in the See House itself an old clergyman approached him with outstretched hand and the words, "I would like you to call bygones just bygones."

"I don't believe I have the honor of knowing you, sir," replied the Indian, with a puzzled but gracious look.

"I am your wife's brother-in-law," said the old clergyman, "the man who would not allow her to be married from my house—that is, married to *you*."

The Indian bit his lip and instinctively stepped backward. Added to his ancestral creed of never

forgiving such injury, came a rush of memory—
the backward-surging picture of his homeless
little sweetheart and all that she had endured.
Then came the memory of his dead mother's
teaching—teaching she had learned from her own
mother, and she in turn from her mother: "Always
forget yourself for *old* people, always honor the
old."

Instantly George Mansion arose—arose above
the prejudices of his blood, above the traditions
of his race, arose to the highest plane a man can
reach—the memory of his mother's teaching.

"I would hardly be here as a lay delegate of
my church were I not willing to let bygones be
bygones," he said, simply, and laid his hand in
that of the old clergyman, about whose eyes
there was moisture, perhaps because this opportunity for peacemaking had come so tardily.

*   *   *   *   *   *   *   *

The little family of the "Grand Mansions"
were now growing to very "big childhood," and
the inevitable day came when Lydia's heart must
bear the wrench of having her firstborn say good-
bye to take his college course. She was not the
type of mother who would keep the boy at home
because of the heartache the good-byes must bring,
but the parting was certainly a hard one, and she
watched his going with a sense of loss that was
almost greater than her pride in him. He had given
evidence of the most remarkable musical talent.
He played classical airs even before he knew a note,
and both his parents were in determined unison

about this talent being cultivated. The following year the oldest daughter also entered college, having had a governess at home for a year, as some preparation. But these changes brought no difference into the home, save that George Mansion's arm grew stronger daily in combat against the old foe. Then came the second attack of the enemy, when six white men beset him from behind, again knocking him insensible, with a heavy blue beech handspike. They broke his hand and three ribs, knocked out his teeth, injured his side and head; then, seizing his pistol, shot at him, the ball fortunately not reaching a vital spot. As his senses swam he felt them drag his poor maimed body into the middle of the road, so it would appear as if horses had trampled him, then he heard them say, "*This* time the devil is dead." But hours afterwards he again arose, again walked home, five interminable miles, again greeted his ever watchful and anxious wife with, "Lydia, they've hurt me once more." Then came weeks of renewed suffering, of renewed care and nursing, of renewed vitality, and at last of conquered health.

These two terrible illnesses seemed to raise Lydia into a peculiar, half-protecting attitude towards him. In many ways she "mothered" him almost as though he were her son—he who had always been the leader, and so strong and self-reliant. After this, when he went forth on his crusades, she watched his going with the haunting fear with which one would watch a child wandering on the edge of a chasm. She waited on him when he returned, served him with the tenderness with which one serves a cripple or a baby. Once he caught her arm, as she carried to him a cup of broth, after he had spent wearisome hours at the same old battle, and turning towards her, said softly: "You are like my mother used to be to me." She did not ask him in what way—she knew—and carried broth to him when next he came home half exhausted. Gradually he now gathered about him a little force of zealous Indians who became enthusiastic to take up arms with him against the whiskey dealers. He took greater precautions in his work, for the growing mist of haunting anxiety in Lydia's eyes began to call to him that there were other claims than those of the nation. His splendid zeal had brought her many a sleepless night, when she knew he was scouring the forests for hidden supplies of the forbidden merchandise, and that a whole army of desperadoes would not deter him from fulfilling his duty of destroying it. He felt, rather than saw, that she never bade him good-bye but that she was prepared not to see him again alive. Added to this he began to suffer as she did—to find that in his good-byes was the fear of never seeing her again. He, who had always been so fearless, was now afraid of the day when he should not return and she would be once more alone.

So he let his younger and eager followers do some of the battling, though he never relaxed his vigilance, never took off his armor, so to speak. But now he spent long days and quiet nights with Lydia and his children. They entertained many guests, for the young people were vigorous and laughter-loving, and George and Lydia never grew old, never grew weary, never grew commonplace. All the year round guests came to the hospitable country house—men and women of culture, of learning, of artistic tastes, of congenial habits. Scientists, authors, artists, all made their pilgrimages to this unique household, where refinement and much luxury, and always a glad welcome from the chief and his English wife, made their visits long remembered. And in some way or other, as their children grew up, those two seemed to come closer together once more. They walked among the trees they had loved in those first bridal days, they rested by the river shore, they wandered over the broad meadows and bypaths of the old estate, they laughed together frequently like children, and always and ever talked of and acted for the good of the Indian people who were so unquestionably the greatest interest in their lives, outside their own children. But one day, when the beautiful estate he was always so proud of was getting ready to smile under the suns of spring, he left her just when she needed him most, for their boys had plunged forward into the world of business in the large cities, and she wanted a strong arm to lean on. It was the only time he failed to respond to her devoted nursing, but now she could not bring him back from the river's brink, as she had so often done before. Cold had settled in all the broken places of his poor body, and he slipped away from her, a sacrifice to his fight against evil on the altar of his nation's good. In his feverish wanderings he returned to the tongue of his childhood, the beautiful, dulcet Mohawk. Then recollecting and commanding himself, he would weakly apologize to Lydia with: "I forgot; I thought it was my mother," and almost his last words were, "It must be by my mother's side," meaning his resting-place. So his valiant spirit went fearlessly forth.

* * * * * * * *

"Do you ever think, dear," said Lydia to her youngest child, some years later, "that you are writing the poetry that always lived in an unexpressed state here in my breast?"

"No, Marmee," answered the girl, who was beginning to mount the ladder of literature, "I never knew you wanted to *write* poetry, although I knew you loved it."

"Indeed, I did," answered the mother, "but I never could find expression for it. I was made just to sing, I often think, but I never had the courage to sing in public. But I did want to write poetry, and now you, dear, are doing it for me. How proud your father would have been of you!"

"Oh, he knows! I'm sure he knows all that I have written," answered the girl, with the sublime faith that youth has in its own convictions. "And if you like my verses, Marmee, I am sure he does, for he knows."

"Perhaps," murmured the older woman. "I often feel that he is very near to us. I never have felt that he is really gone very far away from me."

"Poor little Marmee!" the girl would say to

herself. "She misses him yet. I believe she will always miss him."

Which was the truth. She saw constantly his likeness in all her children, bits of his character, shades of his disposition, reflections of his gifts and talents, hints of his bravery, and she always spoke of these with a commending air, as though they were characteristics to be cultivated, to be valued and fostered.

At first her fear of leaving her children, even to join him, was evident, she so believed in a mother's care and love being a necessity to a child. She had sadly missed it all out of her own strange life, and she felt she *must* live until this youngest daughter grew to be a woman. Perhaps this desire, this mother-love, kept her longer beside her children than she would have stayed without it, for the years rolled on, and her hair whitened, her once springing step halted a little, the glorious blue of her English eyes grew very dreamy, and tender, and wistful. Was she seeing the great Hereafter unfold itself before her as her steps drew nearer and nearer?

And one night the Great Messenger knocked softly at her door, and with a sweet, gentle sigh she turned and followed where he led—joining gladly the father of her children in the land that holds both whites and Indians as one.

And the daughter who writes the verses her mother always felt, but found no words to express, never puts a last line to a story, or a sweet cadence into a poem, but she says to herself as she holds her mother's memory within her heart:

"She knows—she knows."

Catharine of the "Crow's Nest"

*T*HE GREAT transcontinental railway had been
in running order for years before the managers
thereof decided to build a second line across the
Rocky Mountains. But "passes" are few and
far between in those gigantic fastnesses, and the
fearless explorers, followed by the equally fearless
surveyors, were many a toilsome month conquering
the heights, depths and dangers of the "Crow's
Nest Pass."

Eastward stretched the gloriously fertile plains
of southern "Sunny Alberta," westward lay the
limpid blue of the vast and indescribably beautiful
Kootenay Lakes, but between these two arose a
barrier of miles and miles of granite and stone
and rock, over and through which a railway must
be constructed. Tunnels, bridges, grades must be
bored, built and blasted out. It was the work of
science, endurance and indomitable courage. The
summers in the cañons were seething hot, the
winters in the mountains perishingly cold, with
apparently inexhaustible snow clouds circling forever about the rugged peaks—snows in which many
a good, honest laborer was lost until the eagles and
vultures came with the April thaws, and wheeled
slowly above the pulseless sleeper, if indeed the
wolves and mountain lions had permitted him to
lie thus long unmolested. Those were rough and
rugged days, through which equally rough and
rugged men served and suffered to find foundations
whereon to lay those two threads of steel that now

cling like a cobweb to the walls of the wonderful "gap" known as Crow's Nest Pass.

Work progressed steadily, and before winter set in construction camps were built far into "the gap," the furthermost one being close to the base of a majestic mountain, which was also named "The Crow's Nest." It arose beyond the camp with almost overwhelming immensity. Dense forests of Douglas fir and bull pines shouldered their way up one-third of its height, but above the timber line the shaggy, bald rock reared itself thousands of feet skyward, desolate, austere and deserted by all living things; not even the sure-footed mountain goat travelled up those frowning, precipitous heights; no bird rested its wing in that frozen altitude. The mountain arose, distinct, alone, isolated, the most imperial monarch of all that regal Pass.

The construction gang called it "Old Baldy," for after working some months around its base, it began to grow into their lives. Not so, however, with the head engineer from Montreal, who regarded it always with baleful eye, and half laughingly, half seriously, called it his "Jonah."

"Not a thing has gone right since we worked in sight of that old monster," he was heard to say frequently; and it did seem as if there were some truth in it. There had been deaths, accidents and illness among the men. Once, owing to transportation difficulties, the rations were short for days, and the men were in rebellious spirit in consequence. Twice whiskey had been smuggled in, to the utter demoralization of the camp; and one morning, as a last straw, "Cookee" had nearly severed his left hand from his arm with a meat axe. Young Wingate, the head engineer, and Mr. Brown, the foreman, took counsel together. For the three meals of that day they tried three different men out of the gang as "cookees." No one could eat the atrocious food they manufactured. Then Brown bethought himself. "There's an Indian woman living up the cañon that can cook like a French chef," he announced, after a day of unspeakable gnawing beneath his belt. "How about getting her? I've tasted pork and beans at her shack, and flapjacks, and—"

"Get her! get her!" clamored Wingate. "Even if she poisons us, it's better than starving. I'll ride over to-night and offer her big wages."

"How about her staying here?" asked Brown. "The boys are pretty rough and lawless at times, you know."

"Get the axe men to build her a good, roomy shack—the best logs in the place. We'll give her a lock and key for it, and you, Brown, report the very first incivility to her that you hear of," said Wingate, crisply.

That evening Mr. Wingate himself rode over to the cañon; it was a good mile, and the trail was rough in the extreme. He did not dismount when he reached the lonely log lodge, but rapping on the door with the butt of his quirt, he awaited its opening. There was some slight stirring about inside before this occurred; then the door slowly opened, and she stood before him—

88

a rather tall woman, clad in buckskin garments, with a rug made of coyote skins about her shoulders; she wore the beaded leggings and moccasins of her race, and her hair, jet black, hung in ragged plaits about her dark face, from which mournful eyes looked out at the young Montrealer.

Yes, she would go for the wages he offered, she said in halting English; she would come to-morrow at daybreak; she would cook their breakfast.

"Better come to-night," he urged. "The men get down the grade to work very early; breakfast must be on time."

"I be on time," she replied. "I sleep here this night, every night. I not sleep in camp."

Then he told her of the shack he had ordered, and that was even now being built.

She shook her head. "I sleep here every night," she reiterated.

Wingate had met many Indians in his time, so dropped the subject, knowing well that persuasion or argument would be utterly useless.

"All right," he said; "you must do as you like; only remember, an early breakfast to-morrow."

"I 'member," she replied.

He had ridden some twenty yards, when he turned to call back: "Oh, what's your name, please?"

"Catharine," she answered, simply.

"Thank you," he said, and, touching his hat lightly, rode down towards the cañon. Just as he was dipping over its rim he looked back. She was still standing in the doorway, and above and about her were the purple shadows, the awful solitude, of Crow's Nest Mountain.

* * * * * * * *

Catharine had been cooking at the camp for weeks. The meals were good, the men respected her, and she went her way to and from her shack at the cañon as regularly as the world went around. The autumn slipped by, and the nipping frosts of early winter and the depths of early snows were already daily occurrences. The big group of solid log shacks that formed the construction camp were all made weather-tight against the long mountain winter. Trails were beginning to be blocked, streams to freeze, and "Old Baldy" already wore a canopy of snow that reached down to the timber line.

"Catharine," spoke young Wingate, one morning, when the clouds hung low and a soft snow fell, packing heavily on the selfsame snows of the previous night, "you had better make up your mind to occupy the shack here. You won't be able to go to your home much longer now at night; it gets dark so early, and the snows are too heavy."

"I go home at night," she repeated.

"But you can't all winter," he exclaimed. "If there was one single horse we could spare from the grade work, I'd see you got it for your journeys, but there isn't. We're terribly short now; every animal in the Pass is overworked as it is. You'd better not try going home any more."

"I go home at night," she repeated.

Wingate frowned impatiently; then in afterthought he smiled. "All right, Catharine," he said, "but I warn you. You'll have a searchparty out after you some dark morning, and you know it won't be pleasant to be lost in the snows up that cañon."

"But I go home, night-time," she persisted, and that ended the controversy.

But the catastrophe he predicted was inevitable. Morning after morning he would open the door of the shack he occupied with the other officials, and, looking up the white wastes through the grey-blue dawn, he would watch the distances with an anxiety that meant more than a consideration for his breakfast. The woman interested him. She was so silent, so capable, so stubborn. What was behind all this strength of character? What had given that depth of mournfulness to her eyes? Often he had surprised her watching him, with an odd longing in her face; it was something of the expression he could remember his mother wore when she looked at him long, long ago. It was a vague, haunting look that always brought back the one great tragedy of his life—a tragedy he was even now working night and day at his chosen profession to obliterate from his memory, lest he should be forever unmanned—forever a prey to melancholy.

He was still a young man, but when little more than a boy he had married, and for two years was transcendently happy. Then came the cry of "Kootenay Gold" ringing throughout Canada —of the untold wealth of Kootenay mines. Like thousands of others he followed the beckoning of that yellow finger, taking his young wife and baby daughter West with him. The little town of Nelson, crouching on its beautiful hills, its feet laved by the waters of Kootenay Lake, was then in its first robust, active infancy. Here he settled, going out alone on long prospecting expeditions; sometimes he was away a week, sometimes a month, with the lure of the gold forever in his veins, but the laughter of his child, the love of his wife, forever in his heart. Then—the day of that awful home-coming! For three weeks the fascination of searching for the golden pay-streak had held him in the mountains. No one could find him when it happened, and now all they could tell him was the story of an upturned canoe found drifting on the lake, of a woman's light summer shawl caught in the thwarts, of a child's little silken bonnet washed ashore.* The great-hearted men of the West had done their utmost in the search that followed. Miners, missionaries, prospectors, Indians, settlers, gamblers, outlaws, had one and all turned out, for they liked young Wingate, and they adored his loving wife and dainty child. But the search was useless. The wild shores of Kootenay Lake alone held the secret of their resting-place.

Young Wingate faced the East once more. There was but one thing to do with his life— work, *work*, WORK; and the harder, the more difficult, that work, the better. It was this very difficulty that made the engineering on the Crow's Nest Pass so attractive to him. So here he was

*Fact

92

building grades, blasting tunnels, with Catharine's mournful eyes following him daily, as if she divined something of that long-ago sorrow that had shadowed his almost boyish life.

He liked the woman, and his liking quickened his eye to her hardships, his ear to the hint of lagging weariness in her footsteps; so he was the first to notice it the morning she stumped into the cook-house, her feet bound up in furs, her face drawn in agony.

"Catharine," he exclaimed, "your feet have been frozen!"

She looked like a culprit, but answered: "Not much; I get lose in storm las' night."

"I thought this would happen," he said, indignantly. "After this you sleep here."

"I sleep home," she said, doggedly.

"I won't have it," he declared. "I'll cook for the men myself first."

"All right," she replied. "You cookee; I go home—me."

That night there was a terrible storm. The wind howled down the throat of the Pass, and the snow fell like bales of sheep's wool, blanketing the trails and drifting into the railroad cuts until they attained their original level. But after she had cooked supper Catharine started for home as usual. The only unusual thing about it was that the next morning she did not return. It was Sunday, the men's day "off." Wingate ate no breakfast, but after swallowing some strong tea he turned to the foreman. "Mr. Brown, will you come with me to try and hunt up Catharine?" he asked.

"Yes, if we can get beyond the door," assented Brown. "But I doubt if we can make the cañon, sir."

"We'll have a try at it, anyway," said the young engineer. "I almost doubt myself if she made it last night."

"She's a stubborn woman," commented Brown.

"And has her own reasons for it, I suppose," replied Wingate. "But that has nothing to do with her being lost or frozen. If something had not happened I'm sure she would have come to-day, notwithstanding I scolded her yesterday, and told her I'd rather cook myself than let her run such risks. How will we go, Mr. Brown; horses or snowshoes?"

"Shoes," said the foreman decidedly. "That snow'll be above the middle of the biggest horse in the outfit."

So they set forth on their tramp up the slopes, peering right and left as they went for any indication of the absent woman. Wingate's old grief was knocking at his heart once more. A woman lost in the appalling vastness of this great Western land was entering into his life again. It took them a full hour to go that mile, although both were experts on the shoes, but as they reached the rim of the cañon they were rewarded by seeing a thin blue streak of smoke curling up from her lodge "chimney." Wingate sat down in the snows weakly. The relief had unmanned him.

"I didn't know how much I cared," he said,

"until I knew she was safe. She looks at me as my mother used to; her eyes are like mother's, and I loved my mother."

It was a simple, direct speech, but Brown caught its pathos.

"She's a good woman," he blurted out, as they trudged along towards the shack. They knocked on the door. There was no reply. Then just as Wingate suggested forcing it in case she were ill and lying helpless within, a long, low call from the edge of the cañon startled them. They turned and had not followed the direction from which the sound came more than a few yards when they met her coming towards them on snowshoes; in her arms she bore a few faggots, and her face, though smileless, was very welcoming.

She opened the door, bidding them enter. It was quite warm inside, and the air of simple comfort derived from crude benches, tables and shelves, assured them that she had not suffered. Near the fire was drawn a rough home-built couch, and on it lay in heaped disorder a pile of grey blankets. As the two men warmed their hands at the grateful blaze, the blankets stirred. Then a small hand crept out and a small arm tossed the covers a little aside.

"*Catharine*," exclaimed Wingate, "have you a child here?"

"Yes," she said simply.

"How long is it that you have had it here?" he demanded.

"Since before I work at your camp," she replied.

"Whew!" said the foreman, "I now understand why she came home nights."

"To think I never guessed it!" murmured Wingate. Then to Catharine: "Why didn't you bring it into camp and keep it there day and night with you, instead of taking these dangerous tramps night and morning?"

"It is a girl child," she answered.

"Well, what of it?" he asked impatiently.

"Your camp no place for girl child," she replied, looking directly at him. "Your men they rough, they get whiskey sometimes. They fight. They speak bad words, what you call *swear*. I not want her hear that. I not want her see whiskey man."

"Oh, Brown!" said Wingate, turning to his companion. "What a reproach! What a reproach! Here our gang is—the vanguard of the highest civilization, but unfit for association with a little Indian child!"

Brown stood speechless, although in his rough, honest mind he was going over a list of those very "swears" she objected to, but they were mentally directed at the whole outfit of his ruffianly construction gang. He was silently swearing at them for their own shortcomings in that very thing.

The child on the couch stirred again. This time the firelight fell full across the little arm. Wingate stared at it, then his eyes widened. He looked at the woman, then back at the bare arm. It was the arm of a *white* child.

"Catharine, was your husband *white?*" he asked, in a voice that betrayed anxiety.

"I got no husban'," she replied, somewhat defiantly.

"Then—" he began, but his voice faltered.

She came and stood between him and the couch. Something of the look of a she-panther came into her face, her figure, her attitude. Her eyes lost their mournfulness and blazed a black-red at him. Her whole body seemed ready to spring. "You not touch the girl child!" she half snarled. "I not let you touch her; she *mine*, though I have no husban'!"

"I don't want to touch her, Catharine," he said gently, trying to pacify her. "Believe me, I don't want to touch her."

The woman's whole being changed. A thousand mother-lights gleamed from her eyes, a thousand measures of mother-love stormed at her heart. She stepped close, very close to him and laid her small brown hand on his, then drawing him nearer to her said: "Yes, you *do* want to touch her; you not speak truth when you say 'no.' You *do* want to touch her!" With a rapid movement she flung back the blankets, then slipping her bare arm about him she bent his form until he was looking straight into the child's face—a face the living miniature of his own! His eyes, his hair, his small kindly mouth, his fair, perfect skin. He staggered erect.

"Catharine! what does it mean? What does it mean?" he said hoarsely.

"*Your child—*" she half questioned, half affirmed.

"Mine? Mine?" he called, without human understanding in his voice. "Oh, Catharine! Where did you get her?"

"The shores of Kootenay Lake," she answered.

97

"Was—was—she *alone?*" he cried.

The woman looked away, slowly shaking her head, and her voice was very gentle as she replied: "No, she alive a little, but *the other*, whose arms 'round her, she not alive; my people, the Kootenay Indians, and I—we—we bury that other."

For a moment there was a speaking silence, then young Wingate, with the blessed realization that half his world had been saved for him, flung himself on his knees, and, with his arms locked about the little girl, was calling:

"Margie! Margie! Papa's little Margie girl! Do you remember papa? Oh, Margie! Do you? Do you?"

Something dawned in the child's eyes—something akin to a far-off memory. For a moment she looked wonderingly at him, then put her hand up to his forehead and gently pulled a lock of his fair hair that always curled there—an old trick of hers. Then she looked down at his vest pocket, slowly pulled out his watch and held it to her ear. The next minute her arms slipped round his neck.

"Papa," she said, "papa been away from Margie a long time."

Young Wingate was sobbing. He had not noticed that the big, rough foreman had gone out of the shack with tear-dimmed eyes, and had quietly closed the door behind him.

* * * * * * * *

It was evening before Wingate got all the story from Catharine, for she was slow of speech, and found it hard to explain her feelings. But Brown, who had returned alone to the camp in the morning, now came back, packing an immense bundle of all the tinned delicacies he could find, which, truth to tell, were few. He knew some words of Kootenay, and led Catharine on to reveal the strange history that sounded like some tale from fairyland. It appeared that the reason Catharine did not attempt to go to the camp that morning was that Margie was not well, so she would not leave her, but in her heart of hearts she knew young Wingate would come searching to her lodge. She loved the child as only an Indian woman can love an adopted child. She longed for him to come when she found Margie was ill, yet dreaded that coming from the depths of her soul. She dreaded the hour he would see the child and take it away. For the moment she looked upon his face, the night he rode over to engage her to cook, months ago, she had known he was Margie's father. The little thing was the perfect mirror of him, and Catharine's strange wild heart rejoiced to find him, yet hid the child from him for very fear of losing it out of her own life.

After finding it almost dead in its dead mother's arms on the shore, the Indians had given it to Catharine for the reason that she could speak some English. They were only a passing band of Kootenays, and as they journeyed on and on, week in and week out, they finally came to Crow's Nest Mountain. Here the child fell ill, so they built Catharine a log shack, and left her with plenty of food, sufficient to last until the railway gang had worked that far up the Pass, when more food would be available. When she had finished the strange history, Wingate looked at her long and lovingly.

"Catharine," he said, "you were almost going to fight me once to-day. You stood between the couch and me like a panther. What changed you so that you led me to my baby girl yourself?"

"I make one last fight to keep her," she said, haltingly. "She mine so long, I want her; I want her till I die. Then I think many times I see your face at camp. It look like sky when sun does not shine—all cloud, no smile, no laugh. I know you think of your baby then. Then I watch you many times. Then after while my heart is sick for you, like you are my own boy, like I am your own mother. I hate see no sun in your face. I think I not good mother to you; if I was good mother I would give you your child; make the sun come in your face. To-day I make last fight to keep the child. She's mine, so long I want her till I die. Then somet'ing in my heart say, 'He's like son to you, as if he your own boy; make him glad—happy. Oh, ver' glad! Be like his own mother. Find him his baby.'"

"Bless the mother heart of her!" growled the big foreman, frowning to keep his face from twitching.

It was twilight when they mounted the horses one of the men had brought up for them to ride home on, Wingate with his treasure-child hugged tightly in his arms. Words were powerless to thank the woman who had saved half his world for him. His voice choked when he tried, but

100

she understood, and her woman's heart was very, very full.

Just as they reached the rim of the cañon Wingate turned and looked back. His arms tightened about little Margie as ,his eyes rested on Catharine—as once before she was standing in the doorway, alone; alone, and above and about her were the purple shadows, the awful solitude of Crow's Nest Mountain.

"Brown!" he called. "Hold on, Brown! I *can't do it! I can't leave her like that!"*

He wheeled his horse about and, plunging back through the snow, rode again to her door. Her eyes radiated as she looked at him. Years had been wiped from his face since the morning. He was a laughing boy once more.

"You are right," he said, "I cannot keep my little girl in that rough camp. You said it was no place for a girl child. You are right. I will send her into Calgary until my survey is over. Catharine, will you go with her, take care of her, nurse her, guard her for me? You said I was as your own son; will you be that good mother to me that you want to be? Will you do this for your white boy?"

He had never seen her smile before. A moment ago her heart had been breaking, but now she knew with a great gladness that she was not only going to keep and care for Margie, but that this laughing boy would be as a son to her for all time. No wonder that Catharine of the Crow's Nest smiled!

A Red Girl's Reasoning

"*B*E PRETTY good to her, Charlie, my boy, or she'll balk sure as shooting."

That was what old Jimmy Robinson said to his brand new son-in-law, while they waited for the bride to reappear.

"Oh! you bet, there's no danger of much else. I'll be good to her, help me Heaven," replied Charlie McDonald, brightly.

"Yes, of course you will," answered the old man, "but don't you forget, there's a good big bit of her mother in her, and," closing his left eye significantly, "you don't understand these Indians as I do."

"But I'm just as fond of them, Mr. Robinson," Charlie said assertively, "and I get on with them too, now, don't I?"

"Yes, pretty well for a town boy; but when you have lived forty years among these people, as I have done; when you have had your wife as long as I have had mine—for there's no getting over it, Christine's disposition is as native as her mother's, every bit—and perhaps when you've owned for eighteen years a daughter as dutiful, as loving, as fearless, and, alas! as obstinate as that little piece you are stealing away from me to-day—I tell you, youngster, you'll know more than you know now. It is kindness for kindness, bullet for bullet, blood for blood. Remember, what you are, she will be," and the old Hudson Bay trader scrutinized Charlie McDonald's face like a detective.

102

It was a happy, fair face, good to look at, with a certain ripple of dimples somewhere about the mouth, and eyes that laughed out the very sunniness of their owner's soul. There was not a severe nor yet a weak line anywhere. He was a well-meaning young fellow, happily dispositioned, and a great favorite with the tribe at Robinson's Post, whither he had gone in the service of the Department of Agriculture, to assist the local agent through the tedium of a long census-taking.

As a boy he had had the Indian relic-hunting craze, as a youth he had studied Indian archæology and folk-lore, as a man he consummated his predilections for Indianology by loving, winning and marrying the quiet little daughter of the English trader, who himself had married a native woman some twenty years ago. The country was all backwoods, and the Post miles and miles from even the semblance of civilization, and the lonely young Englishman's heart had gone out to the girl who, apart from speaking a very few words of English, was utterly uncivilized and uncultured, but had withal that marvellously innate refinement so universally possessed by the higher tribes of North American Indians.

Like all her race, observant, intuitive, having a horror of ridicule, consequently quick at acquirement and teachable in mental and social habits, she had developed from absolute pagan indifference into a sweet, elderly Christian woman, whose broken English, quiet manner, and still handsome copper-colored face, were the joy of old Robinson's declining years.

103

He had given their daughter Christine all the advantages of his own learning—which, if truthfully told, was not universal; but the girl had a fair common education, and the native adaptability to progress.

She belonged to neither and still to both types of the cultured Indian. The solemn, silent, almost heavy manner of the one so commingled with the gesticulating Frenchiness and vivacity of the other, that one unfamiliar with native Canadian life would find it difficult to determine her nationality.

She looked very pretty to Charles McDonald's loving eyes, as she reappeared in the doorway, holding her mother's hand and saying some happy words of farewell. Personally she looked much the same as her sisters, all Canada through, who are the offspring of red and white parentage— olive-complexioned, grey-eyed, black-haired, with figure slight and delicate, and the wistful, unfathomable expression in her whole face that turns one so heart-sick as they glance at the young Indians of to-day—it is the forerunner too frequently of "the white man's disease," consumption —but McDonald was pathetically in love, and thought her the most beautiful woman he had ever seen in his life.

There had not been much of a wedding ceremony. The priest had cantered through the service in Latin, pronounced the benediction in English, and congratulated the "happy couple" in Indian, as a compliment to the assembled tribe in the little amateur structure that did service at the post as a sanctuary.

104

But the knot was tied as firmly and indissolubly as if all Charlie McDonald's swell city friends had crushed themselves up against the chancel to congratulate him, and in his heart he was deeply thankful to escape the flower-pelting, white gloves, rice-throwing, and ponderous stupidity of a breakfast, and indeed all the regulation gimcracks of the usual marriage celebrations, and it was with a hand trembling with absolute happiness that he assisted his little Indian wife into the old muddy buckboard that, hitched to an underbred-looking pony, was to convey them over the first stages of their journey. Then came more adieus, some handclasping, old Jimmy Robinson looking very serious just at the last, Mrs. Jimmy, stout, stolid, betraying nothing of visible emotion, and then the pony, roughshod and shaggy, trudged on, while mutual handwaves were kept up until the old Hudson's Bay Post dropped out of sight, and the buckboard with its lightsome load of hearts, deliriously happy, jogged on over the uneven trail.

* * * * * * * *

She was "all the rage" that winter at the provincial capital. The men called her a "deuced fine little woman." The ladies said she was "just the sweetest wildflower." Whereas she was really but an ordinary, pale, dark girl who spoke slowly and with a strong accent, who danced fairly well, sang acceptably, and never stirred outside the door without her husband.

Charlie was proud of her; he was proud that she had "taken" so well among his friends, proud that she bore herself so complacently in the drawing-rooms of the wives of pompous Government officials, but doubly proud of her almost abject devotion to him. If ever human being was worshipped that being was Charlie McDonald; it could scarcely have been otherwise, for the almost godlike strength of his passion for that little wife of his would have mastered and melted a far more invincible citadel than an already affectionate woman's heart.

Favorites socially, McDonald and his wife went everywhere. In fashionable circles she was "new" —a potent charm to acquire popularity, and the little velvet-clad figure was always the centre of interest among all the women in the room. She always dressed in velvet. No woman in Canada, has she but the faintest dash of native blood in her veins, but loves velvets and silks. As beef to the Englishman, wine to the Frenchman, fads to the Yankee, so are velvet and silk to the Indian girl, be she wild as prairie grass, be she on the borders of civilization, or, having stepped within its boundary, mounted the steps of culture even under its superficial heights.

"Such a dolling little appil blossom," said the wife of a local M.P., who brushed up her etiquette and English once a year at Ottawa. "Does she always laugh so sweetly, and gobble you up with those great big grey eyes of hers, when you are togetheah at home, Mr. McDonald? If so, I should think youah pooah brothah would feel himself terribly *de trop*."

He laughed lightly. "Yes, Mrs. Stuart, there are not two of Christie; she is the same at home and abroad, and as for Joe, he doesn't mind us a bit; he's no end fond of her."

"I'm very glad he is. I always fancied he did not care for her, d'you know."

If ever a blunt woman existed it was Mrs. Stuart. She really meant nothing, but her remark bothered Charlie. He was fond of his brother, and jealous for Christie's popularity. So that night when he and Joe were having a pipe he said:

"I've never asked you yet what you thought of her, Joe." A brief pause, then Joe spoke. "I'm glad she loves you."

"Why?"

"Because that girl has but two possibilities regarding humanity—love or hate."

"Humph! Does she love or hate *you?*"

"Ask her."

"You talk bosh. If she hated you, you'd get out. If she loved you I'd *make* you get out."

Joe McDonald whistled a little, then laughed.

"Now that we are on the subject, I might as well ask—honestly, old man, wouldn't you and Christie prefer keeping house alone to having me always around?"

"Nonsense, sheer nonsense. Why, thunder, man, Christie's no end fond of you, and as for me— you surely don't want assurances from me?"

"No, but I often think a young couple—"

"Young couple be blowed! After a while when they want you and your old surveying chains, and spindle-legged tripod telescope kickshaws, farther west, I venture to say the little woman will cry her eyes out—won't you, Christie?"

107

This last in a higher tone, as through clouds of tobacco smoke he caught sight of his wife passing the doorway.

She entered. "Oh, no, I would not cry; I never do cry, but I would be heart-sore to lose you, Joe, and apart from that"—a little wickedly—"you may come in handy for an exchange some day, as Charlie does always say when he hoards up duplicate relics."

"Are Charlie and I duplicates?"

"Well—not exactly"—her head a little to one side, and eyeing them both merrily, while she slipped softly on to the arm of her husband's chair—"but, in the event of Charlie's failing me"—everyone laughed then. The "some day" that she spoke of was nearer than they thought. It came about in this wise.

There was a dance at the Lieutenant-Governor's, and the world and his wife were there. The nobs were in great feather that night, particularly the women, who flaunted about in new gowns and much splendor. Christie McDonald had a new gown also, but wore it with the utmost unconcern, and if she heard any of the flattering remarks made about her she at least appeared to disregard them.

"I never dreamed you could wear blue so splendidly," said Captain Logan, as they sat out a dance together.

"Indeed she can, though," interposed Mrs. Stuart, halting in one of her gracious sweeps down the room with her husband's private secretary.

"Don't shout so, captain. I can hear every

108

sentence you uttah—of course Mrs. McDonald
can wear blue—she has a morning gown of cadet
blue that she is a picture in."

"You are both very kind," said Christie. "I
like blue; it is the color of all the Hudson's Bay
posts, and the factor's residence is always decorated
in blue."

"Is it really? How interesting—do tell us
some more of your old home, Mrs. McDonald; you
so seldom speak of your life at the post, and we
fellows so often wish to hear of it all," said Logan
eagerly.

"Why do you not ask me of it, then?"

"Well—er, I'm sure I don't know; I'm fully
interested in the Ind—in your people—your
mother's people, I mean, but it always seems so
personal, I suppose; and—a—a—"

"Perhaps you are, like all other white people,
afraid to mention my nationality to me."

The captain winced, and Mrs. Stuart laughed
uneasily. Joe McDonald was not far off, and he
was listening, and chuckling, and saying to himself,
"That's you, Christie, lay 'em out; it won't hurt
'em to know how they appear once in a while."

"Well, Captain Logan," she was saying, "what
is it you would like to hear—of my people, or my
parents, or myself?"

"All, all, my dear," cried Mrs. Stuart clamor-
ously. "I'll speak for him—tell us of yourself
and your mother—your father is delightful, I
am sure—but then he is only an ordinary Englishman, not half as interesting as a foreigner, or—
or, perhaps I should say, a native."

Christie laughed. "Yes," she said, "my father often teases my mother now about how *very* native she was when he married her; then, how could she have been otherwise? She did not know a word of English, and there was not another English-speaking person besides my father and his two companions within sixty miles."

"Two companions, eh? one a Catholic priest and the other a wine merchant, I suppose, and with your father in the Hudson's Bay, they were good representatives of the pioneers in the New World," remarked Logan, waggishly.

"Oh, no, they were all Hudson's Bay men. There were no rumsellers and no missionaries in that part of the country then."

Mrs. Stuart looked puzzled. "*No missionaries?*" she repeated with an odd intonation.

Christie's insight was quick. There was a peculiar expression of interrogation in the eyes of her listeners, and the girl's blood leapt angrily up into her temples as she said hurriedly, "I know what you mean; I know what you are thinking. You are wondering how my parents were married—"

"Well—er, my dear, it seems peculiar—if there was no priest, and no magistrate, why—a—" Mrs. Stuart paused awkwardly.

"The marriage was performed by Indian rites," said Christie.

"Oh, do tell me about it; is the ceremony very interesting and quaint—are your chieftains anything like Buddhist priests?" It was Logan who spoke.

110

"Why, no," said the girl in amazement at that gentleman's ignorance. "There is no ceremony at all, save a feast. The two people just agree to live only with and for each other, and the man takes his wife to his home, just as you do. There is no ritual to bind them; they need none; an Indian's word was his law in those days, you know."

Mrs. Stuart stepped backwards. "Ah!" was all she said. Logan removed his eye-glass and stared blankly at Christie. "And did McDonald marry you in this singular fashion?" he questioned.

"Oh, no, we were married by Father O'Leary. Why do you ask?"

"Because if he had, I'd have blown his brains out to-morrow."

Mrs. Stuart's partner, who had hitherto been silent, coughed and began to twirl his cuff stud nervously, but nobody took any notice of him. Christie had risen, slowly, ominously—risen, with the dignity and pride of an empress.

"Captain Logan," she said, "what do you dare to say to me? What do you dare to mean? Do you presume to think it would not have been lawful for Charlie to marry me according to my people's rites? Do you for one instant dare to question that my parents were not as legally—"

"Don't, dear, don't," interrupted Mrs. Stuart hurriedly; "it is bad enough now, goodness knows; don't make—" Then she broke off blindly. Christie's eyes glared at the mumbling woman, at her uneasy partner, at the horrified captain. Then they rested on the McDonald brothers, who stood

111

within earshot, Joe's face scarlet, her husband's white as ashes, with something in his eyes she had never seen before. It was Joe who saved the situation. Stepping quickly across towards his sister-in-law, he offered her his arm, saying, "The next dance is ours, I think, Christie."

Then Logan pulled himself together, and attempted to carry Mrs. Stuart off for the waltz, but for once in her life that lady had lost her head. "It is shocking!" she said, "outrageously shocking! I wonder if they told Mr. McDonald before he married her!" Then looking hurriedly round, she too saw the young husband's face— and knew that they had not.

"Humph! deuced nice kettle of fish—poor old Charlie has always thought so much of honorable birth."

Logan thought he spoke in an undertone, but "poor old Charlie" heard him. He followed his wife and brother across the room. "Joe," he said, "will you see that a trap is called?" Then to Christie, "Joe will see that you get home all right." He wheeled on his heel then and left the ball-room.

Joe *did* see.

He tucked a poor, shivering, pallid little woman into a cab, and wound her bare throat up in the scarlet velvet cloak that was hanging uselessly over her arm. She crouched down beside him, saying, "I am so cold, Joe; I am so cold," but she did not seem to know enough to wrap herself up. Joe felt all through this long drive that nothing this side of Heaven would be so good

112

as to die, and he was glad when the poor little voice at his elbow said, "What is he so angry at, Joe?"

"I don't know exactly, dear," he said gently, "but I think it was what you said about this Indian marriage."

"But why should I not have said it? Is there anything wrong about it?" she asked pitifully.

"Nothing, that I can see—there was no other way; but Charlie is very angry, and you must be brave and forgiving with him, Christie, dear."

"But I did never see him like that before, did you?"

"Once."

"When?"

"Oh, at college, one day, a boy tore his prayer-book in half, and threw it into the grate, just to be mean, you know. Our mother had given it to him at his confirmation."

"And did he look so?"

"About, but it all blew over in a day— Charlie's tempers are short and brisk. Just don't take any notice of him; run off to bed, and he'll have forgotten it by the morning."

They reached home at last. Christie said good-night quietly, going directly to her room. Joe went to his room also, filled a pipe and smoked for an hour. Across the passage he could hear her slippered feet pacing up and down, up and down the length of her apartment. There was something panther-like in those restless footfalls, a meaning velvetyness that made him shiver, and again he wished he were dead—or elsewhere.

113

After a time the hall door opened, and some-one came upstairs, along the passage, and to the little woman's room. As he entered, she turned and faced him.

"Christie," he said harshly, "do you know what you have done?"

"Yes," taking a step nearer him, her whole soul springing up into her eyes, "I have angered you, Charlie, and—"

"Angered me? You have disgraced me; and, moreover, you have disgraced yourself and both your parents."

"*Disgraced?*"

"Yes, *disgraced;* you have literally declared to the whole city that your father and mother were never married, and that you are the child of—what shall we call it—love? certainly not legality."

Across the hallway sat Joe McDonald, his blood freezing; but it leapt into every vein like fire at the awful anguish in the little voice that cried simply, "Oh! Charlie!"

"How could you do it, how could you do it, Christie, without shame either for yourself or for me, let alone your parents?"

The voice was like an angry demon's—not a trace was there in it of the yellow-haired, blue-eyed, laughing-lipped boy who had driven away so gaily to the dance five hours before.

"Shame? Why should I be ashamed of the rites of my people any more than you should be ashamed of the customs of yours—of a marriage more sacred and holy than half of your white man's mockeries?"

It was the voice of another nature in the girl—the love and the pleading were dead in it.

"Do you mean to tell me, Charlie—you who have studied my race and their laws for years—do you mean to tell me that, because there was no priest and no magistrate, my mother was not married? Do you mean to say that all my forefathers, for hundreds of years back, have been illegally born? If so, you blacken my ancestry beyond—beyond—beyond all reason."

"No, Christie, I would not be so brutal as that; but your father and mother live in more civilized times. Father O'Leary has been at the post for nearly twenty years. Why was not your father straight enough to have the ceremony performed when he *did* get the chance?"

The girl turned upon him with the face of a fury. "Do you suppose," she almost hissed, "that my mother would be married according to your *white* rites after she had been five years a wife, and I had been born in the meantime? *No*, a thousand times I say, *no*. When the priest came with his notions of Christianizing, and talked to them of re-marriage by the Church, my mother arose and said, "Never—never—I have never had but this one husband; he has had none but me for wife, and to have you re-marry us would be to say as much to the whole world as that we had never been married before.* You

* Fact.

115

go away; *I* do not ask that *your* people be re-married; talk not so to me. I *am* married, and you or the Church cannot do or undo it."

"Your father was a fool not to insist upon the law, and so was the priest."

"Law? *My* people have *no* priest, and my nation cringes not to law. Our priest is purity, and our law is honor. Priest? Was there a *priest* at the most holy marriage known to humanity —that stainless marriage whose offspring is the God you white men told my pagan mother of?"

"Christie—you are *worse* than blasphemous; such a profane remark shows how little you understand the sanctity of the Christian faith—"

"I know what I *do* understand; it is that you are hating me because I told some of the beautiful customs of my people to Mrs. Stuart and those men."

"Pooh! who cares for them? It is not them; the trouble is they won't keep their mouths shut. Logan's a cad and will toss the whole tale about at the club before to-morrow night; and as for the Stuart woman, I'd like to know how I'm going to take you to Ottawa for presentation and the opening, while she is blabbing the whole miserable scandal in every drawing-room, and I'll be pointed out as a romantic fool, and you— as worse; I *can't* understand why your father didn't tell me before we were married; I at least might have warned you to never mention it." Something of recklessness rang up through his voice, just as the panther-likeness crept up from

116

her footsteps and couched itself in hers. She spoke in tones quiet, soft, deadly.

"Before we were married! Oh! Charlie, would it have—made—any—difference?"

"God knows," he said, throwing himself into a chair, his blonde hair rumpled' and wet. It was the only boyish thing about him now.

She walked towards him, then halted in the centre of the room. "Charlie McDonald," she said, and it was as if a stone had spoken, "look up." He raised his head, startled by her tone. There was a threat in her eyes that, had his rage been less courageous, his pride less bitterly wounded, would have cowed him.

"There was no such time as that before our marriage, for we *are not married now*. Stop," she said, outstretching her palms against him as he sprang to his feet, "I tell you we are not married. Why should I recognize the rites of your nation when you do not acknowledge the rites of mine? According to your own words, my parents should have gone through your church ceremony as well as through an Indian contract; according to *my* words, *we* should go through an Indian contract as well as through a church marriage. If their union is illegal, so is ours. If you think my father is living in dishonor with my mother, my people will think I am living in dishonor with you. How do I know when another nation will come and conquer you as you white men conquered us? And they will have another marriage rite to perform, and they will tell us another truth, that you are not

117

my husband, that you are but disgracing and dishonoring me, that you are keeping me here, not as your wife, but as your—your *squaw.*"

The terrible word had never passed her lips before, and the blood stained her face to her very temples. She snatched off her wedding ring and tossed it across the room, saying scornfully, "That thing is as empty to me as the Indian rites to you."

He caught her by the wrists; his small white teeth were locked tightly, his blue eyes blazed into hers.

"Christine, do you dare to doubt my honor towards you? *you,* whom I should have died for; do you *dare* to think I have kept you here, not as my wife, but—"

"Oh, God! You are hurting me; you are breaking my arm," she gasped.

The door was flung open, and Joe McDonald's sinewy hands clinched like vices on his brother's shoulders.

"Charlie, you're mad, mad as the devil. Let go of her this minute."

The girl staggered backwards as the iron fingers loosed her wrists. "Oh, Joe," she cried, "I am not his wife, and he says I am born—nameless."

"Here," said Joe, shoving his brother towards the door. "Go downstairs till you can collect your senses. If ever a being acted like an infernal fool, you're the man."

The young husband looked from one to the other, dazed by his wife's insult, abandoned to

118

a fit of ridiculously childish temper. Blind as he was with passion, he remembered long afterwards seeing them standing there, his brother's face darkened with a scowl of anger—his wife, clad in the mockery of her ball dress, her scarlet velvet cloak half covering her bare brown neck and arms, her eyes like flames of fire, her face like a piece of sculptured greystone.

Without a word he flung himself furiously from the room, and immediately afterwards they heard the heavy hall door bang behind him.

"Can I do anything for you, Christie?" asked her brother-in-law calmly.

"No, thank you—unless—I think I would like a drink of water, please."

He brought her up a goblet filled with wine; her hand did not even tremble as she took it. As for Joe, a demon arose in his soul as he noticed she kept her wrists covered.

"Do you think he will come back?" she said.

"Oh, yes, of course; he'll be all right in the morning. Now go to bed like a good little girl, and—and, I say, Christie, you can call me if you want anything; I'll be right here, you know."

"Thank you, Joe; you are kind—and good."

He returned then to his apartment. His pipe was out, but he picked up a newspaper instead, threw himself into an armchair, and in a half-hour was in the land of dreams.

When Charlie came home in the morning, after a six-mile walk into the country and back again, his foolish anger was dead and buried. Logan's "Poor old Charlie" did not ring so distinctly

119

in his ears. Mrs. Stuart's horrified expression had faded considerably from his recollection. He thought only of that surprisingly tall, dark girl, whose eyes looked like coals, whose voice pierced him like a flint-tipped arrow. Ah, well, they would never quarrel again like that, he told himself. She loved him so, and would forgive him after he had talked quietly to her, and told her what an ass he was. She was simple-minded and awfully ignorant to pitch those old Indian laws at him in her fury, but he could not blame her; oh, no, he could not for one moment blame her. He had been terribly severe and unreasonable, and the horrid McDonald temper had got the better of him; and he loved her so. Oh! he loved her so! She would surely feel that, and forgive him, and— He went straight to his wife's room. The blue velvet evening dress lay on the chair into which he had thrown himself when he doomed his life's happiness by those two words, "God knows." A bunch of dead daffodils and her slippers were on the floor, everything—but Christie.

He went to his brother's bedroom door.

"Joe," he called, rapping nervously thereon; "Joe, wake up; where's Christie, d'you know?"

"Good Lord, no," gasped that youth, springing out of his armchair and opening the door. As he did so a note fell from off the handle. Charlie's face blanched to his very hair while Joe read aloud, his voice weakening at every word:

"DEAR OLD JOE—I went into your room at daylight to get that picture of the Post on your

120

bookshelves. I hope you do not mind, but I kissed your hair while you slept; it was so curly, and yellow, and soft, just like his. Good-bye, Joe.

"CHRISTIE."

And when Joe looked into his brother's face and saw the anguish settle in those laughing blue eyes, the despair that drove the dimples away from that almost girlish mouth; when he realized that this boy was but four-and-twenty years old, and that all his future was perhaps darkened and shadowed for ever, a great, deep sorrow arose in his heart, and he forgot all things, all but the agony that rang up through the voice of the fair, handsome lad as he staggered forward, crying, "Oh! Joe—what shall I do—what shall I do?"

* * * * * * * *

It was months and months before he found her, but during all that time he had never known a hopeless moment; discouraged he often was, but despondent, never. The sunniness of his ever-boyish heart radiated with a warmth that would have flooded a much deeper gloom than that which settled within his eager young life. Suffer? ah! yes, he suffered, not with locked teeth and stony stoicism, not with the masterful self-command, the reserve, the conquered bitterness of the still-water sort of nature, that is supposed to run to such depths. He tried to be bright, and his sweet old boyish self. He would laugh sometimes in a pitiful, pathetic fashion. He took to petting dogs, looking

121

into their large, solemn eyes with his wistful, questioning blue ones; he would kiss them, as women sometimes do, and call them "dear old fellow," in tones that had tears; and once in the course of his travels, while at a little way-station, he discovered a huge St. Bernard imprisoned by some mischance in an empty freight car; the animal was nearly dead from starvation, and it seemed to salve his own sick heart to rescue back the dog's life. Nobody claimed the big starving creature, the train hands knew nothing of its owner, and gladly handed it over to its deliverer. "Hudson," he called it, and afterwards when Joe McDonald would relate the story of his brother's life he invariably terminated it with, "And I really believe that big lumbering brute saved him." From what, he was never known to say.

But all things end, and he heard of her at last. She had never returned to the Post, as he at first thought she would, but had gone to the little town of B——, in Ontario, where she was making her living at embroidery and plain sewing.

The September sun had set redly when at last he reached the outskirts of the town, opened up the wicket gate, and walked up the weedy, unkept path leading to the cottage where she lodged.

Even through the twilight, he could see her there, leaning on the rail of the verandah—oddly enough she had about her shoulders the scarlet velvet cloak she wore when he had flung himself so madly from the room that night.

The moment the lad saw her his heart swelled with a sudden heat, burning moisture leapt into

122

his eyes, and clogged his long, boyish lashes. He bounded up the steps—"Christie," he said, and the word scorched his lips like audible flame.

She turned to him, and for a second stood magnetized by his passionately wistful face; her peculiar greyish eyes seemed to drink the very life of his unquenchable love, though the tears that suddenly sprang into his seemed to absorb every pulse in his body through those hungry, pleading eyes of his that had, oh! so often, been blinded by her kisses when once her whole world lay in their blue depths.

"You will come back to me, Christie, my wife? My wife, you will let me love you again?"

She gave a singular little gasp, and shook her head. "Don't, oh! don't," he cried piteously. "You will come to me, dear? it is all such a bitter mistake—I did not understand. Oh! Christie, I did not understand, and you'll forgive me, and love me again, won't you—won't you?"

"No," said the girl with quick, indrawn breath.

He dashed the back of his hand across his wet eyelids. His lips were growing numb, and he bungled over the monosyllable "Why?"

"I do not like you," she answered quietly.

"God! Oh! God, what is there left?"

She did not appear to hear the heart-break in his voice; she stood like one wrapped in sombre thought; no blaze, no tear, nothing in her eyes; no hardness, no tenderness about her mouth. The wind was blowing her cloak aside, and the only visible human life in her whole body was once when he spoke the muscles of her brown arm seemed to contract.

123

"But, darling, you are mine—*mine*—we are husband and wife! Oh, heaven, you *must* love me, you *must* come to me again."

"You cannot *make* me come," said the icy voice, "neither church, nor law, nor even"—and the voice softened—"nor even love can make a slave of a red girl."

"Heaven forbid it," he faltered. "No, Christie, I will never claim you without your love. What reunion would that be? But, oh, Christie, you are lying to me, you are lying to yourself, you are lying to heaven."

She did not move. If only he could touch her he felt as sure of her yielding as he felt sure there was a hereafter. The memory of times when he had but to lay his hand on her hair to call a most passionate response from her filled his heart with a torture that choked all words before they reached his lips; at the thought of those days he forgot she was unapproachable, forgot how forbidding were her eyes, how stony her lips. Flinging himself forward, his knee on the chair at her side, his face pressed hardly in the folds of the cloak on her shoulder, he clasped his arms about her with a boyish petulance, saying, "Christie, Christie, my little girl wife, I love you, I love you, and you are killing me."

She quivered from head to foot as his fair, wavy hair brushed her neck, his despairing face sank lower until his cheek, hot as fire, rested on the cool, olive flesh of her arm. A warm moisture oozed up through her skin, and as he felt its glow he looked up. Her teeth, white and cold, were

124

locked over her under lip, and her eyes were as grey stones.

Not murderers alone know the agony of a death sentence.

"Is it all useless? all useless, dear?" he said, with lips starving for hers.

"All useless," she repeated. "I have no love for you now. You forfeited me and my heart months ago, when you said *those two words.*"

His arms fell away from her wearily, he arose mechanically, he placed his little grey checked cap on the back of his yellow curls, the old-time laughter was dead in the blue eyes that now looked scared and haunted, the boyishness and the dimples crept away for ever from the lips that quivered like a child's; he turned from her, but she had looked once into his face as the Law Giver must have looked at the land of Canaan outspread at his feet. She watched him go down the long path and through the picket gate, she watched the big yellowish dog that had waited for him lumber up to its feet—stretch—then follow him. She was conscious of but two things, the vengeful lie in her soul, and a little space on her arm that his wet lashes had brushed.

*   *   *   *   *   *   *   *

It was hours afterwards when he reached his room. He had said nothing, done nothing—what use were words or deeds? Old Jimmy Robinson was right; she had "balked" sure enough.

What a bare, hotelish room it was! He tossed off his coat and sat for ten minutes looking blankly

125

at the sputtering gas jet. Then his whole life, desolate as a desert, loomed up before him with appalling distinctness. Throwing himself on the floor beside his bed, with clasped hands and arms outstretched on the white counterpane, he sobbed. he sobbed. "Oh! God, dear God, I thought you loved me; I thought you'd let me have her again, but you must be tired of me, tired of loving me, too. I've nothing left now, nothing! it doesn't seem that I even have you to-night."

He lifted his face then, for his dog, big and clumsy and yellow, was licking at his sleeve.

The Envoy Extraordinary

*T*HERE had been a great deal of trouble in the Norris family, and for weeks old Bill Norris had gone about scowling as blackly as a thunder-cloud, speaking to no one but his wife and daughter, and oftentimes muttering inaudible things that, however, had the tone of invective; and accompanied, as these mutterings were, with a menacing shake of his burly head, old Bill finally grew to be an acquaintance few desired.

Mrs. Norris showed equal, though not similar, signs of mental disturbance; for, womanlike, she clothed her worry in placidity and silence. Her kindly face became drawn and lined; she laughed less frequently. She never went "neighboring" or "buggy-riding" with old Bill now. But the trim farmhouse was just as spotless, just as beautifully kept, the cooking just as wholesome and homelike, the linen as white, the garden as green, the chickens as fat, the geese as noisy, as in the days when her eyes were less grave and her lips unknown to sighs. And what was it all about but the simple matter of a marriage—Sam's marriage? Sam, the big, genial, curly-headed only son of the house of Norris, who saw fit to take unto himself as a life partner tiny, delicate, college-bred Della Kennedy, who taught school over on the Sixth Concession, and knew more about making muslin shirtwaists than cooking for the threshers, could quote from all the mental and moral philosophers, could wrestle with French and Latin

127

verbs, and had memorized half the things Tennyson and Emerson had ever written, but could not milk a cow or churn up a week's supply of butter if the executioner stood ready with his axe to chop off her pretty yellow mop of a head in case she failed. How old Billy stormed when Sam started "keeping company" with her!

"Nice young goslin' fer you to be a-goin' with!" he scowled when Sam would betake himself towards the red gate every evening after chores were done. "Nice gal fer you to bring home to help yer mother; all she'll do is to play May Queen and have the hull lot of us a-trottin' to wait on her. You'll marry a farmer's gal, *I* say, one that's brung up like yerself and yer mother and me, or I tell yer yer shan't have one consarned acre of this place. I'll leave the hull farm to yer sister Jane's man. *She* married somethin' like—decent, stiddy, hard-working man is Sid Sampson, and *he'll* git what land I have to leave."

"I quite know that, dad," Sam blazed forth, irritably; "so does he. That's what he married Janie for—the whole township knows that. He's never given her a kind word, or a holiday, or a new dress, since they were married—eight years. She slaves and toils, and he rich as any man need be; owns three farms already, money in the bank, cattle, horses—everything. But look at Janie; she looks as old as mother. I pity *his* son, if he ever has one. Thank heaven, Janie has no children!"

"Come, come, father—Sam!" a patient voice would interrupt, and Mrs. Norris would appear

128

at the door, vainly endeavoring to make peace. "I'll own up to both of you I'd sooner have a farmer's daughter for mine-in-law than Della Kennedy. But, father, he ain't married yet, and—"

"Ain't married, eh?" blurted in old Bill. "But he's a-goin' to marry her. But I'll tell you both right here, she'll never set foot in my house, ner I in her'n. Sam ken keep her, but what on, I don't know. He gits right out of this here farm the day he marries her, and he don't come back, not while I'm a-livin'."

It was all this that made old Billy Norris morose, and Mrs. Norris silent and patient and laughless, for Sam married the despised "gosling" right at harvest time, when hands were so scarce that farmers wrangled and fought, day in and day out, to get one single man to go into the field.

This was Sam's golden opportunity. His father's fields stood yellow with ripening grain to be cut on the morrow, but he deliberately hired himself out to a neighbor, where he would get good wages to start a little home with; for, farmer-like, old Billy Norris never paid his son wages. Sam was supposed to work for nothing but his clothes and board as reward, and a possible slice of the farm when the old man died, while a good harvest hand gets board and high wages, to boot. This then was the hour to strike, and the morning the grain stood ready for the reaper Sam paused at the kitchen door at sunrise.

"Mother," he said, "I've got to have her. I'm going to marry her to-day, and to-morrow start

129

working for Mr. Willson, who will pay me enough to keep a wife. I'm sorry, mother, but—well, I've got to have her. Some day you'll know her, and you'll love her, I know you will; and if there's ever any children—"

But Mrs. Norris had clutched him by the arm. "Sammy," she whispered, "your father will be raging mad at your going, and harvest hands so scarce. I *know* he'll never let me go near you, never. But if there's ever any children, Sammy, you just come for your mother, and I'll go to you and her *without* his letting."

Then with one of the all too few kisses that are ever given or received in a farmhouse life, she let him go. The storm burst at breakfast time when Sam did not appear, and the poor mother tried to explain his absence, as only a mother will. Old Billy waxed suspicious, then jumped at facts. The marriage was bad enough, but this being left in the lurch at the eleventh hour, his son's valuable help transferred from the home farm to Mr. Willson's, with whom he always quarrelled in church, road, and political matters, was too much.

"But, father, you never paid him wages," ventured the mother.

"Wages? Wages to one's own son, that one has raised and fed and shod from the cradle? Wages, when he knowed he'd come in fer part of the farm when I'd done with it? Who in con-sarnation ever gives their son wages?"

"But, father, you told him if he married her

130

he was never to have the farm—that you'd leave
it to Sid, that he was to get right off the day he
married her"

"An' Sid'll get it—bet yer life he will—fer I
ain't got no son no more. A sneakin' hulk that
leaves me with my wheat standin' an' goes over to
help that Methodist of a Willson is no son of
mine. I ain't never had a son, and you ain't,
neither; remember that, Marthy—don't you ever
let me ketch you goin' a-near them. We're done
with Sam an' his missus. You jes' make a note
of that." And old Billy flung out to his fields
like a general whose forces had fled.

It was but a tiny, two-room shack, away up in
the back lots, that Sam was able to get for Della,
but no wayfarer ever passed up the side road but
they heard her clear, young voice singing like a
thrush; no one ever met Sam but he ceased whistling only to greet them. He proved invaluable
to Mr. Willson, for after the harvest was in and
the threshing over, there was the root crop and
the apple crop, and eventually Mr. Willson hired
him for the entire year. Della, to the surprise
of the neighborhood, kept on with her school until
Christmas.

"She's teachin' instid of keepin' Sam's house,
jes' to git money fer finery, you bet!" sneered old
Billy. But he never knew that every copper for
the extra term was put carefully away, and was
paid out for a whole year's rent in advance on a
grey little two-room house, and paid by a very
proud little yellow-haired bride. She had in-

sisted upon this before her marriage, for she laughingly said, "No wife ever gets her way afterwards."

"I'm not good at butter-making, Sam," she said, "but I *can* make money teaching, and for this first year *I* pay the rent." And she did.

And the sweet, brief year swung on through its seasons, until one brown September morning the faint cry of a little human lamb floated through the open window of the small grey house on the back lots. Sam did not go to Willson's to work that day, but stayed at home, playing the part of a big, joyful, clumsy nurse, his roughened hands gentle and loving, his big rugged heart bursting with happiness. It was twilight, and the grey shadows were creeping into the bare little room, touching with feathery fingers a tangled mop of yellow curls that aureoled a pillowed head that was not now filled with thoughts of Tennyson and Emerson and frilly muslin shirtwaists. That pretty head held but two realities—Sammy, whistling robin-like as he made tea in the kitchen, and the little human lamb hugged up on her arm.

But suddenly the whistling ceased, and Sammy's voice, thrilling with joy, exclaimed:

"Oh, mother!"

"Mrs. Willson sent word to me. Your father's gone to the village, and I ran away, Sammy boy," whispered Mrs. Norris, eagerly. "I just ran away. Where's Della and—the baby?"

"In here, mother, and—bless you for coming!" said the big fellow, stepping softly towards the bedroom. But his mother was there before him,

132

her arms slipping tenderly about the two small beings on the bed.

"It wasn't my fault, daughter," she said, tremulously.

"I know it," faintly smiled Della. "Just these last few hours I know I'd stand by this baby boy of mine here until the Judgment Day, and so I now know it must have nearly broken your heart not to stand by Sammy."

"Well, grandmother!" laughed Sam, "what do you think of the new Norris?"

"Grandmother?" gasped Mrs. Norris. "Why, Sammy, *am* I a *grandmother?* Grandmother to this little sweetheart?" And the proud old arms lifted the wee "new Norris" right up from its mother's arms, and every tiny toe and finger was kissed and crooned over, while Sam slyly winked at Della and managed to whisper, "You'll see, girl, that dad will come around now; but he can just keep out of *our house*. There are two of us that can be harsh. I'm not going to come at *his* first whistle."

Della smiled to herself, but said nothing. Much wisdom had come to her within the last year, within the last day—wisdom not acquired within the covers of books, not yet beneath college roofs, and one truth she had mastered long ago—that

> "To help and to heal a sorrow,
> Love and silence are always best."

But late that night, when Martha Norris returned home, another storm broke above her hapless head. Old Billy sat on the kitchen steps waiting

133

for her, frowning, scowling, muttering. "Where have you been?" he demanded, glaring at her, although some inner instinct told him what her answer would be.

"I've been to Sammy's," she said, in a peculiarly still voice, "and I'm going again to-morrow." Then with shoulders more erect and eyes calmer than they had been for many months, she continued: "And I'm going again the next day and the next. Billy, you and I've got a grandson—a splendid, fair, strong boy, and—"

"What!" snapped old Billy. "A grandson! I got a grandson, an' no person told me before? Not even that there sneak Sam, cuss him! He always was too consarned mean to live. A grandson? I'm a-goin' over termorrer, sure's I'm alive."

"No use for you to go, Billy," said Mrs. Norris, with marvellous diplomacy for such a simple, unworldly farmer's wife to suddenly acquire. "Sammy wouldn't let you set foot on his place. He wouldn't let you put an eye or a finger on that precious baby —not for the whole earth."

"What! Not *me*, the little chap's *grandfather?*" blurted old Billy in a rage. "I'm a-goin' to see that baby, that's all there is to it. I tell yer, I'm a-goin'."

"No use, father; you'll only make things worse," sighed Sam's mother, plaintively; but in her heart laughter gurgled like a spring. To the gift of diplomacy Mrs. Norris was fast adding the art of being an actress. "If you go there Sam'll set the dog on you. I *know* he will, from the way he was talking," she concluded.

"Oh! got a *dog*, have they? Well, I bet they've got no *cow*," sneered Billy. Then after a meaning pause: "I say, Marthy, *have* they got a cow?"

"No," replied Mrs. Norris, shortly.

"*No cow*, an' a sick woman and a baby—*my* grandchild—in the house? Now ain't that jes' like that sneak Sam? They'll jes' kill that baby atween them, they're that igner'nt. Hev they got enny milk fer them two babbling kids, Della an' the baby—my grandchild?"

"No!" snapped Mrs. Norris, while through her mind echoed some terrifying lines she had heard as a child:

> "All liars dwell with him in hell,
> And many more who cursed and swore."

"An' there's that young Shorthorn of ours, Marthy. Couldn't we spare her?" he asked with a pathetic eagerness. "We've got eight other cows to milk. Can't we spare her? If you think Sam'll set the dog on *me*, I'll have her driv over in the mornin'. Jim'll take her."

"I don't think it's any use, Bill; but you can try it," remarked Mrs. Norris, her soul singing within her like a celestial choir.

* * * * * * * *

"Where are you driving that cow to?" yelled Sam from the kitchen door, at sunrise the following morning. "Take her out of there! You're driving her into my yard, right over my cabbages."

But Jim, the Norris' hired man, only grinned, and proceeding with his driving, yelled back:

135

"Cow's yourn, Sam. Yer old man sent it—a present to yer missus and the babby."

"You take and drive that cow back again!" roared Sam. "And tell my dad I won't have hide nor hair of her on my place."

Back went the cow.

"Didn't I tell you?" mourned Mrs. Norris. "Sam's that stubborn and contrary. It's no use, Billy; he just doesn't care for his poor old father nor mother any more."

"By the jumping Jiminy Christmas! I'll *make* him care!" thundered old Billy. "I'm a-goin' ter see that grandchild of mine." Then followed a long silence.

"I say, Marthy, how are they fixed in the house?" he questioned, after many moments of apparently brown study.

"Pretty poor," answered Sam's mother, truthfully this time.

"Got a decent stove, an' bed, an' the like?" he finally asked.

"Stove seems to cook all right, but the bed looks just like straw tick—not much good, I'd say," responded Mrs. Norris, drearily.

"*A straw tick!*" fairly yelled old Billy. "A straw tick fer my grandson ter sleep on? Jim, you fetch that there cow here, right ter the side door."

"What are you going to do?" asked Martha, anxiously.

"I'll show yer!" blurted old Billy. And going to his own room, he dragged off all the pretty patchwork quilts above his neatly-made bed, grabbed up the voluminous feather-bed, staggered with it in his arms down the hall, through the side door, and flung it on to the back of the astonished cow.

"Now you, Jim, drive that there cow over to Sam's, and if you dare bring her back agin, I'll hide yer with the flail till yer can't stand up."

"Me drive that lookin' circus over to Sam's?" sneered Jim. "I'll quit yer place first. Yer kin do it yerself"; and the hired man turned on his lordly heel and slouched over to the barn.

"That'll be the best way, Billy," urged Sam's mother. "Do it yourself."

"I'll do it, too," old Billy growled. "I ain't afraid of no dog on four legs. Git on there, bossy! Git on, I say!" and the ridiculous cavalcade started forth.

For a moment Martha Norris watched the receding figure through blinding tears. "Oh, Sammy, I'm going to have you back again! I'm going to have my boy once more!" she half sobbed. Then sitting down on the doorsill, she laughed like a schoolgirl until the cow with her extraordinary burden, and old Billy in her wake, disappeared up the road.*

From the pillow, pretty Della could just see out of the low window, and her wide young eyes grew wider with amazement as the gate swung open and the "circus," as Jim called it, entered.

"Sammy!" she called, "Sammy! For goodness sake, what's that coming into our yard?"

Instantly Sam was at the door.

*This incident actually occurred on an Ontario farm within the circle of the author's acquaintance.

"Well, if that don't beat anything I ever saw!"
he exclaimed. Then "like mother, like son," he
too, sat down on the doorsill and laughed as only
youth and health and joy can laugh, for, heading
straight for the door was the fat young Shorthorn,
saddled with an enormous feather-bed, and plodding
at her heels was old Billy Norris, grinning sheepishly.

It took just three seconds for the hands of
father and son to meet. "How's my gal an' my
grandson?" asked the old farmer, excitedly.

"Bully, just bully, both of them!" smiled Sam,
proudly. Then more seriously, "Ah, dad, you
old tornado, you! Here you fired thunder at us
for a whole year, pretty near broke my mother's
heart, and made my boy's little mother old before
she ought to be. But you've quit storming now,
dad. I know it from the look of you."

"Quit forever, Sam," replied old Billy, "fer
these mother-wimmen don't never thrive where
there's rough weather, somehow. They're all fer
peace. They're worse than King Edward an'
Teddy Roosevelt fer patchin' up rows, an' if they
can't do it no other way, they jes' hike along with
a baby, sort o' treaty of peace like. Yes, I guess
I thundered some; but, Sam, boy, there ain't a
deal of harm in thunder—but *lightnin'*, now
that's the worst, but I once heard a feller say
that feathers was non-conductive." Then with a
sly smile, "An' Sam, you'd better hustle an' git
the gal an' the baby on ter this here feather-bed,
or they may be in danger of gettin' struck, fer
there's no tellin' but I may jes' start an' storm
thunder an' *lightnin'* this time."

A Pagan in St. Paul's Cathedral

Iroquois Poetess' Impressions in London's Cathedral

*I*T IS a far cry from a wigwam to Westminster, from a prairie trail to the Tower Bridge, and London looks a strange place to the Red Indian whose eyes still see the myriad forest trees, even as they gaze across the Strand, and whose feet still feel the clinging moccasin even among the scores of clicking heels that hurry along the thoroughfares of this camping-ground of the paleface.

So this is the place where dwells the Great White Father, ruler of many lands, lodges, and tribes, in the hollow of whose hands is the peace that rests between the once hostile red man and white. They call him the King of England, but to us, the powerful Iroquois nation of the north, he is always the "Great White Father." For once he came to us in our far-off Canadian reserves, and with his own hand fastened decorations and medals on the buckskin coats of our oldest chiefs, just because they and their fathers used their tomahawks in battle in the cause of England.

So I, one of his loyal allies, have come to see his camp, known to the white man as London, his council which the whites call his Parliament, where his sachems and chiefs make the laws of his tribes, and to see his wigwam, known to the palefaces as Buckingham Palace, but to the red man as the "Tepee of the Great White Father." And this is what I see:

139

WHAT THE INDIAN SEES.

Lifting toward the sky are vast buildings of stone, not the same kind of stone from which my forefathers fashioned their carven pipes and corn-pounders, but a greyer, grimier rock that would not take the polish we give by fingers dipped in sturgeon oil, and long days of friction with fine sand and deer-hide.

I stand outside the great palace wigwam, the huge council-house by the river. My seeing eyes may mark them, but my heart's eyes are looking beyond all this wonderment, back to the land I have left behind me. I picture the tepees by the far Saskatchewan; there the tent poles, too, are lifting skyward, and the smoke ascending through them from the smouldering fires within curls softly on the summer air. Against the blurred sweep of horizon other camps etch their outlines, other bands of red men with their herds of wild cattle have sought the river lands. I hear the untamed hoofs thundering up the prairie trail.

But the prairie sounds are slipping away, and my ears catch other voices that rise above the ceaseless throb about me—voices that are clear, high, and calling; they float across the city like the music of a thousand birds of passage beating their wings through the night, crying and murmuring plaintively as they journey northward. They are the voices of St. Paul's calling, calling me—St. Paul's where the paleface worships the Great Spirit, and through whose portals he hopes to reach the happy hunting grounds.

140

THE GREAT SPIRIT

As I entered its doorways it seemed to me to be the everlasting abiding-place of the white man's Great Spirit.

The music brooded everywhere. It beat in my ears like the far-off cadences of the Sault Ste. Marie rapids, that rise and leap and throb—like a storm hurling through the fir forest—like the distant rising of an Indian war-song; it swept up those mighty archways until the grey dome above me faded, and in its place the stars came out to look down, not on these paleface kneeling worshippers, but on a band of stalwart, sinewy, copper-colored devotees, my own people in my own land, who also assembled to do honor to the Manitou of all nations.

The deep-throated organ and the boys' voices were gone; I heard instead the melancholy incantations of our own pagan religionists. The beautiful dignity of our great sacrificial rites seemed to settle about me, to enwrap me in its garment of solemnity and primitive stateliness.

BEAT OF THE DRUM

The atmosphere pulsed with the beat of the Indian drum, the eerie penetrations of the turtle rattle that set the time of the dancers' feet. Dance? It is not a dance, that marvellously slow, serpentine-like figure with the soft swish, swish of moccasined feet, and the faint jingling of elks'-teeth bracelets, keeping rhythm with every footfall. It is not a

141

dance, but an invocation of motion. Why may we not worship with the graceful movement of our feet? The paleface worships by moving his lips and tongue; the difference is but slight.

The altar-lights of St. Paul's glowed for me no more. In their place flared the camp fires of the Onondaga "long-house," and the resinous scent of the burning pine drifted across the fetid London air. I saw the tall, copper-skinned fire-keeper of the Iroquois council enter, the circle of light flung fitfully against the black surrounding woods. I have seen their white bishops, but none so regal, so august as he. His garb of. fringed buckskin and ermine was no more grotesque than the vestments worn by the white preachers in high places; he did not carry a book or a shining golden symbol, but from his splendid shoulders was suspended a pure white lifeless dog.

Into the red flame the strong hands gently lowered it, scores of reverent, blanketed figures stood silent, awed, for it is the highest, holiest festival of the year. Then the wild, strange chant arose— the great pagan ritual was being intoned by the fire-keeper, his weird, monotonous tones voicing this formula:

"The Great Spirit desires no human sacrifice, but we, His children, must give to Him that which is nearest our hearts and nearest our lives. Only the spotless and stainless can enter into His presence, only that which is purified by fire. So do we offer to Him this spotless, innocent animal —this white dog—a member of our household, a co-habitant of our wigwam, and on the smoke

142

that arises from the purging fires will arise also the thanksgivings of all those who desire that the Great Spirit in His happy hunting grounds will forever smoke His pipe of peace, for peace is between Him and His children for all time."

The mournful voice ceases. Again the hollow pulsing of the Indian drum, the purring, flexible step of cushioned feet. I lift my head, which has been bowed on the chair before me. It is St. Paul's after all—and the clear boy-voices rise above the rich echoes of the organ.

As It Was in the Beginning

*T*HEY account for it by the fact that I am a
Redskin, but I am something else, too—I am a
woman.

I remember the first time I saw him. He came
up the trail with some Hudson's Bay trappers,
and they stopped at the door of my father's tepee.
He seemed even then, fourteen years ago, an old
man; his hair seemed just as thin and white, his
hands just as trembling and fleshless as they were
a month since, when I saw him for what I pray
his God is the last time.

My father sat in the tepee, polishing buffalo
horns and smoking; my mother, wrapped in her
blanket, crouched over her quill-work, on the
buffalo-skin at his side; I was lounging at the
doorway, idling, watching, as I always watched,
the thin, distant line of sky and prairie; wondering,
as I always wondered, what lay beyond it. Then
he came, this gentle old man with his white hair
and thin, pale face. He wore a long black coat,
which I now know was the sign of his office, and
he carried a black leather-covered book, which,
in all the years I have known him, I have never
seen him without.

The trappers explained to my father who he
was, the Great Teacher, the heart's Medicine Man,
the "Blackcoat" we had heard of, who brought
peace where there was war, and the magic of
whose black book brought greater things than all
the Happy Hunting Grounds of our ancestors.

He told us many things that day, for he could speak the Cree tongue, and my father listened, and listened, and when at last they left us, my father said for him to come and sit within the tepee again.

He came, all the time he came, and my father welcomed him, but my mother always sat in silence at work with the quills; my mother never liked the Great "Blackcoat."

His stories fascinated me. I used to listen intently to the tale of the strange new place he called "heaven," of the gold crown, of the white dress, of the great music; and then he would tell of that other strange place—hell. My father and I hated it; we feared it, we dreamt of it, we trembled at it. Oh, if the "Blackcoat" would only cease to talk of it! Now I know he saw its effect upon us, and he used it as a whip to lash us into his new religion, but even then my mother must have known, for each time he left the tepee she would watch him going slowly away across the prairie; then when he was disappearing into the far horizon she would laugh scornfully, and say:

"If the white man made this Blackcoat's hell, let him go to it. It is for the man who found it first. No hell for Indians, just Happy Hunting Grounds. Blackcoat can't scare me."

And then, after weeks had passed, one day as he stood at the tepee door he laid his white, old hand on my head and said to my father: "Give me this little girl, chief. Let me take her to the mission school; let me keep her, and teach her of the great God and His eternal heaven. She will

145

grow to be a noble woman, and return perhaps to bring her people to the Christ."

My mother's eyes snapped. "No," she said. It was the first word she ever spoke to the "Blackcoat." My father sat and smoked. At the end of a half-hour he said:

"I am an old man, Blackcoat. I shall not leave the God of my fathers. I like not your strange God's ways—all of them. I like not His two new places for me when I am dead. Take the child, Blackcoat, and save her from hell."

*   *   *   *   *   *   *   *

The first grief of my life was when we reached the mission. They took my buckskin dress off, saying I was now a little Christian girl and must dress like all the white people at the mission. Oh, how I hated that stiff new calico dress and those leather shoes! But, little as I was, I said nothing, only thought of the time when I should be grown, and do as my mother did, and wear the buckskins and the blanket.

My next serious grief was when I began to speak the English, that they forbade me to use any Cree words whatever. The rule of the school was that any child heard using its native tongue must get a slight punishment. I never understood it, I cannot understand it now, why the use of my dear Cree tongue could be a matter for correction or an action deserving punishment.

She was strict, the matron of the school, but only justly so, for she had a heart and a face like her brother's, the "Blackcoat." I had long

146

since ceased to call him that. The trappers at the post called him "St. Paul," because, they told me, of his self-sacrificing life, his kindly deeds, his rarely beautiful old face; so I, too, called him "St. Paul," though oftener "Father Paul," though he never liked the latter title, for he was a Protestant. But as I was his pet, his darling of the whole school, he let me speak of him as I would, knowing it was but my heart speaking in love. His sister was a widow, and mother to a laughing yellow-haired little boy of about my own age, who was my constant playmate and who taught me much of English in his own childish way. I used to be fond of this child, just as I was fond of his mother and of his uncle, my "Father Paul," but as my girlhood passed away, as womanhood came upon me, I got strangely wearied of them all; I longed, oh, God, how I longed for the old wild life! It came with my womanhood, with my years.

What mattered it to me now that they had taught me all their ways?—their tricks of dress, their reading, their writing, their books. What mattered it that "Father Paul" loved me, that the traders at the post called me pretty, that I was a pet of all, from the factor to the poorest trapper in the service? I wanted my own people, my own old life, my blood called out for it, but they always said I must not return to my father's tepee. I heard them talk amongst themselves of keeping me away from pagan influences; they told each other that if I returned to the prairies, the tepees, I would degenerate, slip back to paganism, as other girls had done; marry, perhaps, with

147

a pagan—and all their years of labor and teaching would be lost.

I said nothing, but I waited. And then one night the feeling overcame me. I was in the Hudson's Bay store when an Indian came in from the north with a large pack of buckskin. As they unrolled it a dash of its insinuating odor filled the store. I went over and leaned above the skins a second, then buried my face in them, swallowing, drinking the fragrance of them, that went to my head like wine. Oh, the wild wonder of that wood-smoked tan, the subtilty of it, the untamed smell of it! I drank it into my lungs, my innermost being was saturated with it, till my mind reeled and my heart seemed twisted with a physical agony. My childhood recollections rushed upon me, devoured me. I left the store in a strange, calm frenzy, and going rapidly to the mission house I confronted my Father Paul and demanded to be allowed to go "home," if only for a day. He received the request with the same refusal and the same gentle sigh that I had so often been greeted with, but *this* time the desire, the smoke-tan, the heart-ache, never lessened.

Night after night I would steal away by myself and go to the border of the village to watch the sun set in the foothills, to gaze at the far line of sky and prairie, to long and long for my father's lodge. And Laurence—always Laurence —my fair-haired, laughing, child playmate, would come calling and calling for me: "Esther, where are you? We miss you; come in, Esther, come in with me." And if I did not turn at once to him

148

and follow, he would come and place his strong hands on my shoulders and laugh into my eyes and say, "Truant, truant, Esther; can't *we* make you happy?"

My old child playmate had vanished years ago. He was a tall, slender young man now, handsome as a young chief, but with laughing blue eyes, and always those yellow curls about his temples. He was my solace in my half-exile, my comrade, my brother, until one night it was, "Esther, Esther, can't *I* make you happy?"

I did not answer him; only looked out across the plains and thought of the tepees. He came close, close. He locked his arms about me, and with my face pressed up to his throat he stood silent. I felt the blood from my heart sweep to my very finger-tips. I loved him. O God, how I loved him! In a wild, blind instant it all came, just because he held me so and was whispering brokenly, "Don't leave me, don't leave me, Esther; *my* Esther, my child-love, my playmate, my girl-comrade, my little Cree sweetheart, will you go away to your people, or stay, stay for me, for my arms, as I have you now?"

No more, no more the tepees; no more the wild stretch of prairie, the intoxicating fragrance of the smoke-tanned buckskin; no more the bed of buffalo hide, the soft, silent moccasin; no more the dark faces of my people, the dulcet cadence of the sweet Cree tongue—only this man, this fair, proud, tender man who held me in his arms, in his heart. My soul prayed his great white God, in that moment, that He let me have only this. It

149

was twilight when we re-entered the mission gate. We were both excited, feverish. Father Paul was reading evening prayers in the large room beyond the hallway; his soft, saint-like voice stole beyond the doors, like a benediction upon us. I went noiselessly upstairs to my own room and sat there undisturbed for hours.

The clock downstairs struck one, startling me from my dreams of happiness, and at the same moment a flash of light attracted me. My room was in an angle of the building, and my window looked almost directly down into those of Father Paul's study, into which at that instant he was entering, carrying a lamp. "Why, Laurence," I heard him exclaim, "what are you doing here? I thought, my boy, you were in bed hours ago."

"No, uncle, not in bed, but in dreamland," replied Laurence, arising from the window, where evidently he, too, had spent the night hours as I had done.

Father Paul fumbled about a moment, found his large black book, which for once he seemed to have got separated from, and was turning to leave, when the curious circumstance of Laurence being there at so unusual an hour seemed to strike him anew. "Better go to sleep, my son," he said simply, then added curiously, "Has anything occurred to keep you up?"

Then Laurence spoke: "No, uncle, only—only, I'm happy, that's all."

Father Paul stood irresolute. Then: "It is—?"

"Esther," said Laurence quietly, but he was

at the old man's side, his hand was on the bent old shoulder, his eyes proud and appealing.

Father Paul set the lamp on the table, but, as usual, one hand held that black book, the great text of his life. His face was paler than I had ever seen it—graver.

"Tell me of it," he requested.

I leaned far out of my window and watched them both. I listened with my very heart, for Laurence was telling him of me, of his love, of the new-found joy of that night.

"You have said nothing of marriage to her?" asked Father Paul.

"Well—no; but she surely understands that—"

"Did you speak of *marriage?*" repeated Father Paul, with a harsh ring in his voice that was new to me.

"No, uncle, but—"

"Very well, then; very well."

There was a brief silence. Laurence stood staring at the old man as though he were a stranger; he watched him push a large chair up to the table, slowly seat himself; then mechanically following his movements, he dropped on to a lounge. The old man's head bent low, but his eyes were bright and strangely fascinating. He began:

"Laurence, my boy, your future is the dearest thing to me of all earthly interests. Why, you *can't* marry this girl—no, no, sit, sit until I have finished," he added, with raised voice, as Laurence sprang up, remonstrating. "I have long since decided that you marry well; for instance, the Hudson's Bay factor's daughter."

Laurence broke into a fresh, rollicking laugh. "What, uncle," he said, "little Ida McIntosh? Marry that little yellow-haired fluff ball, that kitten, that pretty little dolly?"

"Stop," said Father Paul. Then, with a low, soft persuasiveness, "She is *white*, Laurence."

My lover started. "Why, uncle, what do you mean?" he faltered.

"Only this, my son: poor Esther comes of uncertain blood; would it do for you—the missionary's nephew, and adopted son, you might say—to marry the daughter of a pagan Indian? Her mother is hopelessly uncivilized; her father has a dash of French somewhere—half-breed, you know, my boy, half-breed." Then, with still lower tone and half-shut, crafty eyes, he added: "The blood is a bad, bad mixture, *you* know that; you know, too, that I am very fond of the girl, poor dear Esther. I have tried to separate her from evil pagan influences; she is the daughter of the Church; I want her to have no other parent; but you never can tell what lurks in *a caged animal that has once been wild.* My whole heart is with the Indian people, my son; my whole heart, my whole life, has been devoted to bringing them to Christ, *but it is a different thing to marry with one of them.*"

His small old eyes were riveted on Laurence like a hawk's on a rat. My heart lay like ice in my bosom.

Laurence, speechless and white, stared at him breathlessly.

"Go away somewhere," the old man was urging;

"to Winnipeg, Toronto, Montreal; forget her, then come back to Ida McIntosh. A union of the Church and the Hudson's Bay will mean great things, and may ultimately result in my life's ambition, the civilization of this entire tribe, that we have worked so long to bring to God."

I listened, sitting like one frozen. Could those words have been uttered by my venerable teacher, by him whom I revered as I would one of the saints in his own black book? Ah, there was no mistaking it. My white father, my life-long friend who pretended to love me, to care for my happiness, was urging the man I worshipped to forget me, to marry with the factor's daughter—because of what? Of my red skin; my good, old, honest pagan mother; my confiding French-Indian father. In a second all the care, the hollow love he had given me since my childhood, were as things that never existed. I hated that old mission priest as I hated his white man's hell. I hated his long, white hair; I hated his thin, white hands; I hated his body, his soul, his voice, his black book—oh, how I hated the very atmosphere of him!

Laurence sat motionless, his face buried in his hands, but the old man continued, "No, no; not the child of that pagan mother; you can't trust her, my son. What would you do with a wife who might any day break from you to return to her prairies and her buckskins? *You can't trust her.*" His eyes grew smaller, more glittering, more fascinating then, and leaning with an odd, secret sort of movement towards Laurence, he almost whispered, "Think of her silent ways, her

153

noiseless step; the girl glides about like an apparition; her quick fingers, her wild longings—I don't know why, but with all my fondness for her, she reminds me sometimes of a strange—*snake*."

Laurence shuddered, lifted his face, and said hoarsely: "You're right, uncle; perhaps I'd better not; I'll go away, I'll forget her, and then—well, then—yes, you are right, it *is* a different thing to marry one of them." The old man arose. His feeble fingers still clasped his black book; his soft white hair clung about his forehead like that of an Apostle; his eyes lost their peering, crafty expression; his bent shoulders resumed the dignity of a minister of the living God; he was the picture of what the traders called him—"St. Paul."

"Good-night, son," he said.

"Good-night, uncle, and thank you for bringing me to myself."

They were the last words I ever heard uttered by either that old arch-fiend or his weak, miserable kinsman. Father Paul turned and left the room. I watched his withered hand—the hand I had so often felt resting on my head in holy benedictions—clasp the door-knob, turn it slowly, then, with bowed head and his pale face wrapped in thought, he left the room—left it with the mad venom of my hate pursuing him like the very Evil One he taught me of.

What were his years of kindness and care now? What did I care for his God, his heaven, his hell? He had robbed me of my native faith, of my parents, of my people, of this last, this life of love that would have made a great, good woman of me. God! how I hated him!

I crept to the closet in my dark little room. I felt for a bundle I had not looked at for years —yes, it was there, the buckskin dress I had worn as a little child when they brought me to the mission. I tucked it under my arm and descended the stairs noiselessly. I would look into the study and speak good-bye to Laurence; then I would—

I pushed open the door. He was lying on the couch where a short time previously he had sat, white and speechless, listening to Father Paul, I moved towards him softly. God in heaven, he was already asleep. As I bent over him the fulness of his perfect beauty impressed me for the first time; his slender form, his curving mouth that almost laughed even in sleep, his fair, tossed hair, his smooth, strong-pulsing throat. God! how I loved him!

Then there arose the picture of the factor's daughter. I hated her. I hated her baby face, her yellow hair, her whitish skin. "She shall not marry him," my soul said. "I will kill him first —kill his beautiful body, his lying, false heart." Something in my heart seemed to speak; it said over and over again, "Kill him, kill him; she will never have him then. Kill him. It will break Father Paul's heart and blight his life. He has killed the best of you, of your womanhood; kill *his* best, his pride, his hope—his sister's son, his nephew Laurence." But how? how?

What had that terrible old man said I was

155

like? A *strange snake.* A snake? The idea wound itself about me like the very coils of a serpent. What was this in the beaded bag of my buckskin dress? this little thing rolled in tan that my mother had given me at parting with the words, "Don't touch much, but some time maybe you want it!" Oh! I knew well enough what it was—a small flint arrow-head dipped in the venom of some *strange snake.*

I knelt beside him and laid my hot lips on his hand. I worshipped him, oh, how, how I worshipped him! Then again the vision of *her* baby face, *her* yellow hair—I scratched his wrist twice with the arrow-tip. A single drop of red blood oozed up; he stirred. I turned the lamp down and slipped out of the room—out of the house.

* * * * * * * *

I dream nightly of the horrors of the white man's hell. Why did they teach me of it, only to fling me into it?

Last night as I crouched beside my mother on the buffalo-hide, Dan Henderson, the trapper, came in to smoke with my father. He said old Father Paul was bowed with grief, that with my disappearance I was suspected, but that there was no proof. Was it not merely a snake bite?

They account for it by the fact that I am a Redskin.

They seem to have forgotten I am a woman.

The Legend of Lilooet Falls

*N*O ONE could possibly mistake the quiet little tap at the door. It could be given by no other hand west of the Rockies save that of my old friend The Klootchman. I dropped a lap full of work and sprang to open the door; for the slanting rains were chill outside, albeit the December grass was green and the great masses of English ivy clung wet and fresh as in summer about the low stone wall that ran between my verandah and the street.

"Kla-how-ya, Tillicum," I greeted, dragging her into the warmth and comfort of my "den," and relieving her of her inseparable basket, and removing her rain-soaked shawl. Before she spoke she gave that peculiar little gesture common to the Indian woman from the Atlantic to the Pacific. She lifted both hands and with each forefinger smoothed gently along her forehead from the parting of her hair to the temples. It is the universal habit of the red woman, and simply means a desire for neatness in her front locks.

I busied myself immediately with the teakettle, for, like all her kind, The Klootchman dearly loves her tea.

The old woman's eyes sparkled as she watched the welcome brewing, while she chatted away in half English, half Chinook, telling me of her doings in all these weeks that I had not seen her. But it was when I handed her a huge old-fashioned breakfast cup fairly brimming with tea as strong as lye that she really described her journeyings.

She had been north to the Skeena River, south to the great "Fair" at Seattle, but, best of all seemingly to her, was her trip into the interior. She had been up the trail to Lillooet in the great "Cariboo" country. It was my turn then to have sparkling eyes, for I traversed that inexpressibly beautiful trail five years ago, and the delight of that journey will remain with me for all time.

"And, oh! Tillicum," I cried, "have your good brown ears actually listened to the call of the falls across the cañon—the Falls of Lillooet?"

"My ears have heard them whisper, laugh, weep," she replied in the Chinook.

"Yes," I answered, "they do all those things. They have magic voices—those dear, far-off falls!"

At the word "magic" her keen eyes snapped, she set her empty cup aside and looked at me solemnly.

"Then you know the story—the strange tale?" she asked almost whisperingly.

I shook my head. This was always the crucial moment with my Klootchman, when her voice lowers, and she asks if you know things. You must be diplomatic, and never question her in turn. If you do her lips will close in unbreakable silence.

"I have heard no story, but I have heard the Falls 'whisper, laugh and weep.' That is enough for me," I said, with seeming indifference.

"What do you see when you look at them from across the cañon?" she asked. "Do they look to you like anything else but falling water?"

I thought for a moment before replying. Memory seemed to hold up an indistinct photograph of towering fir-crested heights, where through a broken ridge of rock a shower of silvery threads cascaded musically down, down, down, until they lost themselves in the mighty Fraser, that hurled itself through the yawning cañon stretched at my feet. I have never seen such slender threads of glowing tissue save on early morning cobwebs at sun-up.

"The Falls look like cobwebs," I said, as the memory touched me. "Millions of fine misty cobwebs woven together."

"Then the legend must be true," she uttered, half to herself. I slipped down on my treasured wolf-skin rug near her chair, and, with hands locked about my knees, sat in silence, knowing it was the one and only way to lure her to speech. She arose, helped herself to more tea, and with the toe of her beaded moccasin idly stroked one of the wolf-skin paws. "Yes," she said, with some decision, "the Indian men of magic say that the falls are cobwebs twisted and braided together."

I nodded, but made no comment; then her voice droned into the broken English, that, much as I love it, I must leave to the reader's imagination. "Indian mothers are strange," she began. I nodded again.

"Yes, they are strange, and there is a strange tie between them and their children. The men of magic say they can *see* that tie, though you and I cannot. It is thin, fine, silvery as a cobweb, but strong as the ropes of wild vine that

159

swing down the great cañons. No storm ever breaks those vines; the tempests that drag the giant firs and cedars up by their roots, snap their branches and break their boles, never break the creeping vines. They may be torn from their strongholds, but in the young months of the summer the vine will climb up, and cling again. *Nothing* breaks it. So is the cobweb tie the Men of Magic see between the Indian mother and her child.

"There was a time when no falls leapt and sang down the heights at Lillooet, and in those days our men were very wild and warlike; but the women were gentle and very beautiful, and they loved and lived and bore children as women have done before, and since.

"But there was one, more gentle, more beautiful than all others of the tribe. 'Be-be,' our people call her; it is the Chinook word for 'a kiss.' None of our people knew her real name; but it was a kiss of hers that made this legend, so as 'Be-be' we speak of her.

"She was a mother-woman, but save for one beautiful girl-child, her family of six were all boys, splendid, brave boys, too, but this one treasured girl-child they called 'Morning-mist.' She was little and frail and beautiful, like the clouds one sees at daybreak circling about the mountain peaks. Her father and her brothers loved her, but the heart of Be-be, her mother, seemed wrapped round and about that misty-eyed child.

"'I love you,' the mother would say many

times a day, as she caught the girl-child in her arms. 'And I love you,' the girl-child would answer, resting for a moment against the warm shoulder. 'Little Flower,' the woman would murmur, 'thou art morning to me, thou art golden mid-day, thou art slumbrous nightfall to my heart.'

"So these two loved and lived, mother and daughter, made for each other, shaped into each other's lives as the moccasin is shaped to the foot.

"Then came that long, shadowed, sunless day, when Be-be, returning from many hours of ollalie picking, her basket filled to the brim with rich fruit, her heart reaching forth to her home even before her swift feet could traverse the trail, found her husband and her boys stunned with a dreadful fear, searching with wild eyes, hurrying feet, and grief-wrung hearts for her little 'Morning-child' who had wandered into the forest while her brothers played—the forest which was deep and dark and dangerous—and had not returned."

The Klootchman's voice ceased. For a long moment she gazed straight before her, then looking at me said:

"You have heard the Falls of Lillooet weep?"

I nodded.

"It is the weeping of that Indian mother, sobbing through the centuries, that you hear." She uttered the words with a cadence of grief in her voice.

"Hours, nights, days, they searched for the Morning-child," she continued. "And each moment of that unending agony to the mother-woman is repeated to-day in the call, the wail, the ever-

161

lasting sobbing of the falls. At night the wolves howled up the cañon. 'God of my fathers, keep safe my Morning-child,' the mother would implore. In the glare of day eagles poised, and vultures wheeled above the forest, their hungry claws, their unblinking eyes, their beaks of greed shining in the sunlight. 'God of my fathers, keep safe my Morning-child' was again wrung from the mother's lips. For one long moon, that dawned, and shone and darkened, that mother's heart lived out its torture. Then one pale daybreak a great fleet of canoes came down the Fraser River. Those that paddled were of a strange tribe, they spoke in a strange tongue, but their hearts were human, and their skins were of the rich copper-color of the Upper Lillooet country. As they steered downstream, running the rapids, braving the whirlpools, they chanted, in monotone:

> "'We have a lost child,
> A beautiful lost child.
> We love this lost child,
> But the heart of the child
> Calls the mother of the child.
> Come and claim this lost child.'

"The music of the chant was most beautiful, but no music in the world of the white man's Tyee could equal that which rang through the heart of Be-be, the Indian mother-woman.

"Heart upon heart, lips upon lips, the Morning-child and the mother caught each other in embrace. The strange tribe told of how they had found the girl-child wandering fearfully in the forest, crouching from the claws of eagles, shrinking from the horror of wolves, but the mother with her regained

162

treasure in her arms begged them to cease their tales. 'I have gone through agonies enough, oh, my friends,' she cried aloud. 'Let me rest from torture now.' Then her people came and made a great feast and potlatch for this strange Upper Lillooet tribe, and at the feast Be-be arose, and, lifting the girl-child to her shoulder, she commanded silence and spoke:

"'O Sagalie Tyee (God of all the earth), You have given back to me my treasure; take my tears, my sobs, my happy laughter, my joy—take the cobweb chains that bind my Morning-child and me—make them sing to others, that they may know my gratitude. O Sagalie Tyee, make them sing.' As she spoke, she kissed the child. At that moment the Falls of Lillooet came like a million cobweb strands, dashing and gleaming down the cañon, sobbing, laughing, weeping, calling, singing. You have listened to them."

The Klootchman's voice was still. Outside, the rains still slanted gently, like a whispering echo of the far-away falls. "Thank you, Tillicum of mine; it is a beautiful legend," I said. She did not reply until, wrapped about in her shawl, she had clasped my hand in good-bye. At the door she paused, "Yes," she said—"and it is true." I smiled to myself. I love my Klootchman. She is so *very* Indian.

Her Majesty's Guest

[AUTHOR'S NOTE—The "Onondaga Jam" oc-
curred late in the seventies, and this tale is founded
upon actual incidents in the life of the author's
father, who was Forest Warden on the Indian
Reserve.]

I HAVE never been a good man, but then I have
never pretended to be one, and perhaps that at
least will count in my favor in the day when the
great dividends are declared.

I have been what is called "well brought up"
and I would give some years of my life to possess
now the money spent on my education; how I
came to drop from what I should have been to
what I am would scarcely interest anyone—if
indeed I were capable of detailing the process,
which I am not. I suppose I just rolled leisurely
down hill like many another fellow.

My friends, however, still credit me with one
virtue; that is an absolute respect for my neighbor's wife, a feeling which, however, does not
extend to his dollars. His money is mine if I
can get it, and to do myself justice I prefer getting
it from him honestly, at least without sufficient
dishonesty to place me behind prison bars.

Some experience has taught me that when a
man is reduced to getting his living, as I do, by
side issues and small deals, there is no better
locality for him to operate than around the borders
of some Indian Reserve.

The pagan Indian is an unsuspicious fool. You
can do him up right and left. The Christian

Indian is as sharp as a fox, and with a little gloved handling he will always go in with you on a few lumber and illicit whiskey deals, which means that you have the confidence of his brethren and their dollars at the same time.

I had outwitted the law for six years. I had smuggled more liquor into the Indian Bush on the Grand River Reserve and drawn more timber out of it to the Hamilton and Brantford markets than any forty dealers put together. Gradually the law thinned the whole lot out—all but me; but I was slippery as an eel and my bottles of whiskey went on, and my loads of ties and timber came off, until every officer and preacher in the place got up and demanded an inspection.

The Government at Ottawa awoke, stretched, yawned, then printed some flaring posters and stuck them around the border villages. The posters were headed by a big print of the British Coat of Arms, and some large type beneath announced terrible fines and heavy imprisonments for anyone caught hauling Indian timber off the Reserve, or hauling whiskey on to it. Then the Government rubbed its fat palms together, settled itself in its easy chair, and snored again.

I? Oh, I went on with my operations.

And at Christmas time Tom Barrett arrived on the scene. Not much of an event, you'd say if you saw him, still less if you heard him. According to himself, he knew everything and could do everything in the known world; he was just twenty-two and as obnoxiously fresh a thing as ever boasted itself before older men.

He was the old missionary's son and had come up from college at Montreal to help his father preach salvation to the Indians on Sundays, and to swagger around week-days in his brand new clerical-cut coat and white tie.

He enjoyed what is called, I believe, "deacon's orders." They tell me he was recently "priested," to use their straight English Church term, and is now parson of a swell city church. Well! they can have him. I'll never split on him, but I could tell them some things about Tom Barrett that would soil his surplice—at least in my opinion, but you never can be sure when even religious people will make a hero out of a rogue.

The first time I ever saw him he came into "Jake's" one night, quite late. We were knocked clean dumb. "Jake's" isn't the place you would count on seeing a clerical-cut coat in.

It's not a thoroughly disreputable place, for Jake has a decent enough Indian wife; but he happens also to have a cellar which has a hard name for illicit-whiskey supplies, though never once has the law, in its numerous and unannounced visits to the shanty, ever succeeded in discovering barrel or bottle. I consider myself a pretty smart man, but Jake is cleverer than I am.

When young Barrett came in that night, there was a clatter of hiding cups. "Hello, boys," he said, and sat down wearily opposite me, leaning his arms on the table between us like one utterly done out.

Jake, it seemed, had the distinction of knowing him; so he said, kind of friendly-like,

"Hello, parson—sick?"

"Sick? Sick nothing," said Barrett, "except sick to death of this place. And don't 'parson' me! I'm 'parson' on Sundays; the rest of the six days I'm Tom Barrett—Tom, if you like."

We were dead silent. For myself, I thought the fellow clean crazy; but the next moment he had turned half around, and with a quick, soft, coaxing movement, for all the world like a woman, he slipped his arm around Jake's shoulders, and said, "Say, Jake, don't let the fellows mind me." Then in a lower tone—"*What have you got to drink?*"

Jake went white-looking and began to talk of some cider he'd got in the cellar; but Barrett interrupted with, "Look here, Jake, just drop that rot; I know all about *you.*" He tipped a half wink at the rest of us, but laid his fingers across his lips. "Come, old man," he wheedled like a girl, "you don't know what it is to be dragged away from college and buried alive in this Indian bush. The governor's good enough, you know— treats me white and all that—but you know what he is on whiskey. I tell you I've got a throat as long and dry as a fence rail—"

No one spoke.

"You'll save my life if you do," he added, crushing a bank note into Jake's hand.

Jake looked at me. The same thought flashed on us both; if we could get this church student on our side—Well! Things would be easy enough and public suspicion never touch us. Jake turned, resurrected the hidden cups, and went down cellar.

"You're Dan McLeod, aren't you?" suggested

Barrett, leaning across the table and looking sharply at me.

"That's me," I said in turn, and sized him up. I didn't like his face; it was the undeniable face of a liar—small, uncertain eyes, set together close like those of a fox, a thin nose, a narrow, womanish chin that accorded with his girlish actions of coaxing, and a mouth I didn't quite understand.

Jake had come up with the bottle, but before he could put it on the table Barrett snatched it like a starving dog would a hunk of meat.

He peered at the label, squinting his foxy eyes, then laughed up at Jake.

"I hope you don't sell the Indians *this*," he said, tapping the capsule.

No, Jake never sold a drop of whiskey to Indians—the law, you know, was very strict and—

"Oh, I don't care whatever else you sell them," said Barrett, "but their red throats would never appreciate fine twelve-year-old like this. Come, boys."

We came.

"So you're Dan McLeod," he continued after the first long pull, "I've heard about you, too. You've got a deck of cards in your pocket— haven't you? Let's have a game."

I looked at him, and though, as I said in the beginning, I'm not a good man, I felt honestly sorry for the old missionary and his wife at that moment.

"It's no use," said the boy, reading my hesitation. "I've broken loose. I must have a slice of the old college life, just for to-night."

168

I decided the half-cut of Indian blood on his mother's side was showing itself; it was just enough to give Tom a good red flavoring and a rare taste for gaming and liquor.

We played until daylight, when Barrett said he must make his sneak home, and reaching for his wide-brimmed, soft felt preacher's hat, left— having pocketed twenty-six of our good dollars, swallowed unnumbered cups of twelve-year-old and won the combined respect of everyone at Jake's.

The next Sunday Jake went to church out of curiosity. He said Tom Barrett "officiated" in a surplice as white as snow and with a face as sinless as your mother's. He preached most eloquently against the terrible evil of the illicit liquor trade, and implored his Indian flock to resist this greatest of all pitfalls. Jake even seemed impressed as he told us.

But Tom Barrett's "breaking loose for once" was like any other man's. Night after night saw him at Jake's, though he never played to win after that first game. As the weeks went on, he got anxious-looking; his clerical coat began to grow seedy, his white ties uncared for; he lost his fresh, cheeky talk, and the climax came late in March when one night I found him at Jake's sitting alone, his face bowed down on the table above his folded arms, and something so disheartened in his attitude that I felt sorry for the boy. Perhaps it was that I was in trouble myself that day; my biggest "deal" of the season had been scented by the officers and the chances were

169

they would come on and seize the five barrels of whiskey I had been as many weeks smuggling into the Reserve. However it was, I put my hand on his shoulder, and told him to brace up, asking at the same time what was wrong.

"Money," he answered, looking up with kind of haggard eyes. "Dan, I must have money. City bills, college debts—everything has rolled up against me. I daren't tell the governor, and he couldn't help me anyway, and I can't go back for another term owing every man in my class." He looked suicidal. And then I made the plunge I'd been thinking on all day.

"Would a hundred dollars be any good to you?" I eyed him hard as I said it, and sat down in my usual place, opposite him.

"Good?" he exclaimed, half rising. "It would be an eternal godsend." His foxy eyes glittered. I thought I detected greed in them; perhaps it was only relief.

I told him it was his if he would only help me, and making sure we were quite alone, I ran off a hurried account of my "deal," then proposed that he should "accidentally" meet the officers near the border, ring in with them as a parson would be likely to do, tell them he suspicioned the whiskey was directly at the opposite side of the Reserve to where I really had stored it, get them wild-goose chasing miles away, and give me a chance to clear the stuff and myself as well; in addition to the hundred I would give him twenty per cent. on the entire deal. He changed color and the sweat stood out on his forehead.

170

"One hundred dollars this time to-morrow night," I said. He didn't move. "And twenty per cent. One hundred dollars this time to-morrow night," I repeated.

He began to weaken. I lit my pipe and looked indifferent, though I knew I was a lost man if he refused—and informed. Suddenly he stretched his hand across the table, impulsively, and closed it over mine. I knew I had him solid then.

"Dan," he choked up, "it's a terrible thing for a divinity student to do; but—" his fingers tightened nervously. "I'm with you!" Then in a moment, "Find some whiskey, Dan. I'm done up."

He soon got braced enough to ask me who was in the deal, and what timber we expected to trade for. When I told him Lige Smith and Jack Jackson were going to help me, he looked scared and asked me if I thought they would split on him. He was so excited I thought him cowardly, but the poor devil had reason enough, I supposed, to want to keep the transaction from the ears of his father, or worse still—the bishop. He seemed easier when I assured him the boys were square, and immensely gratified at the news that I had already traded six quarts of the stuff for over a hundred dollars' worth of cordwood.

"We'll never get it across the river to the markets," he said dolefully. "I came over this morning in a canoe. Ice is all out."

"What about the Onondaga Jam?" I said. He winked.

"That'll do. I'd forgotten it," he answered, and chirped up right away like a kid.

But I hadn't forgotten the Jam. It had been a regular gold-mine to me all that open winter, when the ice froze and thawed every week and finally jammed itself clean to the river bottom in the throat of the bend up at Onondaga, and the next day the thermometer fell to eleven degrees below zero, freezing it into a solid block that bridged the river for traffic, and saved my falling fortunes.

"And where's the whiskey hidden?" he asked after awhile.

"No you don't," I laughed. "Parson or pal, no man living knows or will know where it is till he helps me haul it away. I'll trust none of you."

"I'm not a thief," he pouted.

"No," I said, "but you're blasted hard up, and I don't intend to place temptation in your way."

He laughed good-naturedly and turned the subject aside just as Lige Smith and Jack Jackson came in with an unusual companion that put a stop to further talk. Women were never seen at night time around Jake's; even his wife was invisible, and I got a sort of shock when I saw old Cayuga Joe's girl, Elizabeth, following at the boys' heels. It had been raining and the girl, a full-blood Cayuga, shivered in the damp and crouched beside the stove.

Tom Barrett started when he saw her. His color rose and he began to mark up the table with his thumb nail. I could see he felt his fix. The girl—Indian right through—showed no surprise at seeing him there, but that did not mean

172

she would keep her mouth shut about it next day. Tom was undoubtedly *discovered.*

Notwithstanding her unwelcome presence, however, Jackson managed to whisper to me that the Forest Warden and his officers were alive and bound for the Reserve the following day. But it didn't worry me worth a cent; I knew we were safe as a church with Tom Barrett's clerical coat in our midst. He was coming over to our corner now.

"That hundred's right on the dead square, Dan?" he asked anxiously, taking my arm and moving to the window.

I took a roll of bank notes from my trousers' pocket and with my back to the gang counted out ten tens. I always carry a good wad with me with a view to convenience if I have to make a hurried exit from the scene of my operations.

He shook his head and stood away. "Not till I've earned it, McLeod."

What fools very young men make of themselves sometimes. The girl arose, folding her damp shawl over her head, and made towards the door; but he intercepted her, saying it was late and as their ways lay in the same direction, he would take her home. She shot a quick glance at him and went out. Some little uneasy action of his caught my notice. In a second my suspicions were aroused; the meeting had been arranged, and I knew from what I had seen him to be that the girl was doomed.

It was all very well for me to do up Cayuga Joe—he was the Indian whose hundred dollars'

173

worth of cordwood I owned in lieu of six quarts of bad whiskey—but his women-folks were entitled to be respected at least while I was around. I looked at my watch; it was past midnight. I suddenly got boiling hot clean through.

"Look here, Tom Barrett," I said, "I ain't a saint, as everybody knows; but if you don't treat that girl right, you'll have to square it up with me, d'you understand?"

He threw me a nasty look. "Keep your gallantry for some occasion when it's needed, Dan McLeod," he sneered, and with a laugh I didn't like, he followed the girl out into the rain.

I walked some distance behind them for two miles. When they reached her father's house and went in, I watched her through the small uncurtained window put something on the fire to cook, then arouse her mother, who even at that late hour sat beside the stove smoking a clay pipe. The old woman had apparently met with some accident; her head and shoulders were bound up, and she seemed in pain. Barrett talked with her considerably and once when I caught sight of his face, it was devilish with some black passion I did not recognize. Although I felt sure the girl was now all right for the night, there was something about this meeting I didn't like; so I lay around until just daylight when Jackson and Lige Smith came through the bush as pre-arranged should I not return to Jake's.

It was not long before Elizabeth and Tom came out again and entered a thick little bush behind the shanty. Lige lifted the axe off the woodpile with a knowing look, and we all three followed silently. I was surprised to find it a well beaten and equally well-concealed trail. All my suspicions returned. I knew now that Barrett was a bad lot all round, and as soon as I had quit using him and his coat, I made up my mind to rid my quarters of him; fortunately I knew enough about him to use that knowledge as a whip-lash.

We followed them for something over a mile, when—heaven and hell! The trail opened abruptly on the clearing where lay my recently acquired cordwood with my five barrels of whiskey concealed in its midst.

The girl strode forward, and with the strength of a man, pitched down a dozen sticks with lightning speed.

"There!" she cried, turning to Tom. "There you find him—you find him whiskey. You say you spill. No more my father he's drunk all day, he beat my mother."

I stepped out.

"So, Tom Barrett," I said, "you've played the d——d sneak and hunted it out!"

He fairly jumped at the sound of my voice; then he got white as paper, and then—something came into his face that I never saw before. It was a look like his father's, the old missionary.

"Yes, McLeod," he answered. "And I've hunted *you* out. It's cost me the loss of a whole term at college and a considerable amount of self-respect, but I've got my finger on you now!"

The whole infernal trick burst right in on my intelligence. If I had had a revolver, he would

175

have been a dead man; but border traders nowadays are not desperadoes with bowie knives and hip pockets—

"You surely don't mean to split on me?" I asked.

"I surely don't mean to do anything else," he cheeked back.

"Then, Tom Barrett," I sputtered, raging, "you're the dirtiest cad and the foulest liar that ever drew the breath of life."

"I dare say I am," he said smoothly. Then with rising anger he advanced, peering into my face with his foxy eyes. "And I'll tell you right here, Dan McLeod, I'd be a hundred times a cad, and a thousand times a liar to save the souls and bodies of our Indians from going to hell, through your cursed whiskey."

I have always been a brave man, but I confess I felt childishly scared before the wild, mesmeric power of his eyes. I was unable to move a finger, but I blurted out boastfully: "If it wasn't for your preacher's hat and coat I'd send your sneaking soul to Kingdom Come, right here!"

Instantly he hauled off his coat and tie and stood with clenched fists while his strange eyes fairly spat green fire.

"Now," he fumed, "I've discarded my cloth, Dan McLeod. You've got to deal with a man now, not with a minister."

To save my immortal soul I can't tell why I couldn't stir. I only know that everything seemed to drop out of sight except his two little blazing eyes. I stood like a fool, queered, dead queered right through.

He turned politely to the girl. "You may go, Elizabeth," he said, "and thank you for your assistance." The girl turned and went up the trail without a word.

With the agility of a cat he sprang on to the wood-pile, pitched off enough cordwood to expose my entire "cellar"; then going across to Lige, he coolly took the axe out of his hand. His face was white and set, but his voice was natural enough as he said:

"Now, gentlemen, whoever cares to interrupt me will get the blade of this axe buried in his brain, as heaven is my witness."

I didn't even curse as he split the five barrels into slivers and my well-fought-for whiskey soaked into the slush. Once he lifted his head and looked at me, and the mouth I didn't understand revealed itself; there was something about it like a young Napoleon's.

I never hated a man in my life as I hated Tom Barrett then. That I daren't resist him made it worse. I watched him finish his caddish job, throw down the axe, take his coat over his arm, and leave the clearing without a word.

But no sooner was he out of sight than my devilish temper broke out, and I cursed and blasphemed for half an hour. I'd have his blood if it cost my neck a rope, and that too before he could inform on us. The boys were with me, of course, poor sort of dogs with no grit of their own, and with the axe as my only weapon we left the bush and ran towards the river.

I fairly yelled at my good luck as I reached the high bank. There, a few rods down shore, beside the open water sat Tom Barrett, calling something out to his folks across the river, and from upstream came the deafening thunder of the Onondaga Jam that, loosened by the rain, was shouldering its terrific force downwards with the strength of a million drunken demons.

We had him like a rat in a trap, but his foxy eyes had seen us. He sprang to his feet, hesitated for a fraction of a moment, saw the murder in our faces, then did what any man but a fool would have done—ran.

We were hot on his heels. Fifty yards distant an old dug-out lay hauled up. He ran it down into the water, stared wildly at the oncoming jam, then at us, sprang into the canoe and grabbed the paddle.

I was murderously mad. I whirled the axe above my shoulder and let fly at him. It missed his head by three inches.

He was paddling for dear life now, and, our last chance gone, we stood riveted to the spot, watching him. On the bluff across the river stood his half-blood mother, the raw March wind whipping her skirts about her knees; but her strained, ashen face showed she never felt its chill. Below, with his feet almost in the rapidly rising water, stood the old missionary, his scant grey hair blowing across his eyes that seemed to look out into eternity—a-midstream Tom, paddling

178

with the desperation of death, his head turning every second with the alertness of an animal to gauge the approaching ice-shove.

Even I wished him life then. Twice I thought him caught in the crush, but he was out of it like an arrow, and in another moment he had leapt ashore while above the roar of the grinding jam I heard him cry out with a strange exultation: "Father, I've succeeded. I have had to be a scoundrel and a cad, but *I've trapped them at last!*"

He staggered forward then, sobbing like a child, and the old man's arms closed round him, just as two heavy jaws of ice snatched the dugout, hurled it off shore and splintered it to atoms.

Well! I had made a bad blunder, which I attempted to rectify by reaching Buffalo that night; but Tom Barrett had won the game. I was arrested at Fort Erie, handcuffed, jailed, tried, convicted of attempted assault and illicit whiskey-trading on the Grand River Indian Reserve—and spent the next five years in Kingston Penitentiary, the guest of Her Most Gracious Majesty Queen Victoria.

Mother o' the Men

A Story of the Canadian North-West Mounted Police

*T*HE COMMANDER'S wife stood on the deck of the *North Star* looking at the receding city of Vancouver as if to photograph within her eyes and heart every detail of its wonderful beauty—its clustering, sisterly houses, its holly hedges, its ivied walls, its emerald lawns, its teeming streets and towering spires. She seemed to realize that this was the end of the civilized trail; that henceforth, for many years, her sight would know only the unbroken line of icy ridge and sky of the northernmost outposts of the great Dominion. To her hand clung a little boy of ten, and about her hovered some twenty young fellows, gay in the scarlet tunics, the flashing buffalo-head buttons, that bespoke the soldierly uniform of the Canadian North-West Mounted Police. They were the first detachment bound for the Yukon, and were under her husband's command.

She was the only woman in the "company." The major had purposely selected unmarried men for his staff, for in the early nineties the Arctic was no place for a woman. But when the Government at Ottawa saw fit to commission Major Lysle to face the frozen North, and with a handful of men build and garrison a fort at the rim of the Polar Seas, Mrs. Lysle quietly remarked, "I shall accompany you, so shall the boy," and the major blessed her in his heart, for had she not so decided, it would mean absolute separation

180

from wife and child for from three to five years, as in those days no railways, no telegraph lines, stretched their pulsing fingers into the Klondyke. One mail went in, one mail came out, each year— that was all.

"It's good-bye, Graham lad," said one of the scarlet-coated soldiers, tossing the little boy to his back. "Look your longest at those paved streets, and the green, green things. There'll be months of just snow away up there," and he nodded towards the north.

"Oh, but father says it won't be lonely at all up there," asserted the child. "He says I'll grow *terribly* big in a few years; that people always grow in the North, and maybe I'll soon be able to wear buffalo buttons and have stripes on my sleeve like you"; and the childish fingers traced the outline of the sergeant's chevrons.

"I hope, dear, that you shall do all that, soon," said Mrs. Lysle; "but first you must *win* those stripes, my boy, and if you win them as the sergeant did, mother shall be very proud of you."

At which, the said sergeant hastily set the boy down, and, with confusion written all over his strong young face, made some excuse to disappear, for no man in the world is as shy or modest about his deeds of valor as is a North-West "Mounted."

"Won't you tell me, mother, how Sergeant Black got those stripes on his sleeve?" begged the boy.

"Perhaps to-night, son, when you are in bed— just before mother says good-night—we'll see. But look! there is the city, fading, fading." Then

181

after a short silence: "There, Graham, it has
gone."

"But isn't that it 'way over there, mother?"
persisted the boy. "I see the sun shining on the
roofs."

Mrs. Lysle shook her head. "No, dearie; that
is the snow on the mountain peaks. The city has
—gone."

But far into the twilight she yet stood watching
the purple sea, the dove-grey coast. Her world
was with her—the man she had chosen for her
life partner, and the little boy that belonged to
them both—but there are times even in the life of
a wife and mother when her soul rebels at cutting
herself off from her womenkind, and all that
environment of social life among women means,
even if the act itself is voluntary on her part.
It was a relief, then, from her rather sombre musing
at the ship's rail, when the major lightly placed both
hands on her shoulders and said, "Grahamie has
toddled off to the stateroom. The sea air is weight-
ing down his eyelids."

"Sea air?" laughed Mrs. Lysle. "Don't you
believe it, Horace. The young monkey has been
just scampering about the deck with the men
until his little legs are tired out. I'm half afraid
our 'Mounted' boys bid fair to spoil him. I'll
go to him, for I promised him a story to-night."

"Which you would rather perish than not tell
him, if you promised," smiled the major. "You
govern that boy as I do my men, eh, dear?"

"It's the only way to govern boys or soldiers,"
she laughed back from the head of the companion

way. "Then both boy and soldier will keep their promises to you."

The major watched her go below, then said to himself, "She's right—she's always right. She was right to come north, and bring him, too. But I am a coward, for I daren't tell her she'll have to part from him, or from me, some day. He will have to be sent to the front again; he can't grow up unlearned, untaught, and there are no schools in our Arctic world, and she must go with him, or stay with me; but I can't tell her. Yes, I'm a coward." But Major Lysle was the only person in all the world who would have thought or said so.

"And will you tell me how Sergeant Black won his stripes, mother, before I go to sleep?" begged Graham.

"Yes, little 'North-West,'" she replied, using the pet name the men in barracks frequently called the child. "It's just a wee story of one man fighting it out alone—just alone, single-handed —with no reinforcements but his own courage, his own self-reliance."

"That's what father says, isn't it, mother, to just do things yourself?" asked the boy.

"That's it, dear, and that is what Sergeant Black did. He was only corporal then, and he was dispatched from headquarters to arrest some desperate horse thieves who were trying to drive a magnificent bunch of animals across the boundary line into the United States, and then sell them. These men were breaking two laws. They had not only stolen the horses, but were trying to evade the American Customs. Your father always

183

called them 'The Rapparees,' for they were Irish, and fighters, and known from the Red River to the Rockies as plunderers and desperadoes. There was some trouble to the north at the same time; barracks was pretty well thinned; not a man could be spared to help him. But when Corporal Black got his instructions and listened to the commanding officer say, 'If that detachment returns from the Qu'Appelle Valley within twenty-four hours, I'll order them out to assist you, corporal,' the plucky little soldier just stood erect, clicked his heels together, saluted, and replied, 'I can do it alone, sir.'

"'I notice you don't say you *think* you can do it alone,' remarked the officer dryly. He was a lenient man and often conversed with his men.

"'It is not my place to *think*, sir. I've just got to *do*,' replied the corporal, and saluting again, he was gone.

"All that night he galloped up the prairie trail on the track of the thieves, and just before daybreak he sighted them, entrenched in a coulee, where their campfires made no glow, and the neighing horses could not be heard. There were six men all told, busying themselves getting breakfast and staking the animals preparatory to hiding through the day hours, and getting across the boundary line the next night. Both men and beasts were wearied with the long journey, but Corporal Black is the sort of man that *never* wearies in either brain or body. He never hesitated a second. Jerking his rat-skin cap down, covering his face as much as possible, he rode

184

silently around to the south of the encampment, clutched a revolver in each hand, and rode within earshot, then said four words:

"'Stand, or I fire!' If a cyclone had swooped down on them, the thieves could not have been more astounded. But they stood, and stood yards away from their own guns. Then they demanded to know who he was, for of course they thought him a thief like themselves, probably following them to capture their spoil. Then Corporal Black unbuttoned his great-coat and flung it wide open, displaying the brilliant scarlet tunic of our own dear Mounted Police. They needed no other reply. At the point of his revolver he ordered them to unstake the horses. Then not one man was allowed to mount, but, breakfastless and frenzied, they were compelled to walk before him, driving the stolen animals ahead, mile upon mile, league after league.

"Father says it was a strange-looking procession that trudged into barracks. Twenty beautiful, spirited horses, six hangdog-looking thieves, with a single exhausted horse in the rear, on which was mounted an alert, keen-eyed and very hungry young soldier who wore a scarlet tunic and buffalo-head buttons. The next day Corporal Black had another stripe on his sleeve."*

Her voice ceased, and she looked down at her son. The child lay for a moment, wide-eyed and tense. Then some indescribable quality seemed

*The foregoing story is an actual occurrence. The author had the honor of knowing personally the North-West Mounted Policeman who achieved his rank through this action.

to make him momentarily too large, too tall, for the narrow ship's berth. Then:

"And he fought it out *alone*, mother, just alone —single-handed?"

"Yes, Grahamie," she said, softly.

"Fought alone!" he said almost to himself. Then aloud: "Thank you, mother, for telling me that story. Perhaps some day I'll have to fight it out alone, and when I do, I'll try to remember Sergeant Black. Good-night, mother."

"Good-night, my boy."

* * * * * * * *

The long, long winter was doing its worst, and that was unspeakable in its dreariness and its misery. The "Fort" was just about completed before things froze up—narrow, small quarters constructed of rough logs, surrounded by a stockade —but above its roof the Union Jack floated, and beneath it flashed the scarlet tunics, the buffalo-head buttons, the clanking spurs of as brave a band of men, "queened over" by as courageous a woman, as ever Gibraltar or the Throne Room knew.

As time went on the major's wife began to find herself "Mother o' the Men" (as an old Klondyker named her), as well as of her own boy. Those blizzard-blown, snow-hardened, ice-toughened soldiers went to her for everything—sympathy, assistance, advice—for in that lonely outpost military lines were less strictly drawn, and she could oftentimes do for the men what would be considered amazingly unofficial, were those little humane kindnesses done in barracks at Regina

186

or Macleod or Calgary. She nursed the men through every illness, preparing the food herself for the invalids. She attended to many a frozen face and foot and finger. She smoothed out their differences, inspirited them when they grew discouraged, talked to them of their own people, so that their home ties should not be entirely severed because they could write letters or receive them but once a year. But there were days when the sight of a woman's face would have been a glimpse of paradise to her, days when she almost wildly regretted her boy had not been a girl— just a little sweet-voiced girl, a thing of her own sex and kind. But it always seemed at these moments that Grahamie would providentially rush in to her with some glad story of sport or adventure, and she would snatch him tightly in her arms and say, "No, no, boy of mine, I don't want even a girlie, if I may only keep you." And once when her thoughts had been more than usually traitorous in wishing he had been a girl, the child seemed to divine some idea of her struggle; for a moment his firm little fingers caught her hand encouragingly, and he said in a whisper, "Are you fighting it out alone, mother—just single-handed?"

"Just single-handed, dearest," she replied.

Then he scampered away, but paused to call back gravely, "Remember Sergeant Black, mother."

"Yes, Grahamie, I'll try to," she replied brightly. At that moment he was the lesser child of the two.

And so the winter crept slowly on, and the brief, brilliant summer flitted in, then out, like

187

a golden dream. The second snows were upon the little fort, the second Christmas, the second long, long weeks and months of the new year. An unspoken horror was staring them all in the face: navigation did not open when expected, and supplies were running low, pitifully low. The smoked and dried meats, the canned things, flour, sealed lard, oatmeal, hard-tack, dried fruits—*everything* was slowly but inevitably giving out day upon day. Before and behind them stretched hummocks of trailless snow. Not an Indian, not a dog train, not even a wild animal, had set foot in that waste for weeks. In early March the major's wife had hidden a single package of gelatine, a single tin of dried beef, and a single half pound of cornstarch. "If sickness comes to my boys" (she did not say boy), "I shall at least have saved these," she told herself, in justification of her act. "A sick man cannot live on beans." But now they were down to beans—just beans and lard boiled together. Then a day dawned when there was not even a spoonful of lard left. "Beans straight!"—it was the death knell, for beans straight—beans without grease—kill the strongest man in a brief span of days. Oh, that the ice bridges would melt, the seas open, the ships come!

But that night the men at mess had beans with unlimited grease, its peculiar flavor peppered and spiced out of it. Life, life was to be theirs even yet! What had renewed it?

But one of the men had caught something on his fork and extracted it from the food on his plate. It was an overlooked *wick*. The major's

wife had begun to boil up the tallow candles.*
But the cheer that shook that rough log roof
came right from hearts that blessed her, and
brought her to the door of the men's mess-room.
The men were on their feet instantly. "A light
has broken upon us, or rather *within* us, Mrs.
Lysle!" cried a self-selected spokesman.

"Illuminating, isn't it, boys?" She laughed,
then turned away, for the cheers and tears were
very close together.

Then one day when even starving stomachs
almost revolted at the continued coarse mixture,
a ribbon of blue proclaimed the open sea, and
into those waters swept the longed-for ship. Yet,
strangely enough, that night the "Mother o' the
Men" wept a storm of tears, the only tears she
had yielded to in those long five years. For
with its blessing of food the ship had her hold
bursting with liquors and wines, the hideous commerce that invades the pioneer places of the
earth. Should the already weakened, ill-fed and
scurvy-threatened garrison break into those supplies, all the labor and patience and mothering of
this courageous woman would be useless, for
after a bean diet in the Northern latitudes, whiskey
is deadly to brain and body, and the victim maddens
or dies.

"You are crying, mother, and the ship here at
last!" said Grahamie's voice at her shoulder.
"Crying when we are all so happy."

"Mother is a little upset, dear. You must try
to forget you ever saw her eyes wet."

* Fact.

189

"I'll forget," said the boy with a finality she could not question. "The ship is so full of good things, mother. We'll think of that, and—forget, won't we?" he added.

"*All* the things in the ship are not good, Grahamie, boy. If they were, mother would not cry," she said.

"I see," he said, but stole from her side with a strained, puzzled look in his young eyes.

Outside he was met by a laughing, joyous dozen of men. One swung the child to his shoulder, shouting, "Hurrah, little 'North-West!' Hurrah! we are all coming to pay tribute to your mother. Look at the dainties we have got for her from the ship!"

"I'm afraid you can't see mother just now," said the boy. "Mother is a little upset. You see, the ship is so full of good things—but then, *all* the things in the ship are not good. If they were, mother would not cry." In the last words he unconsciously imitated his mother's voice.

A profound silence enveloped the men. Then one spoke. "She'll never have cause to cry about anything *I* do, boys."

"Nor I!" "Nor I!" "Nor I!" rang out voice after voice.

"Run back, you blessed little 'North-West,' and tell mother not to be scared for the boys. We'll stand by her to a man. She'll never regret that ship's coming in," said the gallant soldier, slipping the boy to the ground. And to the credit of the men who wore buffalo-head buttons, she never did.

And in all her Yukon years the major's wife had but one more heartache. That agonizing winter had taught her many things, but the bitterest knowledge to come to her was the fact that her boy must be sent "to the front." To be sure, he was growing up the pet of all the police; he was becoming manlier, sturdier, more self-reliant every day. But education he *must* have, and another winter of such deprivation and horror he was too young, too tender, to endure. It was then that the battle arose in her heart. The boy was to be sent to college. Was it her place to accompany him to the distant South-east, to live by herself alone in the college town, just to be near him and watch over his young life, or was it here with her pioneer soldier husband, and his little isolated garrison of "boys" whom she had mothered for two years?

The inevitable day came when she had to shut her teeth and watch Grahamie go aboard the southward-bound vessel alone, in the care of a policeman who was returning on sick leave—to watch him stand at the rail, his little face growing dimmer and more shadowy as the sea widened between them—watch him through tearless, courageous eyes, then turn away with the hopelessness of knowing that for one entire endless year she must wait for word of his arrival.* But his last brave good-bye words rang through her ears every day of that eternal year. "We'll remember Sergeant Black, won't we, mother? And we'll each fight it out alone, single-handed, and maybe

* Fact.

191

they'll give us a chevron for our sleeves when it's over."

But that night when the barracks was wrapped in gloom over the loss of its boy chum, the surgeon appeared in the men's quarters. "Hello, boys!" he said, none too cheerfully. "Dull doings, I say. I'm busy enough, though, keeping an eye on Madam, the major's lady. She's so deadly quiet, so self-controlled, I'm just a little afraid. I wish something would happen to—well, make her less calm."

"*I'll* 'happen,' doctor," chirped up a genial-looking young chap named O'Keefe. "I'll get sick and threaten to die. You say it's serious; she'll be all interest and medicine spoons, and making me jelly inside an hour."

The surgeon eyed him sternly, then: "O'Keefe," he said, "you're the cleverest man I ever came across in the force, and I've been in it eleven years. But, man alive! what have you been doing to yourself? Overwork, no food—why, man, you're sick; look as if you had fever and a touch of pneumonia. You're a very sick man. Go to bed at once—at once, I say!"

O'Keefe looked the surgeon in the eye, winked meaningly, and O'Keefe turned in, although it was but early afternoon. At six o'clock an orderly stood at the door of the major's quarters. Mrs. Lysle was standing on the steps, her eyes fixed on the far horizon across which a ship had melted away.

"Beg pardon, madam," said the orderly, saluting, "but young O'Keefe is very ill. We have had

192

the surgeon, but the—the—pain's getting worse. He's just yelling with agony."

"I'll go at once, orderly. I should have been told before," she replied; and burying her own heartache, she hurried to the men's quarters. Her anxious eyes sought the surgeon's. "Oh, doctor!" she said, "this poor fellow must be looked after. What can I do to help?"

"Everything, Mrs. Lysle," gruffed the surgeon with a professional air. "He is very ill. He must be kept wrapped in hot linseed poultices and—"

"Oh, I say, doctor," remonstrated poor O'Keefe, "I'm not that bad."

"You're a very sick man," scowled the surgeon. "Now, Mrs. Lysle has graciously offered to help nurse you. She'll see that you have hot fomentations every half-hour. I'll drop in twice a day to see how you are getting along." And with that miserable prospect before him, poor O'Keefe watched the surgeon disappear.

"I simply *had* to order those half-hour fomentations, old man," apologized the surgeon that night. "You see, she must be kept busy—just kept at it every minute we can make her do so. Do you think you can stand it?"

"Of course I can," fumed the victim. "But for goodness' sake, don't put me on sick rations! I'll die, sure, if you do."

"I've ordered you the best the commissariat boasts—heaps of meat, butter, even eggs, my boy. Think of it—*eggs*—you lucky young Turk!" laughed the surgeon.

Then followed nights and days of torture. The

193

"boys" would line up to the "sick-room" four times daily, and blandly ask how he was.

"How *am* I?" young O'Keefe would bellow. "How *am* I? I'm well and strong enough to brain every one of you fellows, surgeon included, when I get out of this!"

"But when *are* you going to get out? When will you be out of danger?" they would chuckle.

"Just when I see that haunted look go out of her eyes, and not till then!" he would roar.

And he kept his word. He was really weak when he got up, and pretended to be weaker, but the lines of acute self-control had left Mrs. Lysle's face, the suffering had gone from her eyes, the day the noble O'Keefe took his first solid meal in her presence.

Even the major never discovered that worthy bit of deception. But a year later, when the mail went out, the surgeon sent the entire story to Graham, who, in writing to his mother the following year, perplexed her greatly by saying:

". . . But there are three men in the force I love better than anyone in the world except you, mother. The first, of course, is father, the others, Sergeant Black and Private O'Keefe."

"Why O'Keefe?" she asked herself.

But loyal little "North-West" never told her.

The Nest Builder

"*W*ELL! if some women aren't born just to laugh!" remarked the station agent's wife. "Have you seen that round-faced woman in the waiting-room?"

"No," replied the agent. "I've been too busy; I've had to help unload freight. I heard some children in there, though; they were playing and laughing to beat the band."

"*Nine* of them, John! *Nine* of them, and the oldest just twelve!" gasped his wife. "Why, I'd be crazy if I were in her place. She's come all the way from Grey or Bruce in Ontario—I forget which—with not a soul to help her with that flock. Three of them are almost babies. The smallest one is a darling—just sits on the bench in there and dimples and gurgles and grins all the time."

"Hasn't she got a husband?" asked John.

"Of course," asserted his wife. "But that's just the problem now, or rather he's the problem. He came to Manitoba a year ago, and was working right here in this town. He doesn't seem to have had much luck, and left last week for some ranch away back of Brandon, she now finds out; she must have crossed his letter as she came out. She expected to find him here, and now she is in that waiting-room with nine children, no money to go further, or to go to a hotel even, and—and she's—well, she's just good-natured and smiling, and not a bit worried. As I say, some women are born just to laugh."

195

"Have they anything to eat?" asked the agent, anxiously.

"Stacks of it—a huge hamper. But I took the children what milk we had, and made her take a cup of good hot tea. She *would* pay me, however, I couldn't stop her. But I noticed she has mighty little change in her purse, and she said she had no money, and said it with a round, untroubled, smiling face." The agent's wife spoke the last words almost with envy.

"I'll try and locate the husband," said the agent.

"Yes, she'll get his address to-night, she says," explained the wife; "but no one knows when he will get here. Most likely he's twenty miles away from Brandon, and they will have to send out for him."

Which eventually proved to be the case; and three days elapsed before the husband and father was able to reach the little border town where his wife and ample family had been installed as residents of the general waiting-room of a small, scantily-equipped station. No beds, no washing conveniences, no table, no chairs; just the wall seats, with a roof above them and the pump water at the end of the platform to drink from and dabble in. The distressed man arrived, harassed and anxious, only to be met by a round-faced, laughing wife and nine round-faced, laughing children, who all made sport of their "camping" experience, and assured him they could have "stood it" a little longer, if need be.

But they slept in beds that night—glorious,

196

feathery beds, that were in reality but solid hemp mattresses—in the cheapest lodging-house in town. Then began the home-building. Henderson had secured a quarter section of land ànd made two payments on it when his wife and children arrived, with all their "settlers' effects" in a freight car, which truth to tell, were meagre enough. They had never really owned a home in the East, and when, with saving and selling, she managed to follow her husband into the promising world of Manitoba, she determined to possess a home, no matter how crude, how small, how remote. So Henderson hired horses and "teamed" out sufficient lumber and tar-paper to erect a shack which measured exactly eighteen by twelve feet, then sodded the roof in true Manitoba style, and into this cramped abode Mrs. Henderson stowed her household goods and nine small children. With the stove, table, chairs, tubs and trunks, there was room for but one bed to be put up. Poor, unresourceful Henderson surveyed the crowded shack helplessly, but that round-faced, smiling wife of his was not a particle discouraged. "We'll just build in two sets of bunks, on each end of the house," she laughed. "The children won't mind sleeping on 'shelves,' for the bread-winners must have the bed."

So they economized space with a dozen such little plans, and all through the unpacking and settling and arranging, she would say every hour or two, "Oh, it's a little crowded and stuffy, but it's *ours*—it's *home*," until Henderson and the children caught something of her inspiration, and the sod-roof shack became "home" in the sweetest sense of the word.

There are some people who "make" time for everything, and this remarkable mother was one. That winter she baked bread for every English bachelor ranchman within ten miles. She did their washing and ironing, and never neglected her own, either. She knitted socks for them, and made and sold quantities of Saskatoon berry jam. When spring came she had over fifty dollars of her own, with which she promptly bought a cow. Then late in March they made a small first payment on a team of horses, and "broke land" for the first time, plowing and seeding a few acres of virgin prairie and getting a start.

But her quaintest invention to utilize every resource possible was a novel scheme for chicken-raising. One morning the children came in greatly excited over finding a wild duck's nest in the nearby "slough." Mrs. Henderson told them to be very careful not to frighten the bird, but to go back and search every foot of the grassy edges and try to discover other nests. They succeeded in finding three. That day a neighboring English rancher, driving past on his way to Brandon, twenty miles distant, called out, "Want anything from town, Mrs. Henderson?"

"Eggs, just eggs, if you will bring them, like a good boy," she answered, running out to the trail to meet him.

"Why, you *are* luxurious to-day, and eggs at fifty cents a dozen," he exclaimed.

"Never mind," she replied, "they're not nearly

so luxurious as chickens. You just bring me a dozen and a half. Pay *any* price, but be sure they are fresh, new laid, right off the nest. Now just insist on that, or we shall quarrel." And with a menacing shake of a forefinger and a customary laugh, she handed him a precious bank note to pay for the treasures.

The next day Mrs. Henderson adroitly substituted hen's eggs for the wild ducks' own, and the shy, pretty water fowls, returning from their morning's swim, never discovered the fraud.*

"Six eggs under three sitters—eighteen chicks, if we're lucky enough to have secured fertile eggs," mused Mrs. Henderson. "Oh, well, we'll see." And they *did* see. They saw exactly eighteen fluffy, peeping chicks, whose timid little mothers could not understand why their broods disappeared one by one from the long, wet grasses surrounding the nest. But in a warm canton-flannel-lined basket near the Hendersons' stove the young arrivals chirped and picked at warm meal as sturdily as if hatched in a coop by a commonplace barnyard "Biddy." And every one of those chicks lived and grew and fattened into a splendid flock, and the following spring they began sitting on their own eggs. But the good-hearted woman, in relating the story, would always say that she felt like a thief and a robber whenever she thought of that shy, harmless little wild duck who never had the satisfaction of seeing her brood swim in the "slough."

All this happened more than twenty years ago,

* Fact.

yet when I met Mrs. Henderson last summer, as she was journeying to Prince Albert to visit a married daughter, her wonderfully youthful face was as round and smiling as if she had never battled through the years in a hand-to-hand fight to secure a home in the pioneer days of Manitoba. She is well off now, and lives no more in the twelve-by-eighteen-foot bunk-house, but when I asked her how she accomplished so much, she replied, "I just jollied things along, and laughed over the hard places. It makes them easier then."

So perhaps the station agent's wife was really right, after all, when she remarked that "some women were just born to laugh."

The Tenas Klootchman*

*T*HIS story came to me from the lips of Maarda herself. It was hard to realize, while looking at her placid and happy face, that Maarda had ever been a mother of sorrows, but the healing of a wounded heart oftentimes leaves a light like that of a benediction on a receptive face, and Maarda's countenance held something greater than beauty, something more like lovableness, than any other quality.

We sat together on the deck of the little steamer throughout the long violet twilight, that seems loath to leave the channels and rocky shores of the Upper Pacific in June time. We had dropped easily into conversation, for nothing so readily helps one to an introduction as does the friendly atmosphere of the extreme West, and I had paved the way by greeting her in the Chinook, to which she responded with a sincere and friendly handclasp.

Dinner on the small coast-wise steamers is almost a function. It is the turning-point of the day, and is served English fashion, in the evening. The passengers "dress" a little for it, eat the meal leisurely and with relish. People who perhaps have exchanged no conversation during the day, now relax, and fraternize with their fellow men and women.

I purposely secured a seat at the dining-table beside Maarda. Even she had gone through a simple "dressing" for dinner, having smoothed her satiny black hair, knotted a brilliant silk

*In Chinook language "Tenas Klootchman" means "girl baby."

201

handkerchief about her throat, and laid aside her large, heavy plaid shawl, revealing a fine delaine gown of green, bordered with two flat rows of black silk velvet ribbon. That silk velvet ribbon, and the fashion in which it was applied, would have bespoken her nationality, even had her dark copper-colored face failed to do so.

The average Indian woman adores silk and velvet, and will have none of cotton, and these decorations must be in symmetrical rows, not designs. She holds that the fabric is in itself excellent enough. Why twist it and cut it into figures that would only make it less lovely?

We chatted a little during dinner. Maarda told me that she and her husband lived at the Squamish River, some thirty-five miles north of Vancouver City, but when I asked if they had any children, she did not reply, but almost instantly called my attention to a passing vessel seen through the porthole. I took the hint, and said no more of family matters, but talked of the fishing and the prospects of a good sockeye run this season.

Afterwards, however, while I stood alone on deck watching the sun set over the rim of the Pacific, I felt a feathery touch on my arm. I turned to see Maarda, once more enveloped in her shawl, and holding two deck stools. She beckoned with a quick uplift of her chin, and said, "We'll sit together here, with no one about us, and I'll tell you of the child." And this was her story:

She was the most beautiful little Tenas Klootchman a mother could wish for, bright, laughing, pretty as a spring flower, but—just as frail. Such tiny hands, such buds of feet! One felt that they must never take her out of her cradle basket for fear that, like a flower stem, she would snap asunder and her little head droop like a blossom.

But Maarda's skilful fingers had woven and plaited and colored the daintiest cradle basket in the entire river district for this little woodland daughter. She had fished long and late with her husband, so that the canner's money would purchase silk "blankets" to enwrap her treasure; she had beaded cradle bands to strap the wee body securely in its cosy resting-nest. Ah, it was such a basket, fit for an English princess to sleep in! Everything about it was fine, soft, delicate, and everything born of her mother-love.

So, for weeks, for even months, the little Tenas Klootchman laughed and smiled, waked and slept, dreamed and dimpled in her pretty playhouse. Then one day, in the hot, dry summer, there was no smile. The dimples did not play. The little flower paled, the small face grew smaller, the tiny hands tinier; and one morning, when the birds awoke in the forests of the Squamish, the eyes of the little Tenas Klootchman remained closed.

They put her to sleep under the giant cedars, the lulling, singing firs, the whispering pines that must now be her lullaby, instead of her mother's voice crooning the child-songs of the Pacific, that tell of baby foxes and gamboling baby wolves and bright-eyed baby birds. Nothing

remained to Maarda but an empty little cradle
basket, but smoothly-folded silken "blankets,"
but disused beaded bands. Often at nightfall she
would stand alone, and watch the sun dip into
the far waters, leaving the world as grey and
colorless as her own life; she would outstretch her
arms—pitifully empty arms—towards the west,
and beneath her voice again croon the lullabies of
the Pacific, telling of the baby foxes, the soft,
furry baby wolves, and the little downy fledglings
in the nests. Once in an agony of loneliness she
sang these things aloud, but her husband heard
her, and his face turned grey and drawn, and
her soul told her she must not be heard again
singing these things aloud.

And one evening a little steamer came into
harbor. Many Indians came ashore from it, as
the fishing season had begun. Among others was
a young woman over whose face the finger of illness
had traced shadows and lines of suffering. In
her arms she held a baby, a beautiful, chubby,
round-faced, healthy child that seemed too heavy
for her wasted form to support. She looked
about her wistfully, evidently seeking a face that
was not there, and as the steamer pulled out of
the harbor, she sat down weakly on the wharf,
laid the child across her lap, and buried her face
in her hands. Maarda touched her shoulder.

"Who do you look for?" she asked.

"For my brother Luke 'Alaska,'" replied the
woman. "I am ill, my husband is dead, my
brother will take care of me; he's a good man."

"Luke 'Alaska,'" said Maarda. What had she

heard of Luke "Alaska"? Why, of course, he
was one of the men her own husband had taken
a hundred miles up the coast as axeman on a surveying party, but she dared not tell this sick
woman. She only said: "You had better come
with me. My husband is away, but in a day or two
he will be able to get news to your brother. I'll
take care of you till they come."

The woman arose gratefully, then swayed
unsteadily under the weight of the child. Maarda's
arms were flung out, yearningly, longingly, towards
the baby.

"Where is your cradle basket to carry him
in?" she asked, looking about among the boxes
and bales of merchandise the steamer had left on
the wharf.

"I have no cradle basket. I was too weak to
make one, too poor to buy one. I have *nothing*,"
said the woman.

"Then let me carry him," said Maarda. "It's
quite a walk to my place; he's too heavy for you."

The woman yielded the child gratefully, saying,
"It's not a boy, but a Tenas Klootchman."

Maarda could hardly believe her senses. That
splendid, sturdy, plump, big baby a Tenas Klootchman! For a moment her heart surged with bitterness. Why had her own little girl been so frail,
so flower-like? But with the touch of that warm
baby body, the bitterness faded. She walked slowly,
fitting her steps to those of the sick woman, and
jealously lengthening the time wherein she could
hold and hug the baby in her yearning arms.

The woman was almost exhausted when they

reached Maarda's home, but strong tea and hot, wholesome food revived her; but fever burned brightly in her cheeks and eyes. The woman was very ill, extremely ill. Maarda said, "You must go to bed, and as soon as you are there, I will take the canoe and go for a doctor. It is two or three miles, but you stay resting, and I'll bring him. We will put the Tenas Klootchman beside you in—" she hesitated. Her glance travelled up to the wall above, where a beautiful empty cradle basket hung, with folded silken "blankets" and disused beaded bands.

The woman's gaze followed hers, a light of beautiful understanding pierced the fever glare of her eyes, she stretched out her hot hand protestingly, and said, "Don't put her in—that. Keep that, it is yours. She is used to being rolled only in my shawl."

But Maarda had already lifted the basket down, and was tenderly arranging the wrappings. Suddenly her hands halted, she seemed to see a wee flower face looking up to her like the blossom of a russet-brown pansy. She turned abruptly, and, going to the door, looked out speechlessly on the stretch of sea and sky glimmering through the tree trunks.

For a time she stood. Then across the silence broke the little murmuring sound of a baby half crooning, half crying, indoors, the little cradle-less baby that, homeless, had entered her home. Maarda returned, and, lifting the basket, again arranged the wrappings. "The Tenas Klootchman

206

shall have this cradle," she said, gently. The sick woman turned her face to the wall and sobbed.

It was growing dark when Maarda left her guests, and entered her canoe on the quest for a doctor. The clouds hung low, and a fine, slanting rain fell, from which she protected herself as best she could with a shawl about her shoulders, crossed in front, with each end tucked into her belt beneath her arms—Indian-fashion. Around rocks and boulders, headlands and crags, she paddled, her little craft riding the waves like a cork, but pitching and plunging with every stroke. By and by the wind veered, and blew head on, and now and again she shipped water; her skirts began dragging heavily about her wet ankles, and her moccasins were drenched. The wind increased, and she discarded her shawl to afford greater freedom to her arm-play. The rain drove and slanted across her shoulders and head, and her thick hair was dripping with sea moisture and the downpour.

Sometimes she thought of beaching the canoe and seeking shelter until daylight. Then she again saw those fever-haunted eyes of the stranger who was within her gates, again heard the half wail of the Tenas Klootchman in her own baby's cradle basket, and at the sound she turned her back on the possible safety of shelter, and forged ahead.

It was a wearied woman who finally knocked at the doctor's door and bade him hasten. But his strong man's arm found the return journey comparatively easy paddling. The wind helped him, and Maarda also plied her bow paddle, frequently urging him to hasten.

It was dawn when they entered her home. The sick woman moaned, and the child fretted for food. The doctor bent above his patient, shaking his head ruefully as Maarda built the fire, and attended to the child's needs before she gave thought to changing her drenched garments. All day she attended her charges, cooked, toiled, watched, forgetting her night of storm and sleeplessness in the greater anxieties of ministering to others. The doctor came and went between her home and the village, but always with that solemn headshake, that spoke so much more forcibly than words.

"She shall not die!" declared Maarda. "The Tenas Klootchman needs her, she shall not die!" But the woman grew feebler daily, her eyes grew brighter, her cheeks burned with deeper scarlet.

"We must fight for it now," said the doctor. And Maarda and he fought the dread enemy hour after hour, day after day.

Bereft of its mother's care, the Tenas Klootchman turned to Maarda, laughed to her, crowed to her, until her lonely heart embraced the child as a still evening embraces a tempestuous day. Once she had a long, terrible fight with herself. She had begun to feel her ownership in the little thing, had begun to regard it as her right to tend and pet it. Her heart called out for it; and she wanted it for her very own. She began to feel a savage, tigerish joy in thinking—aye, *knowing*

208

that it really would belong to her and to her alone soon—very soon.

When this sensation first revealed itself to her, the doctor was there—had even told her the woman could not recover. Maarda's gloriously womanly soul was horrified at itself. She left the doctor in charge, and went to the shore, fighting out this outrageous gladness, strangling it—killing it.

She returned, a sanctified being, with every faculty in her body, every sympathy of her heart, every energy of her mind devoted to bringing this woman back from the jaws of death. She greeted the end of it all with a sorrowing, half-breaking heart, for she had learned to love the woman she had envied, and to weep for the little child who lay so helplessly against her unselfish heart.

A beautifully lucid half-hour came to the fever-stricken one just before the Call to the Great Beyond!

"Maarda," she said, "you have been a good Tillicum to me, and I can give you nothing for all your care, your kindness—unless—" Her eyes wandered to her child peacefully sleeping in the delicately-woven basket. Maarda saw the look, her heart leaped with a great joy. Did the woman wish to give the child to her? She dared not ask for it. Suppose Luke "Alaska" wanted it. His wife loved children, though she had four of her own in their home far inland. Then the sick woman spoke:

"Your cradle basket and your heart were empty before I came. Will you keep my Tenas

209

Klootchman as your own?—to fill them both
again?"

Maarda promised. "Mine was a Tenas
Klootchman, too," she said.

"Then I will go to her, and be her mother,
wherever she is, in the Spirit Islands they tell us
of," said the woman. "We will be but exchanging
our babies, after all."

When morning dawned, the woman did not
awake.

*   *   *   *   *   *   *   *

Maarda had finished her story, but the recollections had saddened her eyes, and for a time
we both sat on the deck in the violet twilight
without exchanging a word.

"Then the little Tenas Klootchman is yours
now?" I asked.

A sudden radiance suffused her face, all trace
of melancholy vanished. She fairly scintillated
happiness.

"Mine!" she said. "All mine! Luke 'Alaska'
and his wife said she was more mine than theirs,
that I must keep her as my own. My husband
rejoiced to see the cradle basket filled, and to hear
me laugh as I used to."

"How I should like to see the baby!" I began.

"You shall," she interrupted. Then with a
proud, half-roguish expression, she added:

"She is so strong, so well, so heavy; she sleeps
a great deal, and wakes laughing and hungry."

As night fell, an ancient Indian woman came
up the companion-way. In her arms she carried

a beautifully-woven basket cradle, within which nestled a round-cheeked, smiling-eyed baby. Across its little forehead hung locks of black, straight hair, and its sturdy limbs were vainly endeavoring to free themselves from the lacing of the "blankets." Maarda took the basket, with an expression on her face that was transfiguring.

"Yes, this is my little Tenas Klootchman," she said, as she unlaced the bands, then lifted the plump little creature out on to her lap.

Soon afterwards the steamer touched an obscure little harbor, and Maarda, who was to join her husband there, left me, with a happy good-night. As she was going below, she faltered, and turned back to me. "I think sometimes," she said, quietly, "the Great Spirit thought my baby would feel motherless in the far Spirit Islands, so He gave her the woman I nursed for a mother; and He knew I was childless, and He gave me this child for my daughter. Do you think I am right? Do you understand?"

"Yes," I said, "I think you are right, and I understand."

Once more she smiled radiantly, and turning, descended the companionway. I caught a last glimpse of her on the wharf. She was greeting her husband, her face a mirror of happiness. About the delicately-woven basket cradle she had half pulled her heavy plaid shawl, beneath which the two rows of black velvet ribbon bordering her skirt proclaimed once more her nationality.

The Derelict

CRAGSTONE had committed what his world called a crime—an inexcusable offence that caused him to be shunned by society and estranged from his father's house. He had proved a failure.

Not one of his whole family connections could say unto the others, "I told you so," when he turned out badly.

They had all predicted that he was born for great things, then to discover that they had over-estimated him was irritating, it told against their discernment, it was unflattering, and they thought him inconsiderate.

So, in addition to his failure, Cragstone had to face the fact that he had made himself unpopular among his kin.

As a boy, he had been the pride of his family, as a youth, its hope of fame and fortune; he was clever, handsome, inventive, original, everything that society and his kind admired, but he criminally fooled them and their expectations, and they never forgave him for it.

He had dabbled in music, literature, law, every-thing—always with semi-success and brilliant promise; he had even tried the stage, playing the Provinces for an entire season; then, ultimately sinking into mediocrity in all these occupations, he returned to London, a hopelessly useless, a pitiably gifted man. His chilly little aristocratic mother always spoke of him as "poor, dear Charles." His brothers, clubmen all, graciously alluded to him with, "deuced hard luck, poor Charlie." His father never mentioned his name.

Then he went into "The Church," sailed for Canada, idled about for a few weeks, when one of the great colonial bishops, not knowing what else to do with him, packed him off north as a missionary to the Indians.

And, after four years of disheartening labor amongst a semi-civilized people, came this girl Lydia into his life. This girl of the mixed parentage, the English father, who had been swept northward with the rush of lumber trading, the Chippewa mother, who had been tossed to his arms by the tide of circumstances. The girl was a strange composition of both, a type of mixed blood, pale, dark, slender, with the slim hands, the marvellously beautiful teeth of her mother's people, the ambition, the small tender mouth, the utter fearlessness of the English race. But the strange, laughless eyes, the silent step, the hard sense of honor, proclaimed her far more the daughter of red blood than of white.

And, with the perversity of his kind, Cragstone loved her; he meant to marry her because he knew that he should not. What a monstrous thing it would be if he did! He, the shepherd of this half-civilized flock, the modern John Baptist; he, the voice of the great Anglican Church crying in this wilderness, how could he wed with this Indian girl who had been a common serving-maid in a house in Penetanguishene, and been dismissed therefrom with an accusation of theft that she could never prove untrue? How could he bring this reproach upon the Church? Why, the marriage would have no precedent; and yet he loved her, loved her sweet, silent ways, her listening attitudes, her clear, brown, consumptive-suggesting skin. She was the only thing in all the irksome mission life that had responded to him, had encouraged him to struggle anew for the spiritual welfare of this poor red race. Of course, in Penetanguishene they had told him she was irreclaimable, a thief, with ready lies to cover her crimes; for that very reason he felt tender towards her, she was so sinful, so pathetically human.

He could have mastered himself, perhaps, had she not responded, had he not seen the laughless eyes laugh alone for him, had she not once when a momentary insanity possessed them both confessed in words her love for him as he had done to her. But now? Well, now only this horrible tale of theft and untruth hung between them like a veil; now even with his arms locked about her, his eyes drowned in hers, his ears caught the whispers of calumny, his thoughts were perforated with the horror of his Bishop's censure, and these things rushed between his soul and hers, like some bridgeless deep he might not cross, and so his lonely life went on.

And then one night his sweet humanity, his grand, strong love rose up, battled with him, and conquered. He cast his pharisaical ideas, and the Church's "I am better than thou," aside forever; he would go now, to-night, he would ask her to be his wife, to have and to hold from this day forward, for better, for worse, for—

A shadow fell across the doorway of his simple home; it was August Beaver, the trapper, with the urgent request that he would come across to French Island at once, for old "Medicine" Joe was there, dying, and wished to see the minister. At another time Cragstone would have felt sympathetic, now he was only irritated; he wanted to find Lydia, to look in her laughless eyes, to feel her fingers in his hair, to tell her he did not care if she were a hundred times a thief, that he loved her, loved her, loved her, and he would marry her despite the Church, despite—

"Joe, he's near dead, you come now?" broke in August's voice. Cragstone turned impatiently, got his prayer-book, followed the trapper, took his place in the canoe, and paddled in silence up the bay.

The moon arose, large, limpid, flooding the cabin with a wondrous light, and making more wan the features of a dying man, whose fever-wasted form lay on some lynx skins on the floor.

Cragstone was reading from the Book of Common Prayer the exquisite service of the Visitation of the Sick. Outside, the loons clanged up the waterways, the herons called across the islands, but no human things ventured up the wilds. Inside, the sick man lay, beside him August Beaver holding a rude lantern, while Cragstone's matchless voice repeated the Anglican formula. A spasm, an uplifted hand, and Cragstone paused. Was the end coming even before a benediction? But the dying man was addressing Beaver in Chippewa, whispering and choking out the words in his death struggle.

215

"He says he's bad man," spoke Beaver. A horrible, humorous sensation swept over Cragstone; he hated himself for it, but at college he had always ridiculed death-bed confessions; but in a second that feeling had vanished, he bent his handsome, fair face above the copper-colored countenance of the dying man. "Joe," he said, with that ineffable tenderness that had always drawn human hearts to him; "Joe, tell me before I pronounce the Absolution, how you have been 'bad'?"

"I steal three times," came the answer. "Oncet horses, two of them from farmer near Barrie. Oncet twenty fox-skins at North Bay; station man he in jail for those fox-skins now. Oncet gold watch from doctor at Penetanguishene."

The prayer-book rattled from Cragstone's hands and fell to the floor.

"Tell me about this watch," he mumbled. "How did you come to do it?"

"I liffe at the doctor's; I take care his horse, long time; old River's gal, Lydia, she work there too; they say she steal it; I sell to trader, the doctor he nefer know, he think Lydia."

Cragstone was white to the lips. "Joe," he faltered, "you are dying; do you regret this sin, are you sorry?"

An indistinct "yes" was all; death was claiming him rapidly.

But a great, white, purified love had swept over the young clergyman. The girl he worshipped could never now be a reproach to his calling, she was proved blameless as a baby, and out of his

216

great human love arose the divine calling, the Christ-like sense of forgiveness, the God-like forgetfulness of injury and suffering done to his and to him, and once more his soft, rich voice broke the stillness of the Northern night, as the Anglican absolution of the dying fell from his lips in merciful tenderness:

"O Lord Jesus Christ, who hath left power to His Church to absolve all sinners who truly repent and believe in Him, of His great mercy forgive thee thine offences, and by His authority committed to me I absolve thee from all thy sins in the name of the Father, and of the Son, and of the Holy Ghost. Amen."

Beaver was holding the lantern close to the penitent's face; Cragstone, kneeling beside him, saw that the end had come already, and, after making the sign of the Cross on the dead Indian's forehead, the young priest arose and went silently out into the night.

* * * * * * * *

The sun was slipping down into the far horizon, fretted by the inimitable wonder of islands that throng the Georgian Bay; the blood-colored skies, the purpling clouds, the extravagant beauty of a Northern sunset hung in the west like the trailing robes of royalty, soundless in their flaring, their fading; soundless as the unbroken wilds which lay bathed in the loneliness of a dying day.

But on the color-flooded shore stood two, blind to the purple, the scarlet, the gold, blind to all else save the tense straining of the other's eyes;

217

deaf to nature's unsung anthem, hearing only the other's voice. Cragstone stood transfixed with consternation. The memory of the past week of unutterable joy lay blasted with the awfulness of this moment, the memory of even that first day—when he had stood with his arms about her, had told her how he had declared her reclaimed name far and wide, how even Penetanguishene knew now that she had suffered blamelessly, how his own heart throbbed suffocatingly with the honor, the delight of being the poor means through which she had been righted in the accusing eyes of their little world, and that now she would be his wife, his sweet, helping wife, and she had been great enough not to remind him that he had not asked her to be his wife until her name was proved blameless, and he was great enough not to make excuse of the resolve he had set out upon just when August Beaver came to turn the current of his life.

But he had other eyes to face to-night, eyes that blurred the past, that burned themselves into his being—the condemning, justly and righteously indignant eyes of his Bishop—while his numb heart, rather than his ears, listened to the words that fell from the prelate's lips like curses on his soul, like the door that would shut him forever outside the holy place.

"What have you done, you pretended servant of the living God? What use is this you have made of your Holy Orders? You hear the confessions of a dying man, you absolve and you bless him, and come away from the poor dead thief to shout his crimes in the ears of the world, to dishonor him, to be a discredit to your calling. Who could trust again such a man as you have proved to be—faithless to himself, faithless to his Church, faithless to his God?"

But Cragstone was on the sands at his accuser's feet. "Oh! my lord," he cried, "I meant only to save the name of a poor, mistrusted girl, selfishly, perhaps, but I would have done the same thing just for humanity's sake had it been another to whom injustice was done."

"Your plea of justice is worse than weak; to save the good name of the living is it just to rob the dead?"

The Bishop's voice was like iron.

"I did not realize I was a priest, I only knew I was a *man*," and with these words Cragstone arose and looked fearlessly, even proudly, at the one who stood his judge.

"Is it not better, my lord, to serve the living than the dead?"

"And bring reproach upon your Church?" said the Bishop, sternly.

It was the first thought Cragstone ever had of his official crime; he staggered under the horror of it, and the little, dark, silent figure, that had followed them unseen, realized in her hiding amid the shadows that the man who had lifted her into the light was himself being thrust down into irremediable darkness. But Cragstone only saw the Bishop looking at him as from a supreme height, he only felt the final stinging lash in the words: "When a man disregards the most sacred offices of his God, he will hardly reverence the claims

219

of justice of a simple woman who knows not his world, and if he so easily flings his God away for a woman, just so easily will he fling her away for other gods."

And Lydia, with eyes that blazed like flame, watched the Bishop turn and walk frigidly up the sands, his indignation against this outrager of the Church declaring itself in every footfall.

Cragstone flung himself down, burying his face in his hands. What a wreck he had made of life! He saw his future, loveless, for no woman would trust him now; even the one whose name he had saved would probably be more unforgiving than the Church; it was the way with women when a man abandoned God and honor for them; and this nameless but blackest of sins, this falsity to one poor dying sinner, would stand between him and heaven forever, though through that very crime he had saved a fellow being. Where was the justice of it?

The purple had died from out the western sky, the waters of the Georgian Bay lay colorless at his feet, night was covering the world and stealing with inky blackness into his soul.

She crept out of her hiding-place, and, coming, gently touched his tumbled fair hair; but he shrank from her, crying: "Lydia, my girl, my girl, I am not for a good woman now! I, who thought you an outcast, a thief, not worthy to be my wife, to-night I am not an outcast of man alone, but of God."

But what cared she for his official crimes? She was a woman. Her arms were about him, her lips on his; and he who had, until now, been a portless derelict, who had vainly sought a haven in art, an anchorage in the service of God, had drifted at last into the world's most sheltered harbor— a woman's love.

But, of course, the Bishop took away his gown.

Abbreviations Used in
Notes to Text

BCHSM—Brant County Historical Society and Museum,
Brantford, Ontario.

DIA—Department of Indian Affairs, Canada

MM—The Moccasin Maker

PAC—Public Archives of Canada

NOTES TO TEXT

Prepared by A. LaVonne Brown Ruoff

"MY MOTHER"

In 1908, Pauline began work on this four-part serial, originally published in *The Mother's Magazine*, volume 4, in 1909: 4 (April): 9–11, 40; 5 (May): 7–9, 14; 6 (June): 10–12; 7 (July): 15–18.

Publication information about the stories and essay in *The Moccasin Maker* is given where known.

23—Pauline's maternal grandfather was Henry Charles Howells (b. 1784), son of Thomas Howells and Susannah Beasley Howells of Hay, Wales. His brother was Joseph Howells, father of William Cooper and grandfather of the American author William Dean Howells. In 1805 Henry married Mary Best, who bore him thirteen children before her death in 1828. The 1814 Bristol directory refers to Henry as a "writing Master" living in the fashionable area of St. James Place, Bristol. William Dean Howells describes him as living in "worldly state at Bristol before coming to America" (*Years of My Youth* 11–12). In 1815, he took over the Kingsdown Preparatory Boarding School located in that area, a "Classical and Commercial Academy" for boys five to eleven (Fairs 40). Henry ran this school until 1827. In 1827, Henry sold his school and purchased the "West Bank Academy" in the suburb of Cotham, which he ran until 1831. He married his second wife, Harriet Joyner, in 1829. Two years later, he migrated with his family first to Worthington, northeast of Columbus, Ohio, where his daughter Mary Best Rogers (b. 1807) and her husband the Reverend Robert Vashon Rogers, an Anglican minister, were living. Henry then moved to Putnam, now part of Zanesville, Muskingum County, in

223

southeastern Ohio. His account of his experiences in this first immigration is contained in his *Letters from Ohio, Containing Advice to Emigrants, Who Intend to Settle in the United States of America* (Bristol, England: Wright and Bagnall, 1832).

Later he moved to Pittsburgh, Pennsylvania, where he ran a boys' boarding school (Fairs 40–41). The 1837 *Harris' Pittsburgh Business Directory* lists an H. D. Howells as a real estate and money agent, with an office at St. Clair Street (55). According to Fairs, Henry returned to Bristol in 1837, where his nineteenth child was born in 1839 and where he spent the money remaining from his first wife's estate (41). However, the notice of Eliza Beulah Howells's marriage to the Reverend Adam Elliot on 17 June 1839, Trinity Church, Pittsburgh, describes Henry Charles as "formerly of Bristol, England" (excerpt from *The Church*; rpt. Reid, *Marriage Notices of Ontario* 151).

His wife, Harriet Joyner Howells, died in February 1842 in Allegheny, Pennsylvania. Eight months later Henry married her friend Hannah Kell, who had nursed Harriet until she died. There is no information as to where they were married. Five children were born of this union. Records regarding Howells's return to America are confused, the date being variously given as 1844 and 1850. The notice of Eliza Beulah's marriage suggests that he may have returned as early as 1839. Evelyn Johnson's account of her mother's journey to the Six Nations Reserve indicates that Emily left Cincinnati in 1845, which supports a date prior to that year (Keen and McKeon 1:39). The *Index to the 1850 Federal Population Census of Ohio* lists a Henry C. Howells as residing in Butler County, Hamilton Township. This is contiguous to Hamilton County, where Cincinnati is located. Following his return to America, Henry Charles eventually settled in Eagleswood, New Jersey. His death date is variously given as 1854, 1855, and 1863 (Fairs 41 and Howells family genealogy).

23—Lydia Bestman] The pseudonym for Emily Susanna

Howells Johnson (1824–98). "Bestman" derives from the name of Emily's mother, Mary Best. When her mother died, Emily was four, not two as Pauline indicates (Keller 12–13). After her father's remarriage, Emily was sent to boarding school in Southampton (Keen and McKeon 1:40). **24—Mr.** Bestman . . . a very narrow religionist,] Henry Charles Howells was a fervent abolitionist, who immigrated to the United States and settled in Ohio to work to free the slaves. During the 1830s and 1840s, Ohio was a hotbed of abolitionist activity. Because Ohio bordered the slave state of Kentucky and because many Ohioans opposed slavery, the state was one of the main escape routes for runaway slaves. In Putnam, Henry worked zealously for the abolitionist cause. According to Evelyn Johnson, he operated a station on the Underground Railroad, hiding in his attic as many as twenty-one slaves at a time (Keen and McKeon 1:39–40). In June 1833 he opened his home to the first meeting of what became the Muskingum County Emancipation Society to Promote the Abolition of Slavery and of Oppressive Laws. Henry not only helped draw up the organization's constitution but also served as one of its representatives to the state abolition convention held in Putnam in April 1835. At that convention he was a member of the committee to draw up a petition to be presented to Congress. Local antagonism to this convention was so strong that rowdies attacked the building where the convention was held and threatened to burn the homes of Howells and other abolitionists (Everhart 146–48; Schneider 200–2; *Proceedings of the Ohio Anti-Slavery Convention . . . Putnam . . . 1835* 4, 5).

Such hostility did not deter either the society or Henry. Both he and his daughter Hepzibah Maria (b. 1813) were delegates from Putnam to the first anniversary convention held in April 1836 near Granville, Licking County (Price 179).

Little is known about Henry's career and his involvement in the antislavery movement after this date. Following his second emigration to America, he evidently settled near Cincinnati, Ohio. Located just across the river from Kentucky, Cincinnati was one of the first stops on the Underground Railroad and a center of abolitionist activity in the state.

25—Elizabeth] Eliza Beulah Howells Elliot, was born in 1819 and died on 8 December 1849. See the notation in Emily Johnson's hand in the margin of a newspaper clipping of the poem "I Am Weary!" which reads "E. B. E.—Dec 8th. 1849" (BCHSM). This reference to Eliza Beulah's death is confirmed by the notice in the Toronto *Patriot* on 19 December 1849, which gives her age as 31 (*Ontario Register* 5 [1981]: 60). (Information also supplied by J. Ross Elliot from "Burials," the Parish Register, St. John's, Tuscarora, 1829 – 67, V. P. Cronyn Memorial Archives, Huron College, University of Western Ontario. See also Howells family genealogy. Keller incorrectly gives the date as 1850 [15]).

28—The Rev. Adam Elliot (1802–78). Ordained in 1832, Adam Elliot served for five years as a missionary for the Society for Converting and Civilizing the Indians in the area north and east of York, serving both the white settlers and Ojibwa Indians. His journals of his missionary work from 28 June 1833 to June 1835 are contained in Waddilove, *The Stewart Missions* 29–75. In 1838 he accepted a position with the New England Company station near Brantford and took over the mission church at Tuscarora in March of that year. On 17 June 1839, he married Eliza Beulah Howells in Trinity Church, Pittsburg, Pennsylvania (*Marriage Notices of Ontario* 151). They had four children: Mary Margaret, born 10 December 1840, buried 14 June 1854; Henry Christopher, born 23 April 1843, died 5 November 1847; Charles O'Reilly, born c. June 1845, died 22 December 1847 (aged two years and six months); Emily Charlotte Eliza, born c. 1 July 1847, died 14 August 1848 (aged thirteen months and two weeks) (Reid, *Death Notices of Ontario* 246, 248, 251, and information supplied by J. Ross Elliot from "Baptisms" and "Burials," Parish Register, St. John's, Tuscarora, 1829–67, V. P. Cronyn Memorial Archives, Huron College, University of Western Ontario). Elliot later married Charlotte Racey in 1856. He died in 1878 and was buried in the cemetery of Holy Trinity Church, Onondaga, Ontario. Following his death, the Tuscarora Mission Church was closed and the congregation absorbed by churches on the Tuscarora side of the river. During Elliot's lifetime, the mission's territory, between the mouth of Fairchild's Creek and the present village of Middleport, was then principally occupied by Tuscaroras. (Millman, 10 [1871–80]: 269–70; Waldie, "Middleport Once Important for Grand River Navigation," 12 June 1943, and "Methodists Founded Mission at Salt Springs Long Ago," 28 April 1944, articles from unidentified newspapers in Johnson Coll., BCHSM. Mrs. Marie Elliot Locke, Vallejo, CA, and her daughter, Mrs. Lawrence Crumb, Eugene, OR, also have information on the various branches of the Elliot family.)

28— "Only thirty,"] Elliot was thirty-nine when he married Eliza, who was twenty, not seventeen as Pauline suggests on p. 29.

28—after the marriage ceremony] Pauline telescopes time here. Emily spent as many of her growing years as possible visiting married brothers and sisters, especially Mary Best Rogers and her husband the Reverend Robert Vashon Rogers, who had settled in Bytown, Ottawa, and later in Kingston, Ontario. Pauline describes Lydia as thirteen when her sister married and took her to Canada (30–31). Actually, Emily was twenty-one years old when she joined the Elliot household in 1845, approximately six years after the couple's marriage (Keen and McKeon 1: 24; Keller 12).

30— "Mr. George Mansion,"] George H. M. Johnson (1816–84). George learned English from his father, Smoke Johnson, who was determined that his son should have better advantages than he. George also attended for several years the New England Company school in Brantford run by the Reverend Abraham Nelles. After his return to the reserve, George became both pupil and assistant to the Reverend Adam Elliot, with whom he lived. George mastered English by translating Elliot's sermons into Mohawk. Impressed with George's knowledge of six Iroquois languages, Elliot made the young man his interpreter. In 1840, George was formally appointed interpreter for the English church missions on the reserve and accompanied Elliot on his rounds.

By referring to George as a "boy," Pauline makes her father younger than he actually was. She indicates that he was twenty-four when he succeeded to the hereditary title and when he proposed to Emily (38). However, he was already twenty-nine when the two first met (Keller 12).

The name "Mansion" is derived from the personal name given George after he built Chiefswood: Onwanonsyshon, meaning "He who has the great mansion." It was the name by which he was best known on the reserve (Hale, "Chief George H. M. Johnson—Onwanonsyshon" 140).

See also Evelyn Johnson, "Grandfather and Father of E. Pauline Johnson" 44–47 and Leighton, "Johnson, George Henry Martin (Onwanonsyshon)" 451–53).

33—the position of Government interpreter in the Council of the great 'Six Nations,'] George was officially confirmed as interpreter in January 1860. See the letter from Richard J. Pennefather, superintendent-general of Indian Affairs, to David Thorburn, superintendent, dated 19 January 1860, PAC, DIA, Record Group 10, Vol. 840.80. Weaver indicates that the superintendent depended on the interpreter to present their directives and information to the council and to receive chiefs' decisions. Usually a chief, the interpreter was a government employee appointed by the Indian administration and paid a salary from band funds (528).

33–34—through the death of an uncle . . . speaker of the Council, held the elder title,] During the War of 1812, young John Smoke Johnson (1792–1886), who had fought beside the famed Mohawk chief Joseph Brant, distinguished himself by leading an Iroquois attempt to burn the city of Buffalo. Impressed by his leadership and anxious to have an intermediary within the Grand Council, the British forced the Iroquois Grand Council to make John a Pine-Tree chief, a non-hereditary title bestowed as a recognition of achievement. The council also made him speaker and conferred on him the title "Sakayengwaraton." Known as Smoke Johnson because the rough translation of Sakayengwaraton is "Disappearing Mist," he was highly respected for his ability as an orator and for his knowledge of Mohawk traditions. On the Reserve, he and the descendants of his marriage to Helen Martin were known as the "Smoke Johnsons." In 1858, he was appointed the first permanent speaker, and the position was institutionalized (Weaver 528). George could not have inherited his father's chieftaincy both because it was non-hereditary and because Iroquois hereditary titles descended only through the maternal line.

MacRay incorrectly identifies him as a member of the Wolf Clan (*Pauline Johnson and her Friends* 10); he belonged to the Bear Clan. For biographical information, see particularly Evelyn Johnson, "Chief John Smoke Johnson," "Grandfather and Father of E. Pauline Johnson," and "The Martin Settlement." See also, Leighton, "Johnson, John."

Hale ("Chief George H. M. Johnson—Onwanonsyshon" 136) incorrectly states that George inherited the title from Helen Martin Johnson's brother "Henry," an error repeated by Garland (20–21) and Keller (15). However, Evelyn Johnson makes clear that he inherited it from his uncle "Jacob" Martin ("Grandfather and Father of E. Pauline Johnson" 46). According to Weaver, Jacob is also listed as the holder of the title in the history of its succession from 1776–1915 contained in the letter dated 26 June 1915 from Mrs. Mary (W. J.) Hill, matron to James

C. Elliott's election to the title that year. The title descended through the matrons of the Wolf Clan (Weaver field notes).

The date of George's election as chief is unclear. In a letter to J. B. Clench, published in the *Hamilton Spectator* on 17 October 1849, George gave his title as "Chief Warrior" (copy in Johnson Coll., BCHSM). Strongly objecting to George's letter, the Council of the Six Nations made clear in minutes of their meeting on 31 October 1849 that his letter reflected only his own sentiments, not those of the council. They also stated emphatically that, although he had *"assumed the rank of Chief Warrior,"* he was *"not a Chief."* See PAC, DIA, Record Group 10, Vol. 818. 408–9.

Hale indicates that George became chief while serving as "church interpreter," a position to which he was appointed in 1840 ("Chief George H. M. Johnson—Onwanonsyshon" 136). Both in "My Mother" and in "Mothers of a Great Red Race," Pauline states that he was the official government interpreter, a position to which he was not appointed until 1860 (*The Mother's Magazine* 3 [January 1908]: 5). Weaver suggests that his election as chief occurred around 1855. The Grand Council Minutes of 22 August 1856 refer to him as a chief (PAC, DIA, Record Group 10, Vol. 833, Nos. 186–87). No record of the controversy over George's chieftaincy exists in the minutes of the Grand Council of the Grand River Reserve. Although the collected correspondence of the superintendent of the Six Nations Reserve at Grand River contains some minutes of council meetings, it does not contain minutes for all years nor for all meetings within a given year. However, the absence of such a record leads Weaver to conclude that it occurred in a clan meeting, before the nomination was submitted to the council as a whole (telephone conversation with the editor, 12 December 1985). In 1924, the council abandoned the traditional organization consisting of hereditary chiefs and adopted instead an elected council (Weaver 533).

35—Chief George Mansion's mother Helen Martin Johnson (d. 1866). Also known as Nellie, she married John Smoke Johnson in 1815. George Johnson indicated that the name was spelled Martyn. See Evelyn Johnson, "Chief John Smoke Johnson" 109 and "Grandfather and Father of E. Pauline Johnson" 44).

35–36—She was "Chief Matron" . . . called him to the happy hunting grounds.] Among the Mohawks and other Iroquoian tribes, the basic kin group was a matrilineal lineage, which Hewitt, in *A Constitutional League of Peace in the Stone Age of America*, describes as "all the male and the female progeny of a woman, and also the progeny of a woman and of all her female descendants, tracing descent of blood in the female line and of such other persons as may have been adopted into it" (530). These lineages formed groups headed by a matriarch and combined with other lineages to constitute a clan, usually given the name of an animal. The chief woman or clan matriarch derived her position from age and membership in the chiefly line. Possessing great power, the matriarch selected clan officials, coordinated the economic activity of female clan members, decided on adoption of captives, and warned errant chiefs to mend their ways or be deposed by the matriarchs. Both Pauline's paternal great-grandmother and grandmother were matrons of the Wolf Clan. The presence of the same clans within each tribe was crucial to harmony between the tribes in the confederacy. Any disharmony among member tribes would have united clan members, regardless of tribe.

The three original Iroquois clans were the Wolf, to which both Brant and George Johnson belonged; the Tortoise; and the Bear, to which Smoke Johnson belonged (Hale, *Rites of the Iroquois* 53). The government in each tribe consisted of a council made up of clan chiefs; matriarchs, who dominated clan government; and Pine Tree chiefs, who represented the warriors. Clan government allotted land, supervised field labor, maintained wampum treasuries, and settled judicial disputes between clan members. Chiefs ordered and regulated feasts, public games, care for the poor and helpless, negotiations with other clans, and compensations for crimes (Noon 28–30, 36–39).

Cf. Pauline's comments on the power of Iroquois women versus that of English women (published in "The Lodge of the Law-Makers," *London Daily Express*, Summer 1906, n.p.):

I have heard that the daughters of this vast city cry out for a voice in the Parliament of this land. There is no need for an Iroquois woman to clamour for recognition in our councils; she has had it for upwards of four centuries. The highest title known to us is that of the 'chief matron.' It is borne by the eldest woman of each of the noble families.

From her cradle-board she is taught to judge men and their intellectual qualities, their aptness for public life, and their integrity, so that when he who bears the title leaves his seat in council to join the league-makers in the happy hunting grounds she can use her wisdom and her learning in nominating his fittest successor. She must bestow the title upon one of his kinsmen, one of the blood royal, so that the heritage is unbroken, so, perhaps, she passes by the inadequate eldest son and nominates the capable younger one. Thus is the council given the brain and blood of the nation.

The old and powerful chiefs-in-council never attempt to question her decision; her appointment is final and at the 'condoling council,' when he is installed, and his title conferred as he first takes his seat, the chief matron may, if she so desires, enter the council-house and publicly make an address to the chiefs, braves, and warriors assembled, and she is listened to not only with attention, but respect.

There are fifty matrons possessing this right in the Iroquois Confederacy. I have not heard of fifty white women even among those of noble birth who may speak and be listened to in the lodge of the law-makers here.

Cf. also her comments on the power of Iroquois women

in "Mothers of a Great Red Race" (*The Mother's Magazine* 3 [January 1908]: 5, 14).

For a general introduction to the Iroquois and Mohawks, see the following essays in *The Northeast*, ed. Trigger, vol. 15 of *Handbook of North American Indians*: Tooker, "The League of the Iroquois: Its History, Politics, and Ritual" and "Iroquois Since 1820"; Fenton and Tooker, "Mohawk"; and Weaver, "Six Nations of the Grand River, Ontario."

37—"those dogs of Senecas"] Mrs. Mansion's antagonism to the Senecas may be based on the fact that most of this tribe remained in New York when, in the winter and spring of 1784–85, bands of Iroquois resettled in Canada. The group of approximately 1,600 consisted of 450 Mohawks, 380 Cayugas, 200 Onondagas, 125 Tuscaroras, 75 Senecas, and a few Oneidas. They were accompanied by a handful of other Indians, such as the Delawares, Tutelos, and Nanticokes (Noon 16–18; Johnson xl).

46—Like most Indians, he was recklessly extravagant, . . . less expenditure.] Chiefswood is now being restored to its original elegance. A square house with a central hallway leading from a front and back door, it contained on the first floor a living and dining room, an office where George conducted tribal business, and an additional room. A polished walnut staircase led to the second floor that contained a master bedroom overlooking the river and ravine at the back of the house, a formal parlor, schoolroom, and bedroom. As the family grew, the formal parlor was moved downstairs and all the second-floor rooms became bedrooms. On the third floor was a large garret, where the children played on rainy days.

George had a cabinetmaker construct some of the furniture. Evelyn recalled that "all the rooms were elegantly papered. The parlor was furnished in the height of fashion, dominated by a big square rosewood piano draped with a scarlet blanket. Red rich curtains matched the roses that patterned the black velvet carpet. There were two carved walnut ottomans covered with green and yellow silk and mahogany chairs upholstered in grey damask" (Keen and McKeon 1: 43).

48—Her sister, with whom she never had anything in common,] Emily had planned to be married at the home of her sister Mary Rogers in Kingston, Ontario (Keen and McKeon 1: 43).

51—"good husband"] The Reverend Robert Vashon Rogers (1802–86). Rogers was made a deacon in 1826 at St. Martins in the Fields and took orders in 1828 in the parish church of Bishopshope. He emigrated to Worthington, Ohio, where he was joined by the Henry Charles Howells family in 1832. That year he and Mary Best Howells were married in Ohio. By 1836 Rogers had been appointed rector of Richmond in the Anglican Diocese of Ontario, in the Kingston area, where he was licensed to the St. James Church. In 1839 he was appointed headmaster of the Midland District School and Chaplain of the Kingston, Ontario, Penitentiary in 1839. He was made rural dean of the Redland deanery in 1860. From 1869 to 1871, he served as rector of Norfolk, Victoria County, in the Huron Diocese. His son, also Robert Vashon Rogers, was a prominent lawyer in Kingston, doing much of the law work for the Anglican Diocese (Howells family genealogy; Clergy Register, Anglican Diocese of Ontario Archives).

According to Evelyn, her mother had hoped Rogers would marry her and George at St. George's Church, Kingston (Keen and McKeon 1: 43).

52—the major's wife] Emily took refuge in the home of her close friend Jane Harvey, who arranged for George and Emily to be married on 27 August 1853 at St. Mark's Church, Barriefield, Ontario (Keen and McKeon 1: 43).

58—their new home] Once again Pauline telescopes time. Following their marriage, Emily and George returned to the Tuscarora parsonage, where they lived with the Reverend Mr. Elliot until Chiefswood was finished. They did not move into their new home until December 1856 (Keen and McKeon 1: 44), by which time they were the parents of two children: Henry Beverly (b. 1854) and Eliza Helen Charlotte (b. 1856), called Evelyn or Eva.

64–65—Evils had begun to creep . . . degradation of the Indian souls.] Hale indicates that after George was installed in his offices as interpreter and warden for the government and as member of the Six Nations Council, one of his first priorities was to get rid of the gangs of "white ruffians who then hung about the Reserve, corrupting and impoverishing the Indians by the illicit sale of liquor, and by combining with the more ignorant among them to rob the Reserve of its valuable store of timber" ("Chief George H. M. Johnson—Onwanonsyshon" 138).

That George's policies and lifestyle were not always popular among the Grand River Iroquois is clear from a holograph fragment by Emily, dated 19 February 1860, in which she indicates that in council the chiefs told her husband "that they are the managers of the affairs of their people and do just what they like about their people's affair & Interest they are licensed to cut their own timber & to build Large houses like the Interpreter himself [.]" (Holograph in Johnson Coll., BCHSM).

68—Little moccasin . . . in length.] Evelyn Johnson described the moccasin to J. S. Row, 27 May 1924, as being "about two or three inches long, perfect in make and saved as a white woman saves her first baby's shoes" (quoted in Keller 286, n.13). Pauline bequeathed the moccasin to the Museum of the City of Vancouver (Keller 272).

69—These children were reared . . . not of hers.] Cf. Pauline's "From the Child's Viewpoint," *The Mother's Magazine*, Pt. 1, 5 (May 1910): 30–31; Pt. 2. 5 (June 1910): 60–62, in which she describes her mother's method of child-raising. In Part 1, Pauline says that her mother encouraged her to subdue irritation or annoyance by engaging in vigorous activity. Emily also taught them to disguise their bashfulness with "a peculiar, cold reserve, that made our schoolfellows call us 'stuck-up,' and our neighbors' children mock us as 'proudy' " (1: 30). Pauline characterized her mother as "abnormally sensitive, prone to melancholy or extreme jollity, and, according to her own statement, was high tempered" (1: 30). Pauline regretted her mother never taught her children, who inherited her sensitivity, some sense of humor.

70—Their tastes and distastes . . . imitations.] Cf. "From the Child's Viewpoint," Pt 1: "In my childhood's home not a coarse or vulgar word was ever allowed to be spoken, no story of questionable color was ever told or repeated. I have frequently heard my mother say that, in all her married life, our father never made a single remark or spoke the smallest word to her that he could not have uttered in a roomful of ladies and gentlemen" (31).

Regarding her mother's emphasis on propriety and grooming, Evelyn recalled that she was always beautifully groomed from the moment she arose, "'even to her collar, cuffs, and broach.'" Emily taught her daughters to change to fresh dresses every afternoon, whether or not callers were expected. She also instructed them, "'Never say a person is sick—say he is ill. At dinner always break your bread—never bite it. Never turn in the street to look behind, no matter whether at a person or object. Never tip your soup plate to get the last of the contents, and always leave a little at the bottom . . .'" (Keen and McKeon 1: 44).

72—Once, soon after his marriage, a special review of the British troops . . . as they wheeled past.] See the description of this review in the *Toronto Daily Telegram*, 27 September 1867, written on the same day of the event: "In the center of the staff was no less a personage than Onwanonsyshon, Chief of the Six Nation Indians, in aboriginal costume and all the glory of war paint and feathers, in whose honour, we understand, the review was held." Following the review and accompanying mock battle, George proceeded with the troops through the "more prominent streets of the city back to the barracks. A noticeable feature of the procession was the Indian Chief with his fantastic head dress and native costume and strongly contrasting with the military array which with [*sic*] he was surrounded" (copy in Johnson Coll., BCHSM).

72—And when King Edward of England visited Canada as Prince of Wales, . . . for the British Crown.] Edward VI (1841–1910). On his way to Niagara Falls during his 1860 Canadian tour, Albert Edward, then Prince of Wales, briefly stopped in Brantford on 14 September. While there, he visited the Mohawk Chapel and autographed the Bible given by Queen Anne. The accounts of the prince's brief visit do not refer to his visit to the chapel. See Cornwallis 141–42, Cellem 305, and *Journal of the Progress of . . . the Prince of Wales . . .* 62. For an account of the Canadian tour by the Prince of Wales, see Lee 1: 88–97.

72—when Prince Arthur of Connaught . . . bestowing the title.] Arthur William Patrick Albert, first duke of Connaught and Strathearn and third son of Queen Victoria and Prince Albert. He entered the British army in 1868 and served in Canada during the Red River Rebellion and the Fenian raid of 1870. The duke was governor-general of Canada from 1911 to 1916.

For Pauline's account of this ceremony, see "The Duke of Connaught as Chief of the Iroquois Indians," *The Daily Province Magazine* (2 July 1910), 4; copy in Mills Lib., McMaster, Box 8.33. Pauline stressed that the young prince, later Duke of Connaught, was the only living white man with the undisputed right to the title of "Chief of the Six Nations of Indians." He received the title on 1 October 1869, during his first trip to Canada. Bestowing this title on a white man was a break with Iroquois tradition, which held that the Iroquois Council should consist of only fifty chiefs. Only the Duke of Connaught received such a title, conferred through ancient ritual and the participation of three clans. He was given the title of Kavakoudge or "Sun flying from east to west under the guidance of the Great Spirit" (4). Pauline's description of the ceremony is based on the newspaper article on the event published in Toronto on 2 October 1869, which the duke sent to her father with the notation: "Onwanonsyshon, with kind regards from your brother chief, 'Arthur.' " (4).

During Pauline's final illness, the duke, then governor-general of Canada, visited her at Bute Hospital on 20 September 1912. The chair he sat on was decorated with the red blanket on which he had knelt many years before during the ceremony that made him a chief. The duke not only agreed to allow Pauline to dedicate *Flint and Feather* to him but subsequently helped to arrange for the formal approval of Pauline's request to be buried in Stanley Park (Keller 263–64).

72—Even Bismarck, . . . sent a few kindly words, with his own photograph, ...] According to Hector Charlesworth, a German friend of George's sent Bismarck a photograph of the chief, attired in full regalia. Deeply interested in North America, Bismarck was so delighted that he reciprocated with an autographed portrait and letter (*Candid Chronicles* 1:99).

74–5—when George Mansion's mother . . . Happy Hunting Grounds.] Helen Martin Johnson died in 1866.

76–81—Then one night the blow fell. . . . "they've hurt me once more."] A notation inside the cover of George's prayerbook reads: "January 21st 1865, attacked by John Mills 5:30 p.m., Middleport, Ont. 2nd attack by six white men, Oct. 11, 1873, 2 a.m." (quoted in Waldie, "The Iroquois Poetess, Pauline Johnson" 73). According to the account in the *Brantford Weekly Expositor* 27 January 1865, Johnson and Mills, a tavern keeper from Onondaga, left Challand's Hotel, Middleport, at the same time. Without warning, Mills struck Johnson with something like a skull cracker and then savagely kicked him about the head, breaking his jaw and inflicting internal injuries. Irish Johnson joined in the assault. Mills evidently attacked George because he opposed granting a liquor license to the tavern owner, who sold whiskey to the Indians ("Murderous Assault" 3. See also "Diabolical Outrage," *Hamilton Daily Spectator and Journal of Commerce*, 26 January 1865: 2). According to Evelyn, the weapon was a lead ball in heavy elastic. Both of George's jaws were broken and his head was horribly battered and bruised. Although Evelyn indicates that only one of the men was caught and sentenced to five years in the Kingston, the newspapers state that both men were arrested. As a result of this assault, George bore permanent scars and endured severe bouts of neuralgia for the rest of his life (Keen and McKeon 1: 44).

On 17 October 1873, the *Brantford Weekly Expositor* reported that on the previous Friday, on the Delaware line of the Grand River Reserve, George was "shamefully beaten by Rid. McCloy, Alex. McCloy, Geo. Gorman and John Wilson, all whites. The Chief was cut and bruised and left for dead." After stopping the men, George ordered them to unload the wood they had taken from the reserve (Untitled 3). The *Hamilton Daily Spectator*, evening edition, 15 October 1873, reported that one of George's assailants shot him with his own revolver, the ball passing through his coat and vest. They also inflicted on George severe head injuries, a broken finger, and contusions on the side ("Outrage at Brantford" 3). Evelyn indicates that the criminals responsible for the second attack were caught and imprisoned. Critically ill, George was unable to get around for months (Keen and McKeon 1: 49; see also Hale, "Chief George H. M. Johnson—Onwanonsyshon" 139).

A third attack occurred on 16 April 1878. An unidentified newspaper, dateline "Brantford," reported on Friday, 26 April 1878, that George was attacked again on the evening of the 16th by "a notorious Indian named Joshua Turkey *alias* Williams. It is high time that the participants in such outrages be made an example of, as we believe this is the third assault upon the Chief within the last few years" (n.p.; copy in Johnson Coll., BCHSM; see also "Aggravated Assault," *Brantford Weekly Expositor*, 26 April 1878, 9). George never resumed his old way of life after this attack. He took little part in Senate affairs and was often too unwell to carry out his government duties as interpreter and liaison to Superintendent Jasper T. Gilkison (Keller 39).

80–81—firstborn say good bye to take his college course. . . . the oldest daughter also entered college,] Henry Beverly entered Hellmuth College in London, Ontario; Evelyn went to Hellmuth Ladies College a year later (Keller 32).

83—All the year round guests . . . made their visits long remembered.] Among the distinguished visitors to Chiefswood whom Evelyn remembers were the governor-general of Canada, Lord and Lady Dufferin, who visited on 25 August 1874, the Marquis of Lorne (later Duke of Argyll), and his Lady the Princess Louise, daughter of Queen Victoria who visited in 1879 (Keen and McKeon 1: 49; Foster 28; Keller 28). According to Charlesworth, other visitors included the soldiers Sir William Butler and Sir Garnet Wolseley. Many actors and actresses visiting Brantford were entertained at Chiefswood as well: "Among her [Pauline's] closest friends were the once famous Belgian artiste, Hortense Rhea, the delightful English comedienne, Rosina Vokes, and the lovely American actress, Belle Archer, ..." (1: 99–100). Hale notes that the many visitors to Chiefswood "came away delighted with a reception in which Indian hospitality had combined with English courtesy and refinement to make the guests feel themselves pleasantly at home." American tourists to Brantford eagerly sought invitations to Chiefswood and sometimes wrote accounts of their experiences for American journals: "the elegant and tasteful Indian home in the tree-embowered mansion, overlooking the wide and winding river, the cordial and dignified chief, the gentle English matron, and the graceful accomplished young 'Indian princesses'—all making a picture as charming as it was novel and unexpected" ("Chief George H. M. Johnson—Onwanonsyshon" 141–42).

84—So his valiant spirit went fearlessly forth.] On 12

February 1884, George had attended a reception for the newly appointed bishop, the Very Reverend Baldwin, in Brantford. After a long drive home in a drenching rain, George became ill with erysipelas on 13 February. Pyaemia or "blood poisoning" set in, and George gradually lost consciousness. He died on 19 February 1884, at the age of 68 (E.S.H.J. holograph note, Johnson Coll., BCHSM; "Chief G. H. M. Johnson," *Brantford Weekly Expositor*. Death Roll. 22 February 1884: 2; "Dead: Chief Johnson, of the Six Nation Indians, Goes to the Happy Hunting Ground," *Hamilton Daily Spectator*, 20 February 1884: 4. See also Hale, "Chief George H. M. Johnson—Onwanonsyshon" 142; Keen and McKeon 1: 49; and Keller 40).

85—"She misses him yet. I believe she will always miss him."] Emily expressed her grief in notes she wrote both about her husband and to him. On 17 May 1884, she noted that "This a.m. I have received the last present my poor dear husband (Chief George H. M. Johnson) bought as a 'surprise' for me on February. He was taken ill on the 13th Feb 1884 and died on the 19th. I often think what fun the poor fellow would have had laughing at me while we may have been looking at those wretched dying & bleeding men. He bought Lord Nelson for me as he knew 'I had *not* much *love* for *old* Bonaparte [.]" George idolized Napoleon, whom Emily disliked intensely.

In 1889 and 1890 she commemorated the anniversary of her marriage to George by making a pilgrimage to his grave and expressed her grief in two short notes. On a black-bordered card, carrying the notation "grass from G. H. Johnson's grave, 1889 & 90," she wrote a signed note to her dead husband dated 27 August 1889: "I walked to the Mohawk this afternoon, to see your grave my dear, lost Husband, and all I could bring away was this bit of grass, which I have tied in the shape of a cross. Simple as it is, it reminds me of things that happened, *long, long ago*."

She recorded her 28 August 1890 visit to his grave in an unsigned note: "This afternoon dearest George, I went to see your grave, it is a long walk for me, but I must try, and go there once a year, as long as I can. I intended going yesterday 27th our wedding day, but visitors came preventing my doing so.

"A little grass again, I brought away. Not many years, and I shall rest by your side, for I am getting old" (Holographs in Johnson Coll., BCHSM).

85—And one night the Great Messenger . . . whites and Indians as one.] Pauline was in Winnipeg when she learned of her mother's critical condition. Because of heavy snow, Pauline's journey to reach her mother took seven days. She arrived only forty-five minutes before her mother, who had lapsed into unconsciousness, died on 23 February 1898 ("Passed Away: Mother of Pauline Johnson Died Last Night After Lengthy Illness," *Brantford Weekly Expositor*, n.d., n.p., and unidentified newspaper, n.d., n.p. E. Pauline Johnson Coll., Mills Library, McMaster University, Box 4, F.3).

"CATHARINE OF THE 'CROW'S NEST' "

The Mother's Magazine 5 (December 1910): 12–13, 29–30. Foster praised this as "a story of many sided appeal" (116).

86—Crow's Nest Pass] Work on the Crow's Nest Railway began on 14 July 1897 in Lethbridge, Alberta (McGregor 150).

87—"The Crow's Nest." It arose . . . all that regal Pass."] Crow's Nest Pass (elevation: 4450 feet) is located in the Rocky Mountains of southern Alberta, west of Lethbridge, between Michel and Coleman. Cf. Pauline's poem "At Crow's Nest Pass," *Canadian Born* (1903) and *Flint and Feather* (1913):

> At Crow's Nest Pass the mountains rend
> Themselves apart, the rivers wend
> A lawless course about their feet,
> And break into torrents beat

In useless fury where they blend
At Crow's Nest Pass.

The nesting eagle, wise, discreet,
Wings up the gorge's lone retreat
And makes some barren crag her friend
At Crow's Nest Pass.

Uncertain clouds, half-high, suspend
Their shifting vapours, and contend
With rocks that suffer not defeat;
And snows, and suns, and mad winds meet
To battle where the cliffs defend
At Crow's Nest Pass.

Pauline's descriptions of Crow's Nest Mountain reflect the influence of Shelley's "Mont Blanc" 3, 60–71.

87—There had been deaths . . . rebellious spirit in consequence.] According to James G. McGregor, there was little sanitation in these camps: "Such lack of supervision and of hospital facilities, combined with the callousness and indifference with which the contractors treated these men and the downright dishonesty to which they resorted, form an unsavoury part of our heritage. Conditions on the Crowsnest [*sic*] Pass Railway were so bad that typhoid swept the contraction camps and many men died." An aroused press and public insisted on an investigation, which led to governmental insistence on better working conditions for the laborers, many of whom were European immigrants (150).

91—untold wealth of Kootenay mines] In 1863 the discovery of gold in the Kootenay region, of southwestern British Columbia, fifty miles north of the United States border, brought hordes of American gold seekers to the area. The rush climaxed in 1865, when five thousand miners came to Fisherville, near the present site of Cranbrook. The rush declined until 1868, when new discoveries on nearby Perry Creek started a second rush. After these mines failed, the rush subsided. By 1872, only a few dozen miners worked the streams of the East Kootenay (Christian, "Abstract" 192–93).

92—little town of Nelson, . . . of Kootenay Lake] Located approximately twenty miles west of Kootenay Lake in southeastern British Columbia, Nelson is considerably west of Crow's Nest Pass.

98—"my people, the Kootenay Indians"] The Kutenai (or Kootenay) are a Plateau tribe whose members live on the Kootenay River, Kootenay Lake, Arrow Lake, and the upper Columbia River in southeastern British Columbia, northern Idaho, and northwestern Montana. They speak an isolate in the Algonquian-Wakashan language family. For information about the Kootenai Indians, see Turney-High.

"A RED GIRL'S REASONING"

In 1892, this story won the *Dominion Magazine*'s first prize for fiction and was published in its February 1893 issue (2.1:19–28). It became a popular part of Pauline's repertoire. She performed it both alone and with her partner Owen Smily, who played Charlie MacDonald. Although there was some discussion about turning it into a play, this was never done (Keller 70, 121, 134).

104—Personally she looked much the same . . . 'the white man's disease,' consumption—] The physical characteristics ascribed to Christine describe Pauline Johnson herself.

"THE ENVOY EXTRAORDINARY"

The Mother's Magazine, 4 (March 1909): 11–13. According to Foster, the story was suggested by one that Walter McRaye told Pauline (116).

Notes to Text

"A PAGAN IN ST. PAUL'S CATHEDRAL"

Written during Pauline's visit to London from June through November 1906, this essay was published in the *London Daily Express* on 3 August 1906 (copy in E. Pauline Johnson Coll., Mills Lib., McMaster, Box 8. 24; see also Keller 215, 224).

142—In their place flared the campfires of the Onondaga "long-house," . . . was suspended a pure white lifeless dog.] An allusion to the ceremony of the "White Dog Sacrifice" practiced among the Onondagas of the Grand River Reserve. It is part of the rites of the new year, which begin on the fifth day of the new moon, around the end of January or early in February. It fulfills the dream of Teharonhiawagon, one of the chief gods of the Iroquois and the embodiment of all animal and plant life on earth, that a sacrificial victim and an offering of tobacco were required to disenchant the life forces in nature and man. The goal of the New Year rites is to revive all life on earth by supplying the Master of Life with what he has dreamed is necessary to his incarnations and to renew through ceremony all the elements thought to secure man's welfare. It was originally a major rite of the Midwinter Ceremony of the five (later Six) Nations Iroquois.

Pauline witnessed the ceremony as a small child accompanied by her father and ethnologist Horatio Hale. She briefly described the ceremony in "The Iroquois of the Grand River," *Harper's Weekly*, 23 June 1894, 587–89. Cf. her detailed description in "The Great New Year White Dog: Sacrifice of the Onondagas," *The Daily Province Magazine*, 14 January 1911 (Box 8.38, E. Pauline Johnson Coll., Mills Library, McMaster University). She also made the ceremony the basis of her story "We-hro's Sacrifice" included in *The Shagganappi* (1913), 96–102, originally published in *Boys World* (January 1907).

For Hale's account of the ceremony he witnessed with Chief Johnson, see "The Iroquois Sacrifice of the White

Dog." See also Hewitt, "White Dog Sacrifice." For contemporary studies of the ceremony, see Blaud and Tooker.

"AS IT WAS IN THE BEGINNING"

146—they forbade me to use any Cree words whatever.]
This was a common rule among church and government schools in the United States and Canada.

A very large group, the Crees live in a vast area of the eastern subarctic, from western Quebec and James Bay, to British Columbia and northern Montana. They speak a dialect of Algonquian. Pauline's reference to the "prairie" on p. 145 indicates that she undoubtedly alludes to the Plains Cree. For information about this group, see Mandelbaum.

148—"Esther"] The Jewish queen of the Persian King Ahasuerus (Xerxes I, 486–65 B.C.) With her cousin and foster father, Mordecai, Esther frustrated the desires of Haman, a favorite of the king, to slay Jews living in the empire. See "The Book of Esther," in the Old Testament of the Bible.

153–4—His eyes grew smaller, more glittering . . . of a strange—*snake.*] Pauline's allusions to snakes combine Biblical, classical, and Indian mythology. Cf. the serpent's seduction of Eve in Genesis 3: 1–5.

Cf. also the myth of Lamia, a snake who took the form of a beautiful woman to entice young men into her embrace in order to devour them. In *Life of Apollonius of Tyana,* Philostratus describes Lamia as a serpent witch who transforms herself into a beautiful woman in order to entrance Lycius. She is destroyed by the sage Apollonius. Keats retells this story in *Lamia.* (See particularly the description of her transformation from serpent to beautiful woman [1: 146–66].) Coleridge also uses the "Lamia" myth in *Christabel.* Geraldine, the Lamia figure, first entrances Christabel and then her father. Geraldine's eyes "glitter bright" (1: 221). She is later described as having "shrunken serpent eyes" (2: 602).

Serpents and dragons are common in Mohawk and Cree mythology of tribes in the Great Lakes area and are especially associated with water. See Speck and Dodge, whose research was conducted at the Grand River Six Nations Reserve in 1944, and Barbeau. According to Barbeau, Lake Ontario, which means "Beautiful Lake," was made in mythic times by the Great Serpent or Dragon as a home for himself and a maiden who fell under his power. Its neighbor, Lake Erie, is named after the mythic Lion or Griffin, often associated with the Serpent or Dragon (82). Barbeau notes that North American Indians not only had a Dragon tradition of their own but also picked up another branch of it from the French-Canadians (83).

"THE LEGEND OF LILLOOET FALLS"

The Mother's Magazine 7 (January 1912): 19, 45.

"Lillooet" means "wild onion" in Salish. One of the four principal Salish tribes, located on the Fraser River in British Columbia, the Lillooet Indians are sometimes divided into the lower (the Douglas and Pemberton Meadows bands) and the upper (all the rest).

Hilda Bryson, Lillooet District Historical Society, indicates that, although there is no falls in the area known as "Lillooet Falls," there are two very beautiful ones known as "Dickey Creek Falls" and "Cayoosh Creek Falls." Both flow into the Fraser River.

I find no other printed version of this legend. For other Lillooet stories see Teit, "The Traditions of the Lillooet Indians of British Columbia." For information about the tribe's culture, see Teit, *The Lillooet Indians*.

The town of Lillooet was founded after the discovery of gold in 1858 on the banks of the Fraser River, where it converges with Cayoosh Creek and the Bridge River. During that period, it was the hub of traffic from the coast to the gold mines farther north on the Carriboo Trail (Harris 8).

Cf. Pauline's well-known poem "The Trail to Lillooet," published in *Flint and Feather* (1912). Both works were inspired by her journey to the town of Lillooet in 1903. On 25 July, Pauline and McRaye left Ashcroft, west of Kamloops in southwestern British Columbia, to travel twenty days by horse and buggy 400 miles along the Cariboo Road, up country to Barkerville. Located near what is now Bowron Lake Provincial Park, Barkerville became famous thirty years earlier as the site of British Columbia's largest gold strike. On the way back. Pauline and McRaye detoured to visit the town of Lillooet (McRaye, *Pauline Johnson and Her Friends* 72 − 74; Keller 201 − 2). Pauline described the journey in one of her most popular travel pieces, "Coaching on the Cariboo Trail," published by *Canadian Magazine* 42 (Feb. 1914): 399–400.

157—Klootchman] Chinook for "woman." A jargon composed of a mixture of elements from various American Indian and some European languages, Chinook was the trade language of the southern Northwest Coast.

157—Kla-how-ya, Tillicum] In Chinook, "Kla-how-ya" means "Good morning," "good evening," or "good-bye." "Tillicum" means "people."

159—towering fir-crested heights, . . . early morning cobwebs at sun-up.] Cf. her description here of her journey through the area near the Fraser River, which winds through Marble Canyon between Clinton and Lillooet: "On the return trip we made a detour of sixty miles westward to Lillooet, on the Upper Fraser River. For miles the trail hangs like a chiffon scarf above the river, which boils through its rock canon, a thousand feet below. For miles the carriage wheels flew along one foot from the edge of this precipice. We climbed Pavilion Mountain, where the trail wound in six distinct loops above us, we galloped every foot of the way down the opposite side, where the trail dropped in six circles below us" (400).

Pauline also used the "cobweb" image in "The Trail to Lillooet":

Trail that winds and trail that wanders, like a cob-
web hanging high,
Just a hazy thread outlining mid-way of the stream
and sky,
Where the Fraser River canyon yawns its pathway
to the sea,
But half the world has shouldered up between its
song and me.
Here, the placid English August, and the sea-en-
circled miles,
There—God's copper-coloured sunshine beating
through the lonely aisles
Where the waterfalls and forest voice for ever their
duet,
And call across the canyon on the trail to Lillooet.
(Lines 9–16)

Pauline's story "Wolf-Brother" in *The Shagganappi* (1913),
88–95, also deals with the Lillooet Indians.

"HER MAJESTY'S GUEST"

Although Foster called this story "the least attractive of the
collection" (116), it accurately reflects dangers Chief
George H. M. Johnson faced as he tried to stop liquor
traffic on the Grand River Reservation. For a description of
the attempts to stop him, see the notes to "My Mother,"
76–81 of *MM*.
   177—Napoleon's] Chief Johnson greatly admired Bonaparte, whom Emily disliked. See the note to 85— "She
misses him yet" of *MM*.

"MOTHER O' THE MEN"

The Mother's Magazine 4 (February 1908): 14–16, 56.
   This is Pauline's only work devoted to the wife of a

North-West Mounted Policeman, although she often alluded to the troopers themselves. For her other works about the Mounted Police, see "Riders of the Plains," *Canadian Born* (1903) and *Flint and Feather* (1912).

180—The commander's wife] Born in Ottawa, Henrietta Armstrong Constantine (1857–1934) was the third daughter of Captain Edward A. Armstrong of Quebec. In 1872, she moved with her family to Winnipeg, where her father was a member of the expedition commanded by Garnet Joseph Wolseley, first viscount. In her parents' Winnipeg home, sixteen-year-old Henrietta married Charles Constantine on 5 November 1873. Constantine was then a lieutenant in the North-West Mounted Police and a member of the Wolseley expedition. The Constantines had three sons, two of whom predeceased their mother.

According to Pauline's partner, McRaye, he and Pauline were frequently the guests of the wives and officers commanding North-West Mounted Police Stations (now the Canadian Mounted Police). Arriving at Fort Saskatchewan on or around 25 May 1903, Pauline and McRaye spent a week with Henrietta and Major Charles Constantine (Keller 200). Pauline's name for her was "Dear Lady of My Friendship" (Going 177). The Constantine's house was full of trophies, nuggets, and furs, given by the miners to Henrietta, "who had won their hearts by her many acts of kindness in that land where woman and her ministering power were respected and loved" (*Pauline Johnson and Her Friends* 88; *Town Hall Tonight* 46). Following the death of her husband in 1912, Henrietta went to live with her son Charles Francis in Kingston.

McRaye described his visit to Henrietta in Kingston shortly before her death when they reminisced about mutual friends: "What a flood of memories she had of Winnipeg after the first rebellion. She had seen the West change from the days of the buffalo to its present populated cities and towns" (*Pauline Johnson and Her Friends* 89). Keller notes that Henrietta became the model for "many of the idealized mothers and wives who populate her later stories" (*Pauline* 200). For accounts of her life, see Going 176–77; "Pioneer Woman of the West," *Winnipeg Evening Tribune* 7 Nov. 1927: n.p.; "Women and their Work," *The Chatelaine*, 4 (Dec. 1931): 38; and Turner 73, 44. See also "Constantine-Armstrong," *The Manitoban*, Marriage Announcement, 8 Nov. 1873: 2; "Widow of Major C. Constantine Passes in East," *Winnipeg Tribune* 19 Feb. 1935: 5; and the following from the *Winnipeg Free Press*: "Constantine," 17 Feb. 1934: 17; "Mrs. H. Constantine, One of the Prairie West's first Pioneer Women, Is Dead" 19 Feb. 1934: 3; "Tribute paid to Mrs. Constantine Paid by Mrs. Colin Campbell," 20 Feb. 1934: 2. Copies of the Winnipeg newspapers in the Manitoba Provincial Archives.

180—a little boy of ten] Charles Francis Constantine (1883–1953), C. F., C.B., D.S.O., only surviving son of Henrietta and Charles Constantine. Francis, a member of the Canadian military service, was awarded the Legion of Honor by France for his service during World War I. He was later stationed at the Royal Military College at Kingston, where he served as professor of artillery and later as commandant. Promoted to the rank of major general in 1934, he served as adjutant general of the Canadian Forces in Ottawa from 1934 to 1938, retiring in 1943. See "Constantine, Maj.-Gen. C. F.," 192–93; Preston, 250 and n.

180—her husband's command] Born in Bradford, Yorkshire, England, Charles Constantine (1849–1912) came to Canada in 1854. He served with the Red River Force from 1870 to 1874, was deputy sheriff of Manitoba, and in 1880 was appointed chief of the Manitoba Provincial Police. After serving as adjutant of the Winnipeg Light Infantry during the North-West Rebellion, Charles was appointed in 1886 as inspector in the North-West Mounted Police.

By 1893 gold mining activity in the Yukon had reached the point that the Canadian government felt it needed to assert its presence. Having surveyed conditions in the Yukon the previous year, Charles began in June 1895 a voyage of 4,800 miles to the Yukon, in command of twenty men selected for their size and for their temperance. The party landed on 24 July 1895, 1,800 miles up the Yukon River, establishing the most northerly military post in the British empire. Accompanying the party were Henrietta and young Francis. Because the wife of Inspector D'Arcy Strickland also accompanied the party, Henrietta was not the only woman as Pauline suggests.

Charles established Fort Constantine on the Forty-Mile River and enforced Canadian law, ending the rule of the miners' meetings. The fort was barely finished by November, when the temperature plunged to almost 50 degrees below zero, huddling there for the next three months. Constantine strove hard to maintain morale during the winter, as monotony drove some of the men to drink. Longstreth describes the choice of Charles to command this post as a "happy one." He was "scrupulously honest, exact and exacting, tenacious, and enormously hard-working, inconsiderate of others if the Force was to be served, . . ." (194). Walter McRaye described Charles as summing up "all the glamorous tradition of that wonderful fighting constabulary . . ." (*Pauline Johnson and Her Friends* 88). According to Keller, Charles supplied Pauline with material for many of her later stories (200).

By spring 1897, Constantine erected Fort Herchmer and abandoned Fort Constantine, made obsolete by the discovery of gold near what became Dawson City. George Washington Carmack, known as Siwash George because of his marriage to the daughter of a Tagish chieftain; his Indian kinsmen Tagish Charlie; and Skookum Jim discovered gold on Rabbit Creek, renamed Bonanza. Henrietta loaned them money to file their claim to the Yukon's richest gold strike (Paterson 61–67; "Mrs. Chas. Constantine" 44). Gold fever brought 30,000 people to the town of only 750, which became Dawson City. In answer to Charles's urgent pleas, the Canadian government sent almost 200 officers and men, well equipped with guns, to maintain order among the miners, most of whom were American. The Constantines remained in Dawson until summer 1898. As a token of the city's appreciation for his diligence and fairness, Charles was presented with a silver plate and a loving cup formed of raw gold nuggets worth $4,000. On 18 June 1898, the Yukon Order of Pioneers paid tribute both to Charles for his sterling integrity, administrative firmness and fairness, and helpful kindness, and to Henrietta, "a most worthy helpmeet in your good work, our rough words cannot express fittingly all we feel" (Longstreth 204).

Charles's work helped establish the fame of the North-West Mounted Police, established in 1873 to maintain law in that area. The Mounted Police were frequently the only administration in these isolated territories. After leaving the Yukon, Charles commanded detachments at Fort Saskatchewan, 1901–05; Lesser Slave Lake, 1905–07; and along the Peace River–Yukon Trail, 1904–07. Charles returned to the Yukon on special duty in 1902; in 1904 he traveled down the Mackenzie River opening posts at McPherson and Herschel Island. In 1905 he commanded a party sent to build the Peace River–Yukon pack trail. Charles died on 5 May 1912 and was buried with a military funeral in Winnipeg.

See "C. Constantine to Be Buried Here," *Winnipeg Telegram* 8 May 1912: n.p.; Longstreth, 194, 204, 238, 257, 263; Paterson, 52–75; Phillips, 88, 130–31; and biographical sketches supplied by the PAC and by the Royal Canadian Mounted Police. The Charles Constantine papers (MG30, E 55, consisting of diaries, files, and letterbooks) are in the PAC. These papers contain little about his personal life.

"THE NEST BUILDER"

The Mother's Magazine, 5 (March 1910), 11, 32.

195—Brandon] A Manitoba town approximately 127 miles west of Winnipeg.

200—Prince Albert] This town is located in north central Saskatchewan.

"THE ENVOY EXTRAORDINARY"

The Mother's Magazine 4 (March 1909): 11–13. According to Foster, this story was told to Pauline while she waited for a train in Saskatchewan (116).

"THE TENAS KLOOTCHMAN"

The Mother's Magazine 6 (August 1911): 12–13.

202—at the Squamish River, some thirty-five miles north of Vancouver City] These directions suggest that Maarda is Squamish, part of the Comox tribe. Located at the Squamish River, Capilano, and North Vancouver, the Comox Squamish speak Coastal Salish. See Duff. For further information about the Squamish, see Barnett.

"THE DERELICT"

213—mother] The Ojibwa (Chippewa, Anishinabe) are numerically the largest tribal group in the United States and Canada. Although they primarily inhabit the western Northern Great Lakes area, they also extend west to Montana, south to Wisconsin and Minnesota, and north to Lake Manitoba. The Ojibwa speak a dialect of the Algonquian language.

For further information about the Ojibwa, see Densmore and Landes.

214—Penetanguishene] A town located in Ontario at the southeastern end of Georgian Bay, which flows into Lake Huron.

216—Barrie] This Ontario town is approximately 27 miles east of Nottawasaga Bay, at the southern end of Georgian Bay, and approximately 29 miles south of Penetanguishene.

216—North Bay] A town at the northeastern corner of Lake Nipissing, Ontario, about halfway between Sudbury and Algonquin Provincial Park.

BIBLIOGRAPHY

Prepared by A. LaVonne Brown Ruoff

Works by E. Pauline Johnson Cited
(excluding the essay and stories reprinted in this volume)

"Coaching on the Cariboo Trail," *Canadian Magazine* 42 (February 1914): 399–400.

Canadian Born. Toronto: Morang, 1903.

"Duke of Connaught as Chief of the Iroquois Indians." *The Daily Province Magazine* 2 July 1910: 4. Copy in E. Pauline Johnson Collection, Mills Memorial Library, McMaster University, Box 8.33.

Flint and Feather. Toronto: Musson, 1912; Markam, Ontario: PaperJacks, 1973.

"The Great New Year White Dog: Sacrifice of the Onondagas." *The Daily Province Magazine* 14 January 1911:16.

"The Iroquois of the Grand River," *Harper's Weekly,* 23 June 1894: 587–89.

Legends of Vancouver. Vancouver: Sunset, 1911; McClelland, 1912, 1961.

"The Lodge of the Law-Makers." *London Daily Express,* Summer 1906, n.d., n.p. E. Pauline Johnson Collection, Mills Memorial Library, McMaster University, Box 8.27.

The Moccasin Maker. Vancouver: Briggs, 1913.

The Shagganappi. Vancouver: Briggs, 1913.

The White Wampum. London: John Lane, The Bodley Head, 1895.

Selected Works by E. Pauline Johnson
Published in *The Mother's Magazine*

"From the Child's Viewpoint." Pt. 1, 5 (May 1910): 30–31; Pt. 2, 5 (June 1910): 60–62.

"The Call of the Skookum Chuck." 5 (April 1910): 14–17.

256

"Catharine of the 'Crow's Nest.' " 5 (Dec. 1910): 12–13, 29–30.
"The Christmas Heart." 4 (Dec. 1909): 13,30.
"The Envoy Extraordinary." 4 (March 1909): 11–13.
"Her Dominion—A Story of 1867, and Canada's Confederation." 2 (July 1907): 10–11, 40.
"The Great Deep Water: A Legend of 'The Flood.' " 7 (Feb. 1912): 35.
"The Gray Archway: A Legend of the Charlotte Islands." 5 (June 1910): 10–11.
"Heroic Indian Mothers." 3 (Sept. 1908): 23–24.
"The Home Comers." 2 (Sept. 1907): 4–6.
"Hoolool of the Totem Poles: A Story of the North Pacific Coast." 6 (Feb. 1911): 12–13, 71.
"How One Resourceful Mother Planned an Inexpensive Outing." 3 (June 1908): 19, 63.
"The Legend of Lillooet Falls." 7 (Jan. 1912): 19, 45.
"The Legend of the Ice Babies." 6 (Nov. 1911): 23–24.
"The Legend of the Seven Swans." 6 (Sept. 1911): 17–18, 32.
"The Legend of the Two Sisters." 4 (Jan. 1909): 12–13.
"The Legend of Siwash Rocks." 5 (Oct. 1910): 10–11.
"The Legend of the Squamish Twins or the Call of Kinship." 5 (July 1910): 16–17.
"The Lost Salmon Run: A Legend of the Pacific Coast." 5 (Aug. 1910): 13–14.
"Mother o' the Men: A Story of the Canadian North West Mounted Police." 4 (Feb. 1908): 14–16, 56.
"Mother of the Motherless." 3 (Nov. 1908): 13, 50.
"My Mother." 4 (1909). Pt. 1 (April): 9–11, 40; Pt. 2 (May): 7–9, 14; Pt. 3 (June): 10–12; Pt. 4 (July): 15–18.
"Mothers of a Great Red Race." 3 (Jan. 1908): 5, 14.
"The Nest-Builder." 5 (March 1910): 11, 32.
"Outdoor Occupations of the Indian Mother and Her Children." 3 (July 1908): 22–23.
"Prayers of the Pagan." 2 (Nov. 1907): 10.
"The Tenas Klootchman." 6 (Aug. 1911): 12–14.

"Winter Indoor Life of the Indian Mother and Children."
3 (Feb. 1908): 5, 42.

Works Cited About E. Pauline Johnson
and the Howells-Johnson-Elliot Families

"Aggravated Assault." *Brantford Weekly Expositor.* 26 April
1878: 1.
*Biographical and Historical Memoirs of Muskingum County,
Ohio.* Chicago: Goodspeed, 1892.
Charlesworth, Hector. *Candid Chronicles.* 2 vols. Toronto:
Macmillan of Canada, 1925.
"Chief G. H. M. Johnson." *Brantford Weekly Expositor.*
Death Roll. 22 Feb. 1884: 5.
"Dead. Chief Johnson, of the Six Nation Indians, Goes to
the Happy Hunting Ground." *Hamilton Daily Spectator
and Journal of Commerce.* 20 Feb. 1884: 4.
Elliot, Adam. "Correspondence of the Rev. Adam Elliot,
to the Rev. C. Mathews, Secretary to the Society for
Converting and Civilizing the Indians." In *The Stewart
Missions; A Series of Letters and Journals* . . . . Ed. Rev.
William J. D. Waddilove. London: 1838. 29–75.
"[Elliot, Eliza Beulah.] 19 Dec. 1849." In *"The Patriot,*
Toronto, 1833–49." *The Ontario Register* 5 (1981): 60.
Fairs, Geoffrey L. "Thomas Howells of Hay and His De-
scendants in America." *The New England Historical and
Genealogical Register* 134 (1980): 27–47.
Foster, Mrs. W. Garland (Anne). *The Mohawk Princess,
Being Some Account of the Life of Teka-hion-wake (E. Pauline
Johnson).* Vancouver: Lion's Gate, 1931.
Gerson, Carole. "Some Notes Concerning Pauline
Johnson." *Canadian Notes & Queries.* 34 (Autumn 1985):
16–19.
Hale, Horatio. "Chief George H. M. Johnson—Onwanon-
syshon: His Life and Work Among the Six Nations."
Magazine of American History 13 (1885): 131–42.

Howells, Henry C. *Letters from Ohio, Containing Advice to Emigrants, Who Intend to Settle in the United States of America.* Bristol: Wright and Bagnall, 1832. Copy in Cincinnati Historical Society.

Howells, William Dean. "Years of My Youth." In *Years of My Youth and Three Essays.* Ed. David J. Nordloh. Vol. 29. *A Selected Edition of W. D. Howells.* Ed. Don L. Cook and David J. Nordloh. Bloomington: Indiana University Press, 1975.

Index to the 1850 Federal Population Census of Ohio. Comp. Ohio Family Historians. Hubbard, OH: TOCON, 1972.

Johnson, Evelyn H. C. "Chief John Smoke Johnson." *Ontario Historical Society, Papers and Records* 12 (1914): 102–13.

——. "Grandfather and Father of E. Pauline Johnson." *Annual Archaeological Report of the Ontario Department of Education,* 36 (1928): 44–47.

——. "The Martin Settlement." *Brant Historical Society Papers,* 11 (1908–11): 55–64.

Keen, Dorothy, and Martha McKeon, as told to Mollie Gillen. "The Story of Pauline Johnson, Canada's Passionate Poet." *Chatelaine,* Pt. 1, 39.2 (February 1966): 39–42, 44, 49; Pt. 2, 39. 3 (March 1966): 95–98, 100.

"[Johnson, George H. M.]." *Brantford Weekly Expositor.* 17 October 1873: 3.

Keller, Betty. *Pauline: A Biography of Pauline Johnson.* Vancouver: Douglas & McIntyre, 1981.

Klinck, Carl F., gen. ed. *Literary History of Canada: Canadian Literature in English.* 2nd ed. 3 vols. Toronto: University of Toronto Press, 1976. 1: 441–42; 2: 264.

Leighton, Douglas. "Johnson, George Henry Martin (Onwanonsyshon)." 1881–1890. Ed. Frances G. Halpenny. *Dictionary of Canadian Biography.* Gen. ed. George W. Brown. 11 vols. Toronto: University of Toronto Press, 1982, 11: 451–53.

——. "Johnson, John (Sakayengwaraton, Shakoyen'karahton, usually known as Smoke Johnson)." 1881–1890.

Ed. Frances G. Halpenny. *Dictionary of Canadian Biography.* Gen. ed. George W. Brown. 11 vols. Toronto: University of Toronto Press, 1982. 11: 453–54.

Logan, J. D., and Donald G. French. *Highways of Canadian Literature.* 2nd ed. Toronto: McClelland and Stewart, 1928, pp. 18, 105, 107, 195 – 209.

Loosley, Elizabeth. "Pauline Johnson, 1861–1913." In *The Clear Spirit: Twenty Canadian Women and their Times.* Ed. Mary Quale Innis. Toronto: University of Toronto Press, 1966. 74–90.

McKay, Isabel Ecclestone. "Pauline Johnson: A Reminiscence." *Canadian Magazine* 41 (July 1913): 273–78.

McRaye, Walter. "East and West with Pauline Johnson." *Canadian Magazine* Pt. 1, 40. 5 (March 1923): 381–89; Pt. 2, 40. 6 (April 1923): 494–502.

———. *Pauline Johnson and Her Friends.* Toronto: Ryerson, 1947. Ryerson, 1947.

———. *Town Hall To-Night.* Toronto: Ryerson, 1929.

Mair, Charles. "Johnson: An Appreciation." *Canadian Magazine* 41.3 (July 1913): 281–83.

Millman, T. R. "Elliot, Adam (Elliott)." *1871–1880.* Ed. Marc LaTerreur. *Dictionary of Canadian Biography.* Gen. ed. George W. Brown. 11 vols. Toronto, 1972. 10: 269–70.

"Murderous Assault." *Hamilton Daily Spectator and Journal of Commerce.* 26 Jan. 1865: 2.

"Outrage at Brantford." *Hamilton Daily Spectator.* Evening ed. 15 Oct. 1873: 3.

"Passed Away. Mother of Pauline Johnson [Emily Howells Johnson] After Lengthy Illness." *Brantford Weekly Expositor.* 24 Feb. 1898: n.p.

Percival, Walter Pilling. *Leading Canadian Poets.* Toronto: Ryerson, 1948.

Price, Robert. "The Ohio Anti-Slavery Convention of 1836." *Ohio State Archaeological and Historical Quarterly* 45 (1936): 173–88.

Proceedings of the Ohio Anti-Slavery Convention, Held at Put-

nam, on the Twenty-Second, Twenty-Third, and Twenty-Fourth of April, 1835. New York: American Anti-Slavery Society, 1835.

Reid, William D., comp. *Death Notices of Ontario*. Lambertville, NJ: Hunterdon House, 1980.

———. *Marriage Notices of Ontario*. Lambertville, NJ: Hunterdon House, 1980.

Rood, Henry. "W. D. Howells, at 75, Talks of Old Literary New York." In *Interviews with William Dean Howells*. Ed. Ulrich Halfmann. *American Literary Realism* 6 (1973): 376–82, 407–8.

"Serious Assault." 26 April 1878. Unidentified newspaper clipping, n.p. Johnson Collection, BCHSM.

Shirk, W. D. *The History and Genealogy of the Thomas, Joseph, and Henrietta (Howells) Powell Families*. Fairfield, Iowa: Ledger, 1918.

Shrive, Norman. "What Happened to Pauline?" *Canadian Literature* 13 (1962): 25–38.

Schneider, Norris F. *Y Bridge City: The Story of Zanesville and Muskingum County, Ohio*. Cleveland: World, 1950.

Sutor, J. Hope. *Past and Present of the City of Zanesville and Muskingum County, Ohio*. Chicago: Clarke, 1905.

Stevenson, Orlando J. *A People's Best*. Toronto: Musson, 1927.

Waldie, Jean H. "The Iroquois Poetess, Pauline Johnson." *Ontario History* 40 (1948): 64–75.

Webling, Peggy. *Peggy: The Story of One Score Years and Ten*. London: Hutchinson, 1924.

Whale, R. R. "A Short Sketch of Chief G. H. M. Johnson of the Six Nations Indians." *Annual Archaeological Report, Ontario Department of Education* 36 (1928): 40–47.

Works Cited about The Constantine Family

Campbell, Mrs. Colin. "Tribute to Mrs. Constantine Paid by Mrs. Colin Campbell." *Winnipeg Free Press*. 20 Feb.

1934: 2.

"Constantine, [Henrietta]." *Winnipeg Free Press*. Obituary. 17 Feb. 1934: 17.

"Constantine-Armstrong." *Manitoban*. Marriage Announcement. 8 Nov. 1873: 2.

"Constantine, Maj.-Gen. C. F." *Canadian Who's Who*. Toronto: International Press, 1948.

"C. Constantine to Be Buried Here." *Winnipeg Telegram*. Obituary. May 1912: n.p.

"Editorial Notes." *R. M. C. Review* 6 (1925): 9–10.

Going, A. M. "A Pioneer Woman of the West [Henrietta Constantine]." *Willisons Monthly*. 3 (October 1927): 176–77.

Longstreth, T. Morris. *The Silent Force, Scenes from the Life of the Mounted Police of Canada*. New York: Century, 1927.

"Mrs. H. Constantine, One of Prairie West's First Pioneer Woman, Is Dead." *Winnipeg Free Press*. 19 Feb. 1934: 3.

"Pioneer Woman of the West [Henrietta Constantine]." *Winnipeg Evening Tribune*. 7 Nov. 1927: n.p.

Ottawa. Public Archives of Canada. Charles Constantine Papers, MG 30, E 55. Diaries, files, and letterbooks.

Paterson, T. W. *Ghost Towns of the Yukon*. Vancouver: Stagecoach, 1977.

Philipps, R. A. J. *Canada's North*. New York: St. Martin's, 1967.

Preston, Richard Arthur. *Canada's RMC: A History of the Royal Military College*. Toronto: University of Toronto, 1969.

Turner, T.A.K. "'Canada's Finest'—The Pioneer Women of the Force." *Scarlet and Gold* 16 (1935): 41–44, 73.

"Widow of Major C. Constantine Passes in East." *Winnipeg Tribune*. 19 Feb. 1934: 5.

"Women and their Work [Henrietta Constantine]." *Chatelaine*, 4 (December 1931): 38.

Collections of Materials Pertaining to
E. Pauline Johnson and Charles Constantine

Brantford, Ontario. BCHSM. Johnson Family Papers: documents, letters, newspaper clippings.

Hamilton, Ontario. Mills Library, McMaster University. E. Pauline Johnson Papers: Largest collection of her works, letters, documents, memorabilia.

———. Walter R. McRaye Papers.

North York, Ontario. North York Public Library. Newton McFaul MacTavish Papers. Letters from Walter McRaye and Charles Mair to McTavish pertaining to Johnson.

Ottawa. PAC, MG 27, 2 D 15. Clifford Sifton Papers: Letters from Johnson dated 1900–01.

———. PAC, MG 30, D 58. Frank Yeigh Papers: Letters and newspaper clippings about Johnson, two poems, and one letter from Johnson.

———. PAC, MG 22 A 14. Gertrude O'Hara Papers: letter from Johnson to Frank Yeigh.

———. PAC, MG 30, E 55. Charles Constantine Papers.

———. PAC, Department of Indian Affairs, Record Group 10. Correspondence of the Superintendent of the Six Nations Reserve.

———. Royal Canadian Mounted Police Archives. History of the Northwest Mounted Police, including material on Charles Constantine.

American Indians: Works Cited and General Sources on Tribes Alluded to in *The Moccasin Maker*

Barbeau, Marius. "The Dragon Myths and Ritual Songs of the Iroquoians." *International Folk Music Journal* 8 (1951): 80–85.

Barnett, H. G. "Gulf of Georgia Salish." *Anthropological Records*. 1 (1939): 221–95.

———. *The Coast Salish of British Columbia*. University of Oregon Monographs, Studies in Anthropology. 4 (1953): 1–333.

Beauchamp, W. M. "The Iroquois Sacrifice of the White Dog." *The American Antiquarian* 7 (1885): 235–39.

Blau, Harold. "The Iroquois White Dog Sacrifice: Its Evolution and Symbolism" *Ethnohistory* 11 (1964): 97–119.

Chadwick, Edward Marion. *The People of the Longhouse.* Toronto: The Church of England Pub. Co. Ltd., 1897.

Densmore, Frances. *Chippewa Customs.* Bulletin, U. S. Bureau of American Ethnology. 26 (1929): 1–204; Minneapolis: Ross and Haines, 1971.

Duff, Wilson. *The Indian History of British Columbia.* Vol. 1. *The Impact of the White Man.* Anthropology in British Columbia, Memoir 5. Victoria, B. C.: Provincial Museum of British Columbia, 1964.

Fenton, William N., and Elizabeth Tooker. "Mohawk." In *Northeast.* Ed. Bruce G. Trigger. Vol. 15 of *Handbook of American Indians.* Ed. William Sturtevant. Washington: Smithsonian, 1978. 466–80.

Hagen, William T. *American Indians.* Rev. ed. The Chicago History of American Civilization. Ed. Daniel J. Boorstin. Chicago: University of Chicago Press, 1979.

Hale, Horatio E. "Chief George H. M. Johnson—Onwanonsyshon: His Life and Work Among the Six Nations." *Magazine of American History.* 13 (1885): 131–42.

———. *Iroquois Book of Rites.* Vol. 2. *Library of Aboriginal American Literature.* Ed. D. G. Brinton. Philadelphia: D. G. Brinton, 1883; rpt. with intro. by William T. Fenton, Toronto: University of Toronto Press, 1965.

———. "The Iroquois Sacrifice of the White Dog." *American Antiquarian* 7 (1889): 7–14.

Hewitt, J. N. B. *A Constitutional League of Peace in the Stone Age of America.* Annual Report, Bureau of Ethnology 1 (1918): 527–45.

———. "White Dog Sacrifice." *Handbook of American Indians North of Mexico.* Ed. Frederick Webb Hodge Bulletin. Bureau of American Ethnology. 30. 2 (1910): 939–44.

Johnston, Charles J., ed. *The Valley of the Six Nations: A Collection of Documents on the Indian Lands of the Grand River.* Toronto: University of Toronto Press, 1964.

Landes, Ruth. *The Ojibwa Woman.* 1938. New York: Norton, 1971.

Mandelbaum, David G. *The Plains Cree.* Anthropological Papers of the American Museum of Natural History. 37 (1940): 155–316.

Mooney, James. *The Ghost-Dance Religion and the Sioux Outbreak of 1890.* Annual Report, Bureau of Ethnology. 14. 2 (1892 – 93). Ed. and abridged. With Intro. by Anthony F. C. Wallace. Classics in Anthropology, ed. Paul Bohannan. Chicago: University of Chicago Press, 1965.

Noon, John A. *Law and Government of the Grand River Iroquois.* Viking Fund Publications in Anthropology, 12. 1949; New York: Johnson, 1964.

Scheick, William J. *The Half-Blood: A Cultural Symbol in 19th-Century American Fiction.* Lexington: University of Kentucky Press, 1979.

Speck, Frank G., and Ernest S. Dodge. "Amphibian and Reptile Lore of the Six Nations Cayuga." *Journal of American Folklore,* 58 (1945): 306–9.

Teit, James A. "Traditions of the Lillooet Indians of British Columbia." *Journal of American Folklore* 25 (1912): 287–371.

Tooker, Elisabeth. "Iroquois." In *The Northeast.* Ed. Bruce G. Trigger. Vol. 15 of *Handbook of North American Indians.* Ed. William C. Sturtevant. Washington: Smithsonian, 1978. 449–65.

———. *The Iroquois Ceremonial of Midwinter.* Syracuse: Syracuse University Press, 1970.

———. "The League of the Iroquois: Its History, Politics, and Ritual." In *The Northeast.* Ed. Bruce G. Trigger. Vol. 15 of *Handbook of North American Indians.* Ed. William C. Sturtevant. Washington: Smithsonian, 1978. 418–41.

Turney-High, Harry H. *Ethnography of the Kutenai.* American Anthropological Association, Memoirs. 56 (1941): 1–201.

Weaver, Sally M. "Six Nations of the Grand River, Ontario." In *The Northeast*. Ed. Bruce G. Trigger. Vol. 15 of *Handbook of North American Indians*. Ed. William C. Sturtevant. Washington: Smithsonian, 1978. 525–36.

Additional Works Cited

Baym, Nina. *Women's Fiction: A Guide to Novels by and about Women in America, 1820–1870*. Ithaca, New York: Cornell University Press, 1978.

Cellem, Robert. *Visit of His Royal Highness the Prince of Wales to the British North American Provinces and United States, in the Year 1860*. Toronto: Rowsell, 1861.

Christian, John Willis. "The Kootenay Gold Rush: The Placer Decade, 1863–1872." Ph.D. dissertation, Washington State University, 1967.

Cornwallis, Kinahan. *Royalty in the New World; or, the Prince of Wales in America*. New York: Doolady, 1860.

Englehart, Gardner. *Journal of the Progress of H. R. H. The Prince of Wales Through British North America; and His Visit to the United States, 10th July to 15th November, 1860*. London: privately printed, ca. 1860.

MacGregor, James G. *A History of Alberta*. Edmonton, Alberta: Hurtig, 1972.

Showalter, Elaine. *A Literature of Their Own: British Women Novelists from Brontë to Lessing*. Princeton: Princeton University Press, 1977.

Shrive, Norman. *Charles Mair: Literary Nationalist*. Toronto: University of Toronto Press, 1965.

266